Zoë Fairbairns was born in 1948. She studied history at St Andrews University and the College of William and Mary in Virginia, USA. *Benefits* is her third novel; it is over ten years since *Live as Family* and *Down* were published. Her play, *Details of Wife*, was performed in Richmond and Brussels in 1973, and she is co-author of *Tales I Tell My Mother*, a collection of short stories published in 1978. She has worked as a freelance journalist since 1973, and has also published poetry and pamphlets. In 1977/8 she was Writer-in-Residence at Rutherford Comprehensive School in London. She lives in London and is at present poetry editor of *Spare Rib* and involved in running the Women's Research and Resources Centre. Her next novel, *Fruits* is an epic saga of four generations of women, also published by Virago.

Benefits, a chilling novel of the future, takes women as its main theme, their relations with men, with each other and with the power of the state. With remarkable irony and compassion, Zoë Fairbairns writes of an all-too-possible future, a world ruled by the cold dictates of superbureaucracy. But there is some hope too – for women, and, through them, for humankind.

BENEFITS

a
novel
by

Zoë Fairbairns

Virago
London

First published by VIRAGO Limited 1979
Ely House, 37 Dover Street, London W1X 4HS

Reprinted 1980, 1981

ISBN 0 86068 112 2 Casebound Edition
ISBN 0 86068 113 0 Paperback Edition

Typeset by Malvern Typesetting Services
and printed in Great Britain by litho
at the Anchor Press Ltd, Tiptree, Essex

Contents

Acknowledgements

This novel would not even have been started without Valerie Miner and her suggestion for the formation of a women writers' group; she and the other members of the group – Sara Maitland, Michele Roberts, Michelene Wandor – revived my interest in writing fiction and gave constant support. As did John Petherbridge who (while not typing the manuscript) always knew the right moment to praise, bully or just put the kettle on again, and never lost interest even when I did. The Greater London Arts Association provided financial support in the form of a C. Day Lewis Fellowship at Rutherford School in North London, where the ever-friendly staff and pupils kept me in touch with reality and alive to the unexpected. And the women of Virago continue to prove that it is possible to be feminists, friends and professional publishers – in the best sense of all those words. My thanks to them and to the many other friends, far too numerous to list, whose interest, encouragement and ideas were so welcome and so important.

Zoë Fairbairns, 1979

PART ONE

1

Summer of Seventy-Six

It was a tall, wide structure, and it stood like a pack of chewing gum, upended in a grudging square of grass on the side of a hill. It was made of glass, grey metal and rough brown brick, and had a depressing but all-too-familiar history. It was one of the last tower blocks to be built in the sixties for London families to live in. By the time it was up, planners, builders and social workers were already losing faith in tower blocks and the families that moved in from the dirty, neighbourly streets being cleared around Collindeane's feet did so without enthusiasm.

Ninety-six flats had meant more than twice that many children; but once the older boys had staked territorial claims to the grass patch, no one young or weak got a look-in. The boys found other sources of fun: filling the lift with bricks, tying door-knockers together, calling in the fire-brigade. Windows got smashed. Families withheld rent and were evicted; or vanished overnight, leaving massive arrears and furniture that had not been paid for. Childish high spirits turned malignant. Paraffin was poured through letterboxes and lit; human shit was left on landings; bricks and planks and crockery were thrown from high windows. Soon anyone with any choice in the matter moved out of the flats, leaving behind only those with no choice. Teenage mothers who looked forty. Drunken, shuffling, unemployed men. Ragged litters of children, yelling as they slithered down the endless banisters or hung from high windows to terrorise passers-by. Old folk with multiple locks on the doors, peering out at the stray dogs that met and fought and mated in the corridors.

Disease entered the flats – pneumonia, gastroenteritis, rumours of typhoid, even a rabies scare – and the council said it would close the flats and pull them down. The local paper declared such waste inexcusable. The council promised to rehabilitate instead, and put up some swings. But before this could be done, the curtain came down on the era of affluence that had spawned and nurtured the British welfare state. The international oil crisis

brought inflation that galloped through dreams, slashed welfare
budgets. There was no money to rehabilitate Collindeane Tower.
The council closed it, rehoused its inmates, nailed wooden planks
across the doorway and tried to pretend they had never built it,
indeed had not noticed it was there – one of the biggest, most
embarrassing statutory nuisances on the London skyline.

Soon after, Collindeane Tower was spotted by a group of
women looking for somewhere to squat and establish a feminist
community. One of them chopped through the planks with her
axe, and they moved in while the council averted its eyes.

Everyone who was in London in the summer of 1976 remembers
the weather. The four-month heatwave brought pleasure at first,
then incredulity, then resignation and unease as the curious
realities of urban drought upset the jocular complacency of
those who would never have believed that Londoners would pray
for rain. People remember what they were doing that summer
in the same way that they can pinpoint their location and activity at the time they heard about the death of President
Kennedy.

From May to September, misty mornings preceded glaring
debilitating days and dry airless nights. The Thames became
unnavigable. Workers went on strike for better ventilation. Grass
browned, trees drooped, earth subsided under foundations and
buildings cracked. Commuters left jackets and cotton cardigans at
home and adhered to each other in packed trains, licking ices.
Umbrella sellers went out of business, shorts were worn in the
staidest of offices, and members of parliament were outraged by
the price of cold drinks in Oxford Street. Day followed incredible
day and still the heat did not let up, still it did not rain. Once or
twice a grey, brooding constipated sky rumbled and flashed and a
few drops of water fell, but you could not call that rain; not when
there was talk of standpipes in the streets and even Buckingham
Palace (it was rumoured) had a sign up in the loo saying 'Don't
pull for a pee.' It rained enough, it was true, to kill the Saturday
of the Lords' Test against Australia (if it had to rain one day of the
year, Londoners told each other wisely, that would be the one) but
that was not enough to break the drought – an almost indecent
word to be used about their city, thought Londoners, to whom
drought meant sandy deserts and cracked farmland in places near
the equator. In unaccustomed chats between strangers, sympathy

for our own farmers (pictured each night on television running dust through their fingers and waving parched roots as if the government ought to do something about it) alternated only with contrived sighs of ecstasy: 'Isn't it glorious?'. Londoners did not really believe in farmers.

Women active in what was then known as the women's liberation movement have other reasons for remembering that summer. One of the major demands of that movement was for a woman's right to abortion on demand. It seemed axiomatic that women could not advance without full control of their fertility; and as things stood, abortion was only allowed when a woman was ill enough, or stressed enough, or rich enough to persuade two doctors ('acting in good faith' the law insisted), to say it would be good for her. And throughout that summer, a Select Committee of MPs, under pressure from organised anti-feminists, was considering ways of making abortions even more difficult to obtain, particularly for those women who sought them merely because they did not wish to be pregnant. The women's liberationists' response to these efforts was to commit themselves, this gleaming summer, to vigorous grassroots campaigning; marches, pickets, petitions, letter-writing, all aimed at showing that parliament (which appeared to have an anti-abortion majority) was out of step with the public on this issue.

The women were interested in another parliamentary fight too: the 'child benefits' issue. The government of the day had a long-standing commitment to making a weekly cash payment to mothers, financing this by increased taxation of fathers; transferring money, as the newspapers liked coyly to put it, 'from wallet to purse'. Unfortunately, at just the time when this scheme was due to come into effect, the government was making a deal with the mighty trade union movement (mighty compared with the organised strength of mothers) that the workers would reduce their pay-demands if the government would reduce taxation. Stalemate. The government had made two contradictory promises, one to women and one to trade unionists, mainly men; and so it was, late in May, that the government flew in the face of its commitment to women's rights and postponed the child benefit scheme indefinitely.

Feminist anger and agitation about this was less vocal and coherent, however, than the response to the Select Committee's threat to abortion rights. Abortion was a simple matter. Anyone who did not approve of abortion did not have to have one, but it should be each individual woman's right to choose. Child benefits, though – that raised other issues. Of course it was monstrous that the organised males of the trade union movement should object to their wives having a right to some of 'their' money, monstrous that sexism should so blatantly coerce government policy. But feminists weren't sure that they wanted men's miserable pay-packets docked to finance child benefits, they weren't sure they wanted to be paid to stay at home and have children, which was how some of them saw it. Shortly after the government announced its decision, a gathering of women sat and argued these points on the roof of Collindeane Tower.

Lynn Byers was thirty-two, short, red-haired and a journalist; she freelanced occasionally for the local paper and had been a vitriolic opponent of the demolition of Collindeane, though privately she had known that all the rehabilitation in the world would not make a 24-storey tower suitable for children to live in. Lynn lived with her husband Derek in a house that they had bought for a song in nearby Seyer Street. The house was cheap partly because it was falling down and partly because Seyer Street was a slum; but it was harmless enough for a healthy couple in their thirties, for whom freedom from a heavy mortgage far outweighed the odd rat.

Lynn had never been in a women's liberation group, though she had felt complete sympathy with the movement insofar as she perceived it from *Spare Rib* and the women's page in the *Guardian*. She'd been on a few marches, usually alone, and was as incensed as anyone about child benefits and the threat to abortion rights. She was in a state of ambivalence herself about having children – the steady advance of the years, Derek's clearly stated (but not harped upon) desire for fatherhood, and her own curiosity and yearning vied with the knowledge of how hard it would be to give up the independence and pride of self-employment and self-support. And political events weighed heavily against having children. The mammoth arrogance of a government closing off women's escape route from unwanted pregnancy while at the same time withholding the tiny improvement that they'd promised in mothers' financial position, made Lynn sweat with rage.

The women in the tower had been friendly enough to Lynn,

particularly in the early days of their occupancy when the weather was still cold and she brought them thermoses of coffee and let them use her bath and her phone; but she never felt fully accepted, partly, she supposed, because she was married and liked her husband (quite apart from loving him); and partly because she earned her living. She had no particular objections to people squatting or drawing social security, which was how most of the women lived, or, for that matter, to the one called Marsha living on money inherited from a dead relative, most of which she had paid into an account to which all the women had access for the refurbishment of the flats. It seemed a perfectly reasonable use for state or private wealth. Nevertheless, Lynn had the feeling that they had the feeling that she disapproved. Or perhaps it was just Marsha. Marsha was new to the group, and, despite having been the one who struck the first blow to the planks boarding up Collindeane with her axe, didn't actually live there. This was partly (she admitted to Lynn one day when no one was listening, obviously seeing her as a partner in the crime of *incomplete commitment*) because she liked to escape to her own place, and partly because she had a boyfriend called David who was a social worker of rather traditional opinions who would not visit her in a women's commune even if he were allowed through the door. Marsha compensated for her assorted guilts by recounting, to anyone who would listen, conversations in which she had rebuked David for his authoritarian and moralistic attitude to his clients, twiddling her long, dark hair, and pouring her money and energy into the flats. In fact, Lynn doubted how far the thing would have got without her; many of the other twenty-odd women seemed to prefer consciousness-raising to clearing out rubble.

Apart from Posy, of course. Posy provided organisation and skills; there seemed nothing she couldn't do from glazing windows to restarting vandalised lavatories. They made a curious couple, Marsha skinny and penitent, Posy blustering and huge.

From the first day the outer windows of the Collindeane squat had been plastered with posters claiming abortion on demand, but political activity had been postponed while a few flats were made habitable. Now Lynn was on her way home from the dust-filled sweaty inferno that central London had become and her spirits lifted to see evidence that they were thinking as she was thinking, and planned action too.

'CHILD BENEFITS PROTEST PLANNING MEETING, ALL WOMEN WELCOME.'

She noted the time and the place (the roof of the tower, what a nice idea) and continued on her way.

Derek was in. He was marking a student's essay on the kitchen table. The table was spotless and the morning's breakfast things wet and draining. *I'm not going to thank you*, she thought, *because that implies it's my job; but it is nice not having to fight you about housework, as so many women do with their of-course-I'm-in-favour-of-women's-lib husbands.*

'Hello. You look awful,' he said.

'Thank you, my dear.'

'Red haired ladies shouldn't go out in this heat. D'you want a bath?'

'Why, do you think I need one?'

He sniffed. 'Definitely.' He buried his nose in her neck. 'Don't tell me . . . Victoria Line to Brixton, then a bus.'

'I'll have that bath.'

'It's run. I picked up your approach on my antennae.'

She sighed as she lowered herself into pleasantly tepid water. 'You are nice to me.' He was sitting on the toilet seat to chat. 'It takes such ages for water to piddle out of these taps.'

He said airily, 'It's all right, you deserve it.'

She started sweating and feeling dirty again almost as soon as she was out of the water, and the cream she put on to soothe her sunburn only picked up dust from the old house. She went to the kitchen and started hulling strawberries.

'The women in the tower,' she said, 'are going to make some kind of protest over child benefits.'

'Over what, dear?'

'Child benefits.'

'Oh that.'

'Oh that. It's only the nub of what women's liberation's all about. Economic control of mothers by men.'

'Rather academic concern to us, wouldn't you say?'

Her hand slipped on her knife and a tiny thread of blood mixed with strawberry juice. She threw the strawberry away, and immediately wondered why she had. She glanced at Derek. He was deep in his essay. The meaning of the remark was clear, but it could have been at any level. It was probably a joke. He was not the man to follow a cryptic sarcasm with a meaningful silence. Such finely-honed weapons were not for him, he was a babe in arms when it came to verbal quarrels.

'Yes, but you're supposed to be an academic. Look, get that junk off the table, unless your student wants food all over his essay.'

Derek looked at her in reproachful surprise. 'It's not a his, it's a her.' And he whistled smugly as he laid the table.

It was a hot, exhausting business, getting to the roof of the tower. The lift, of course, was long dead, and the shaft bricked off; the stairs were endless, though fortunately less fragile than they looked. Footsteps echoed, and even Lynn's healthy, non-smoking lungs were rebelling before she reached the top. She felt beside her the ghosts of arthritic pensioners, and mothers with push-chairs. She peered into derelict flats as she climbed, trying not to wonder about rats or loose bricks or asbestos. The women had attacked the building, they said, like rising damp, but had not yet risen very far. Most of the front doors were open. Here and there were sticks of furniture – a wet armchair with a rusty spring poking through the fabric, cracked white china cups with fabulous crops of ferny mould. She doubted, if she was honest, whether the squat would last, or if it would spread beyond the first floor, and then she doubted herself for doubting the women. Whatever they might lack in realism or resources, they had an indomitable spirit in Posy.

Lynn had felt sorry for Posy the first time she met her, before sharply reminding herself that feminists do not waste pity on other women's looks. But it was true that big, muscular, denim-clad Posy, with her puggish face and mighty strength was the sort who drew sneers about feminism being the last refuge of women who could not attract a man. Not that Posy cared. The women accepted her for herself and her skills, and that was as it should be. Of course, she did have a way of rubbing people up the wrong way, but that was nothing to do with her looks.

Lynn remembered sitting on a dusty floor one wintry day very early in the squat (she'd gone round with curtain material given to her as a wedding present seven years ago) and hearing Posy's tales and plans.

She came from Australia originally, she said – 'where male chauvinism was invented' – but now regarded herself as a woman of the world. At a very early age she'd realised that the only hope for the world in general and women in particular lay in an international female revolution, led by her; she didn't specify precisely where, how or to what end the revolution would be accomplished, but her deep-set, slightly hooded eyes shone when she described the early skirmishes.

'I was in the first women's liberation group that was ever started,' she liked to allege, 'In fact, I seem to remember I thought of the name. It was an anti-war group in California in 'sixty six. We were talking about having a mill-in at the local draft office – '

'A what?' said someone.

'A mill-in, you all go along and mill about and gum up the works. Anyway, we were planning it and one of the guys said, "Could one of you chicks get us some coffee?" and I got up and said, "Chicks, is it? What about women's liberation?"'

'And that was how it all started?'

'Well, more or less.'

Lynn had enjoyed this as well as Posy's other stories (she'd fought the dowry system in India, she'd been on hand in Southern Africa when women guerillas wanted equality with their male comrades, she'd joined Irish women pelting customs officials with pills and condoms to protest against the contraceptive ban in the South) but she'd shared the scepticism she saw in the other women's eyes. If there was one thing they liked less than leaders, it was people seeking personal glory from the collective struggles of sisters. And perhaps, this afternoon of the Child Benefit meeting, she had at last realised this, for when Lynn stepped out on to the sizzling roof Posy was sitting quietly with Marsha and showing no sign of taking command. There were about fifty women, in various stages of sunbathing undress. A few were smoking dope. Lynn slipped in behind Posy; her bulk provided the only shade there was. Everybody was talking at once, so it wasn't clear whether the meeting had begun.

'It's disgusting.'

'Millions for defence, so-called, nothing for us.'

'Women and children first, eh? First for the chop.'

'International Women's Year plus one, and they think the men of this country would go on strike rather than let their wives have money of their own – '

'They would, too.'

'Sisters, we mustn't let this degenerate into an attack on men.'

'Why not?'

'It's what the state wants. It divides the working class.'

'Men divide the working class. What about those right-on trade union brothers who don't tell their wives what they earn?'

'But we don't want money from men. We want it from the government.'

The argument went round and round. Lynn began to feel irritated. Someone would propose something and the next woman would politely and rationally refute it. The original speaker would accept the refutation, then five minutes later make exactly the same point again. No one was even pretending to be in the chair, and everyone who spoke prefaced her remarks with 'Sorry'. There seemed to be no mechanism for making decisions, even if there had been agreement. Posy was brooding silently, her chin on her knees. Lynn glanced at Marsha, who rolled her eyes hopelessly. Lynn rolled hers back. Posy scowled.

'We'll get local union branches to pass motions – '

'Unions! Instruments of male power, just like – '

'What can we do?'

'March – '

'Where to?'

'We don't want child benefits, we want abortion on demand – '

'The whole money system's sick anyway – '

'Look, I belong to NUPE, and – '

Marsha whispered to Lynn, 'You look like I feel.'

'Is it always like this?'

Posy whispered 'Patience, sisters,' and closed her eyes. Meanwhile someone suggested that they break into small groups to discuss how they felt about motherhood. Someone else said that would be a waste of time, but by then the small groups appeared to have formed themselves by spontaneous fission.

Posy gestured for Lynn and Marsha to get together. 'Raise your consciousness, sisters,' she said, 'I've been there.'

'Is two a small group?' Marsha asked anxiously.

'It's as small as they get,' said Posy, 'one is individualism.' Marsha blushed, looked helplessly at Lynn, apparently forgetting that she was a new girl too.

'Have you got any children, Lynn?'

'Hm. Sore point.'

'Oh – sorry.'

'It's okay, it's okay. No, I haven't. Have you?'

The question seemed to amuse Marsha. She said, 'I've never had sex with a man.'

Lynn tried to hide her surprise which, she supposed, was not very well-mannered. *Or with anyone?* she wondered. Many of the

women were openly lesbian, and she'd assumed Posy was, though
not Marsha, who, after all, had a boyfriend. But what the hell?
Thinking in stereotypes, Lynn. Go to the bottom of the class.
Maybe an element too – *go on, don't let yourself off, you really
ought to be doing this out loud* – of liking Marsha so much she
didn't like to think it of her. Facing the thought, she resolved it;
she thought *so what*? and meant it. The weather was glorious, her
skin was getting used to the sun and she felt suddenly very happy
and powerful and sensual, perched on top of a building that the
authorities had put up and then washed their hands of, with a lot
of relaxed, anarchistic, half-dressed women. She felt a lazy smile
uncurl as she caught a glimpse of why women might choose each
other. Derek, poor Derek, seemed suddenly very small and very
far beneath them. The sun shone through Marsha's hair, she
looked like an anxious saint. Posy was eyeing the two of them
thoughtfully.

Lynn spoke fast. 'I'm married. My . . .' (She hesitated. My
Husband sounded like the queen. My Bloke, My Man, My Fella,
were apologetic.) 'Derek wants us to have kids. Well, one,
anyway.'

'And you don't want to?' said Marsha.

'I can't.' It sounded like a serious illness. 'I don't mean physically
can't. I don't know if I can or not. I'm the most efficient con-
traceptor in the world. Textbook. Cap in every night, even when
he's dead on his feet. Sometimes I feel I'm fizzing with fertility and
then I ask him to wear a durex as well, *and* withdraw. It drives
him crazy.'

'So what do you mean, you can't have children?'

'I can't take the decision.'

Lynn's euphoria was gone. She was down again – bored,
almost, at the prospect of having this conversation once more,
even though she'd never discussed it with anyone other than
Derek, and (endlessly) herself. It was impossible to explain to
feminists like Marsha in their mid-twenties how she felt. They
were still intoxicated and belligerent about their freedom not to
have babies. It was going to be interesting when this generation
became old enough to realise it was almost too late for them too.
What would happen? A lovely harvest of strong little girls and
gentle boys with early middle-aged parents? Or a new bitterness, a
politics that saw in their choice just another male plot? 'I can't
take the decision. It would be like voluntary mutilation.'

'You mean birth?'

'No, no. I think that must be amazing. I'm talking about my life, me.' She shrugged, reached for something to say that didn't sound as banal as: 'I'm used to pleasing myself.' She looked around at animated knots of women on the hot roof, as if she would escape.

'So, don't do it. Your husband isn't trying to force you, is he?'

The idea of Derek trying to force anything! 'Let me tell you about my ideal day. It isn't always like this. But sometimes, on an ordinary, working weekday, I lie in bed till nine o'clock and read a novel. Then I get an off-peak train into town, deliver some copy here, go and see a firm there that wants some promotional stuff written, set up some work for next week. Have lunch with someone useful or nice or preferably both. Pop in at some specialist library – you'd be amazed the places you can get into by just looking confident, even military installations at the height of a bomb-scare. Then home to work, or maybe a film. There's nothing so delightful as an afternoon film in the West End. I work out why everyone else is there – she's retired, he's unemployed, they've come in for an illicit grope – me, I've given myself an afternoon off because I feel like it. I work too, of course, but I decide when.'

'Yes, and you get paid for what you do.'

'Oh Marsha, isn't it sordid to bring it down to that?'

'It isn't sordid at all. You don't want to be dependent on your husband.'

'But – but – ' How could she explain about Derek? 'This child benefit thing was a clincher. I was so *bloody* angry – I thought – my God – what woman in her right mind would become a mother, to be treated with such contempt? But it's all excuses. I'm frightened. I've been the go-getting career woman for so long I think I've lost the bits of me that could love a baby, but you *have* to. And that's an oppression in itself. A few weeks ago I thought – the hell with it. I'll show them. I'll have a baby, and survive as me. And then, before I could leap on Derek, I saw a little blind kid. And I thought, Jesus, am I mad? I've been wondering if I could tolerate the sweet brilliant daughter that my fantasies beget – what if I got one of those lolling, slobbering monsters that you see, that grow and grow and never grow up and suck their parents into dry wisps. So I told Derek I had a headache.' Lynn's voice was shaking, and she saw anxiety and guilt on Marsha's face, as if it were *her* fault, for heaven's sake. 'I'm mutilated either way.'

Marsha said slowly and carefully, 'It's only society that makes you think that. A society that values women by their children and nothing else – '

'I am not undervalued, Marsha, and I still want a child.'

There! It was said! The meeting was coming together again, and not a moment too soon. Posy was on her feet and demanding that everyone listen to her.

'We're all angry, right?' The women seemed to have forgotten their dislike of leaders in relief at her air of purpose. 'We're all angry, right?' The women looked angry. Posy had a good sense of timing and her voice shook. 'And we want to take some action. It might not be effective. We know we can't get this appalling betrayal reversed this minute. We know we're dealing with forces that are mightier than ourselves – at the moment.' Lynn glanced at the felt boots that encased Posy's rocklike feet and found it hard to believe that there were mightier forces. 'We want something short, sharp and appropriate to give a keynote to a long-term struggle. Am I right? Right. Now. Tell me what would happen at a car factory, for example. What would happen if the men were promised a pay-rise, and at the last minute management said, sorry, we've changed our minds. What would happen, eh? Would the workers sit around in the sun and have nice chats and smoke joints as I see some of you are doing, just to keep your wits razor-sharp at this watershed of history?' Some of the guilty women grinned sheepishly; others screwed up their faces to draw even deeper on the weedy cigarettes. 'What would they do, eh? Go back to work like good children, and say, oh well, next year?'

Posy singled out a timid woman and glared till she said 'No.'

'What, then? What would they do?'

'Go on strike, I suppose,' someone said.

Posy cupped her hand dramatically to her ear. 'Pardon?'

'Go on strike.'

'On – ?'

'*Strike*.'

'Oh, on *strike*?' She could have made it big as a pantomime dame. 'On strike? They'd go on strike, would they? So what must the mothers do, sisters?'

'Go on strike?'

Posy had mistimed.

'What do you mean?' women demanded.

'Mean? You know what a strike is?'

'Yes, but who against? Against their kids?'

'Against the state.'

Lynn heard an angry voice say, 'Mothers don't work for the state'; it was only when Posy turned and said, 'Wanna bet?' that she realised the voice was hers. Posy went on: 'I think we should organise a mass march of mothers to the Social Security office. When we get there, the mothers'll leave the children for a symbolic hour.'

To Lynn it seemed that all the other women had disappeared; the issue trembled between her and Posy. The idea was simply grotesque.

'What point would you be making?'

'What point? What point?' Posy's lip curled. 'Let's not worry too much about the point. The finer points of socialist-feminist theory, which may not be of too much interest to housewives who were relying on this money and aren't going to get it. Women whose husbands are getting their pay-rises all right but neither know nor care what's happening to food prices and expect them to manage on the same housekeeping money as last year, and oh yes,' she turned on the women in socialist badges, who hadn't said a word, 'that happens, even in the sainted working class. Anyway, let's just do it, hm? And see if the women don't get the *point*, even where we intellectuals fail?'

Lynn got up and made for the stairs. Marsha followed.

'Come back, Lynn.'

'I didn't come here to be attacked. I don't need her.'

'You were quite fierce yourself.'

'Maybe. Well, that's my problem.'

She ran down the long height of the building, her one thought to get back to Derek. But he would be out, damn it, shopping.

She straightened her sun-glasses and came out of the tower into sunlit stillness. Her feet sizzled on the pavement – she must have stepped in something wet. She would go home for a cool drink and a long lie-down. She screwed up her eyes behind her dark lenses. Something caught her attention, red cloth flapping. A black girl was standing by the big sign that proclaimed feminist occupation of the tower. She was short and young, maybe still in her teens. Her dark skin had the slight pallor that might romantically be explained by its being too long in a damp and foggy climate, but was more likely to be the result of the rape of a slave a few generations back. She wore a red scarf on her head, and red cheesecloth draped her body, though whether it was a dress, a skirt and blouse or just bits of material was not clear. She was staring at the notice that claimed 'A Woman's Right to Choose' and Lynn noticed, as a stray breath of wind stirred the stillness of the robes, the clear round bulge of the girl's belly.

'Hello,' Lynn said.

'Hello,' said the girl. She spoke as if half-asleep or drugged; somehow not quite there. Her features moved slowly, exaggeratedly, like a bad actress.

'Did you come for the meeting? They're on the roof.'

The girl shook her head and glanced again at the notice, furtively.

'Do you need an abortion? Is that it?'

'There isn't a baby.' The voice was very definite.

'What's your name?'

'Judy.'

'Have you been to a doctor?'

'I took some pills.'

'Did your doctor give them to you?'

A sheepish grin. 'Don't ask who gave them. I took them all, swallowed them right down. They said if I did there wouldn't be a baby any more. Don't ask where I got the money.'

'Judy, have you been to a proper doctor?'

'There isn't a baby, not now.'

Lynn felt helpless. There quite clearly was a baby, or something, in that stomach. She said, 'Look, there's this charity that I know where you can talk it all over and they'll help with whatever you decide to do.'

'You mean kill the baby?'

Lynn said craftily, 'I thought you said there wasn't one.'

'Is there?'

'It's not exactly a baby – but you do look pregnant.' She put her arm round Judy. 'Don't you? You go to this place I'm telling you about. I don't have the number . . . can I contact you?'

Judy smiled beatifically and shook her head.

'You ring me then. Tomorrow. Here's my number.'

Still smiling, Judy walked away, waddling slightly.

'Don't forget,' Lynn called.

But Judy didn't phone. Next time Lynn saw her was at the demonstration outside the Social Security office. Lynn's compromise between participating and staying away was to persuade the local paper to let her report it. That way her ambivalence could pass as objectivity.

Feminist organisers of a 'strike' by mothers were doubly disappointed today –

Despite hopes of a larger turnout, local women's liberationists were well pleased –

Fifty women and children picketed the local office of the Department of Health and Social Security . . . their original plan for a thousands-strong 'strike' in which mothers would have dumped their children at the office in support of their 'pay claim' was thwarted by Department officials who closed up for the day –

Lynn wondered sadly how many of the women standing about outside the offices were new converts, and how many were organisers. Her interest revived at the appearance of one of her neighbours from Seyer Street, a fat, hot, sad, toothless woman shuffling along with a push-chair, her numerous children swarming round her, fighting, snatching each other's bright gluey sweets, clutching each other's hands. *Ordinary Woman joins women's movement*! Now there was a case for child benefit! The husband, of course, was never in work, but held the male prerogative of receiving every penny of the family's dole money straight into his tobacco-stained fingers.

Lynn stepped forward with her notebook just as Marsha approached the woman to welcome her.

'We're glad to see you.'

The woman, Mrs Hindley, said nothing.

'Do you recognise me? I live in your road,' Lynn tried.

'Hindley's giro hasn't come – '

'Unfortunately, the office is closed – '

'Closed!' The woman looked at her children, at each other's throats like puppies in the dirt. 'Closed!'

'You see, it's a demonstration. Let me explain.'

'I'll have to come back tomorrow. Stop that, you kids.'

'Please stay, it's just your sort of situation – '

But the woman trailed off miserably, the children demanding their turns to share the push-chair with the baby.

Lynn stood and watched a little longer. The women talked to passers-by, and there was much emphatic nodding of heads and signing of petitions.

Public opinion seemed sympathetic, and two hundred signatures were –

One noted non-signator was Mrs Hindley of Seyer Street, who found herself rather inconvenienced by such a large group of women campaigning for her rights –

God damn it Lynn, how cheap! Whose side are you on?

She crossed it out.

She shivered in spite of the sun as a brown figure dressed in red crept into her field of vision. It was Judy, pregnant as ever.

'Hello. Do you want that number?'

Again the slow, ghostly smile. 'It won't be necessary.'

'You've decided to keep the baby?'

'There isn't a baby.'

'All the same, I wish you'd – '

Judy put out her hands and held Lynn as she might hold a child to whom something very important had to be explained.

'There isn't *room* for a baby.'

And she continued her slightly swaying walk towards the demonstrators, who gave her a banner to hold saying 'Child Benefits Now'.

2

After the Summer

The government appointed a minister with special responsibility for the drought. He walked along cracked river-beds with film-crews and measured reservoirs. He was photographed pulling dead roots from dusty earth. He responded with courtesy to suggestions that aboriginal or Red Indian rainmakers be hired by his department. He wrote a lot of letters. And early in September, it rained.

It was as if the skies had grown tired of complaints. I give you a good summer and all you do is moan and appoint ministers. You want rain, do you? Watch this. The skies opened. Rivers and reservoirs overflowed. The umbrella sellers re-appeared – particularly in those parts of the country where domestic water supplies had been cut off and consumers needed shelter while they queued at the standpipes pending re-connection.

Lynn was shopping when the first rain hit her part of London. She'd expected rain when she left the house, but still wore only a light cotton frock and sandals. Big wet drops fell on her skin, burnt so red and leathery that it clashed with the bleached gold of her hair through which drops coursed, sizzling in the dryness. The drops were grey and warm, soft and plump as ripe fruit. She felt her lips smile as she walked. Drops hit the ground and disappeared in the dirt. More followed. She stood still, listening for the blades of grass that would poke up between paving stones and duck down again to spread the news: it's raining. Get your green on.

She looked round for strangers to share her pleasure. The rain was sheeting down now, the sky was rumbling. She wanted to pull off her dress and dance, but smiling at strangers would have to do.

The street was empty. She was astonished. Had the magic that brought the rain spirited away the people? Had a sacrifice been demanded?

They were sheltering. They were escaping from the rain drops into doorways and shops. They were hiding in the bus-shelter and in telephone boxes. They were covering their heads with newspapers, their arms with plastic shopping bags as they ran plish-plash across the zebra and into the post office and Tescos.

'It's not prussic acid, you know,' Lynn muttered spreading her arms to feel the drops falling on their tender undersides.

'Isn't it wonderful?' she glowed in the packed greengrocers. The shelter-seekers moved away. Lynn giggled, patted some shrivelled tomatoes. '*They* know it's wonderful.'

'Please don't touch the tomatoes,' said the assistant.

'I'll take a pound.'

'You can stay and shelter if you want.'

'What from?' Lynn sang.

'Some people.'

'Catch her death of cold.'

'Lives in Seyer Street.'

'Oh *well* –'

She waltzed into an off-licence.

'Bottle of champagne, please.'

'You just got married?'

'Why, do I look miserable?'

Her hair flapped in her face and she sucked water from the rats' tails. She jumped in filling puddles, and grinned at toys abandoned on neat lawns. Windows slammed angrily shut as she passed, and she heard the howls of children thwarted in their play. The sky was grey. The brown grass was springing to life. Trees wept. She turned the corner into Seyer Street. She'd hoped the women in the tower would be doing a rain-dance too, but they were skulking inside – anxious, no doubt, to see if the building was waterproof. 'What if it isn't?' she shouted gaily, her words lost in the beat of the rain, 'it's only water.' She resisted an urge to sing 'Singin' in the Rain', but it was close. She looked down the street.

Six tanned naked Hindley children were carefully mixing dust and water into mud and throwing it at each other. Reaching up to the rain. Rubbing it on themselves, drinking it. They were malnourished, ill-kempt noisy little vandals most of the time, and Lynn kept a weather eye on her windows when they ventured to her end of the street; now she wanted to hug them.

She glanced at their mother, leaning on the gate, watching. Mrs Hindley glared back, defensively. Lynn smiled. Mrs Hindley's lip quivered. 'They're only young once,' she said. She was drenched.

'Derek! De-rek!'

'You don't have to shout.'

'Sorry, didn't see you sitting there. Always got your nose in a book. No good will come of it.'

'Have you been down a well?'

'Derek! It's *raining*!'

'So it is. Ah well, we had it coming.'

'Derek, for heaven's sake. It's redemption, not retribution!'

'Coo, 'ark at 'er,' said Derek, and she clasped wet hands to his face and ran them down the front of his shirt. He protested, 'Stop it, you're wet, I'm trying to read – '

'All right.' She flounced into the kitchen. 'Read, then.' He followed as she knew he would. She brushed him aside and popped the champagne. She took a glass and went to the back door and raised it like a chalice. When it was full she swilled it down and held it up for more. She put the full glass and an empty glass and the champagne bottle on a tray.

'Now where are you off to?'

'A thanksgiving ceremony.' She stopped at the door of the bedroom and barred his way. 'Er, sorry. It's women only.'

'Oh. Okay.'

'However –'

'No, I don't want special treatment.'

' – in view of your long commitment to feminism, you can be an honorary woman.'

'Oh thank you, dear. Thank you very much.'

Lynn's cotton dress struck to her as she tried to pull it over her head, leaving her helpless and muffling the noises she made as Derek started to play the washboard on her ribs.

'You've torn it. Derek! You can sew it up!'

'Hush. You're like an eel.'

'What about your reading, Professor – ? That was so important –'

'You are ruining my career, Jezebel – ' His fingers were all over her and in her and around her. 'You're very wet.'

'I'm raining.'

He stopped. 'You haven't got your cap in.'

She muttered into the pillow, 'It's okay.'

Derek took away his hand and sat up and looked at her. 'Lynn.'

'It's okay, Derek. Please.' *Now, please, before I think. Which of us would be here now if our parents had thought? Which bird or flower or puppy for that matter?*

He put his fingers to his lips. 'Lynn, I don't even know what you're saying. I don't know if you're saying we can take a chance or if you've . . . changed your mind. I must know.' He kissed her. 'And, what's more important, you must.'

'I thought you wanted it!' she shouted, furiously. 'I thought you wanted it!' She got up on her knees and with a strength she didn't usually have, pushed him backwards. He smiled, puzzled, slightly tense still, but not arguing. His penis flopped against his stomach. She reached for the champagne and filled her mouth with it, then put her mouth to him to let him feel the bubbles.

'Lynn – '

She moved up his body, kissed his mouth with foam and bubbles and eased herself on to him. She took her weight on her knees and rose up and down, swigging now from a wine glass, now from a water glass.

Derek said, 'Er, excuse me.'

'Yes?'

'I'm here, you know.'

'Who? Oh yes, you.'

'Is this rape or what?'

'No,' she said, 'it's a woman's right to choose,' and she poured champagne and rainwater all over the two of them and all over the bed and continued to rise up and down and back and forth and round and round until everywhere was flooded and everyone was drowned.

Next day it was still raining. There was nowhere to hang washing and a stain was spreading on the bathroom ceiling. The Hindley kids ambushed passers-by in Seyer Street with water-pistols. Derek was shy and kept starting up conversations on everything except what they were both thinking. At last he said, 'Did you mean it? Because if not – '

Lynn's mouth said, 'I think I did.' She had to mean it. She might be pregnant already. She consulted a calendar and did sums. She might indeed.

Well. That was okay. She could still change her mind. She'd be sensible now. She'd use her cap and her little bombs of sperm-killer and hope that one chance taken had not been fatal. Fatal! What an extraordinary word! Anyway, if it had been – fertile, fateful – she still had the number of the charitable clinic that she kept by the phone for Judy.

Why hadn't Judy rung? Had she changed her mind, feeling in her rounding belly the same movement and certainty that Lynn now felt in her still flat one?

Whatever was in there would barely be visible through a strong lens, yet Lynn knew she could not abort it. It was not the physical details; she'd read the anti-abortionists' propaganda and it left her as cold as a trip to the butcher's. It was something else – something more indulgent, academic, philosophical; the rag-bag of potential that a person could be –

The friends this person will make (some of them now no more than tears of ambivalence in their own mothers' eyes), the events she will create or influence, the kindness she will draw from strangers when she bangs her knee. And the rest she will give to the hardnosed lady with the heart that quakes when she picks up the phone and says 'have you any comment to make on the allegations that you – ?' and sometimes has days of phone-phobia when work simply has to be postponed; a rest for her and a chance for the other one (the one Lynn knew was there because she was always telling her to shut up), the one that says 'what's the matter?' and 'tell me all about it' and listens and does not pounce.

Panicking but elated, Lynn rehearsed to herself the reasons for not carrying this pregnancy to term (if there was a pregnancy) and found them interesting but irrelevant.

Even the government seemed in league.

Under pressure from feminists, poverty campaigners and its own back bench, and faced with innocent disclaimers from the trade union movement, the government had agreed to compromise over child benefits. A very small payment would be made to mothers. It would be financed partly from public funds and partly by taking more tax from fathers. Thus would the promised transfer from wallet to purse take place – but by such slow degrees and in such small amounts and so far into the future that neither purse nor wallet would seriously feel the difference. Lynn felt women had won a victory and had been conned.

When her period started, there was no room for disappointment or relief, she just felt shocked. She'd known she was pregnant, and she'd turned her brain inside out making the child welcome! She willed the familiar ache to go away from her back; she imagined the foetus (a little girl called Jane – *a dull old name, kid, but it seems to be yours; and anyway, you're going to be such a stunner, it won't matter*) successfully fertilised that extraordinary day while the rain bucketed down, but not quite managing to embed in the threadbare lining of her aged mother's womb. Tears squeezed from Lynn's eyes at the thought of Jane clinging to the walls like a climber in a landslide; *hang on Janey, hang on*, – she saw the little bruised fists and heard Jane's last sad cry as her home collapsed and broke up and she was washed out on a tide of blood.

Lynn ran a bath and lowered herself into the water; she watched fascinated as the blood flowed out of her and dispersed into red threads and clouds and whorls, and peered close for a little swimming daughter whom she would rescue with her finger and her thumb.

Derek and she kept on trying. But three more periods came, each on the day and at the hour it was due, and one at the very moment (as far as Lynn could work out without questioning her too closely) that Judy Matthews was delivered (insisting to the last 'there isn't a baby') of a healthy half-white boy called Jim. Judy remained vague and cryptic, but spent a lot of time at Collindeane where the women made her welcome and where Jim was the first customer for a planned creche. No one knew where they lived the rest of the time.

He was a plump, placid boy with a philosophical approach to life, which was just as well; sometimes Judy would appear eager to relinquish him to the care of Lynn or anyone else who was around, and would sit by herself, crooning or asleep or stricken with horror in some private dream into which no one else was allowed, and when she came to she would get up to leave alone, fiercely asserting that she had no baby. Sometimes she left him behind overnight, and then would come beating at the doors in the early morning with overflowing milk and charges of kidnapping. Other days she hugged him to herself, was peaceful, even prayerful; she became obsessed with a mural some women were making of goddesses of ancient religions, and though she would never help paint she would sit cross-legged in her red robes (just thin cotton cloth, even in the depths of winter) and contemplate and nurse her baby, wide-eyed.

Meanwhile Lynn told Derek they should take a break from nightly sex and bought a thermometer and some graph paper. She watched her temperature cruise along at 98.4 for two weeks, then it did a little hop up to 98.7. Derek suggested they should stop doing it with Lynn on top. She lay back with cushions tilting her hips so that the chosen sperm could freewheel to posterity. She tried to think soft maternal thoughts, and was gratified to note that Jim's warm brown body was provoking these in abundance. There was even a day when playing with him caused her to miss a deadline and the manufacturer of plastic curtains for whom she was supposed to be writing a promotion gave her a rocket down the phone and she didn't care a bit. (Fourteen days after the hop in the graph, her period started.) She wondered whether years of thinking tough feminist thoughts could make you sterile. She steered clear of the abortion campaign, put all her energies into Jim and Judy and the creche. An American magazine asked her for an article on 'Male chauvinism, British style.' She declined, and they didn't ask again. She found she was living off Derek and she didn't even mind.

She read the worst baby books she could find, and strolled (menstruating) round the baby departments of shops, desensitising herself to the anger that their hideous commercialism evoked. *It's all right, body, I know what you're thinking, but you can go ahead, no one's pushed me into this, I've decided.* It was winter. Jim was starting to smile at his mother and at all the women, but Lynn liked to think he had a special gummy grin for her.

The cold was making Posy irritable; at least, she said it was the cold, but the women said behind her back that it was the way she had been proved wrong by the squat being so successful without leadership; and Lynn thought Marsha's refusal to move in with Posy and continued attachment to David Laing had something to do with it. Whatever it was, Posy kept ending arguments by saying, 'Do what you want. I'm going back to Australia soon'; and the response 'Oh don't' was wearing thin with use.

Marsha was defensive. She said she only hung around with David for research purposes.

'For heaven's sake, read a book,' Posy snorted.

'He's telling me all about the crisis in the welfare state.'

'Oh yeah, the crisis of capitalism part two.'

'There's no point in talking to you.'

Once Marsha confided to Lynn that she didn't even like David that much; she just respected him and felt a sort of desperate attachment, not because he had any sympathy with the women's movement but more because he hadn't.

'How do you mean?'

'Well – living here – I mean, I don't, but it's the same because I do *live* here, I mean, here is where I live if you see what I mean – it all becomes rather overwhelming. I love living here, I've never felt so free and useful. But it's a bit of a hothouse and it doesn't prove anything, does it?'

'I don't know,' said Lynn.

'I mean, I agree with everything everybody says, but it would be surprising if I didn't, wouldn't it? You're not exactly encouraged to think outside the orthodoxy, are you?'

Lynn smiled to hear her own thoughts so exquisitely expressed.

'I mean, a lot of women would say there isn't an orthodoxy, just because it isn't written down as one, but if you say something you damn soon know whether it's in or out. If I slap my hand over my mouth many more times, I'll stay that way. Don't laugh, you're the same.'

'And where does David Laing fit into all this?'

'It's the arguments we have. The women say social workers are agents of state repression and control. He says his first function is to stop everyone else feeling guilty.'

Lynn sighed. 'He's not wrong either.'

Marsha grabbed at her hair like a lifeline. 'I don't agree with everything he says.'

'Give me an example.'

'He told me about these two women he visits. A forty-year-old spinster and her dreadful mother. The mother's got a stranglehold on the daughter, she never lets her leave home or get married or anything, and now the mother's half-mad and incontinent, doubly incontinent, that means –'

'I know what it means.'

' – yes, well, and even violent sometimes, and every time Dave goes to see them – which he does in his own time, there's nothing he can do – the daughter gets hold of his hand and begs him, *begs* him with tears – to get her mother into a home.'

'And can't he?'

'He says with the cuts there isn't space for old women whose only – *only*! – problem is that they crap on the carpet from time to time and who have able-bodied daughters to care for them at home. He said he once told the daughter that the only way he could help would be if she walked out. Which of course she wouldn't do.'

Lynn looked at Marsha with respect. 'Have you raised that here?'

'Yes, and they said the reason mother's gone insane is probably the stress of being a woman in this society, and the reason the daughter's exploited is because she's been taught to believe it's her role to be exploited, all of which is absolutely true, but we don't have many exploited daughters or senile mothers living here, do we? Do you think I should sleep with David?'

'Good heavens! I mean . . . haven't you already?'

'No.'

'Why?'

'I don't know if I want to.'

'Don't then.'

Marsha sighed. 'He wants it, and I suppose he has a right – '

'Rubbish.'

'No, a right to want it.'

'I suppose he can want what he wants to want, but you don't go to bed with people out of guilt.'

'But if I don't, that'll be out of guilt too.'

'Posy, you mean?'

'I do love her, I see right through her rages. She wants me to go away with her.'

'"To Australia?"' Lynn mocked.

'Oh, more than that, my dear, a world revolutionary cruise. Well, it could be fun. Some people say it's a cop-out to say you're bisexual, all proper feminists are lesbians. I suspect it's a cop-out to give up men when you've never had one.'

'We could always set up a group called the improper feminists.'

'Trouble is, I don't know if I'd be able to join.'

Lynn realised that Judy hadn't been in for over a week. She felt almost bereft; she worried what might have happened to Judy, but she actually missed the little boy. She asked around. None of the women seemed unduly worried; Judy had a right to come and go as she pleased. Lynn wondered if she was the only one to have noticed that Judy had had specific needs: to leave her baby for a while and wander and dream and meditate; to proclaim that she had no baby and to be coaxed patiently back into accepting that she had, that he was lovable and that she was caring for him splendidly, for he seemed to be thriving despite her eccentricities. Lynn also found herself wondering whether her own care might have something to do with it – but who, she wondered, was she mothering?

She confided her unspecified fears in Marsha, but her response was the same as the others: Judy came and went; it was okay. Lynn remained uneasy, and berated herself for not even knowing Judy's address. And when she did finally turn up, Lynn took no pleasure in being proved right to have worried.

It was after a particularly agitated night in which she and Derek had argued themselves into knots of exasperation and hostility, he having said that she ought to see the doctor about her infertility. What did he mean, *her* infertility, she'd retorted, and he'd said, sorry, of course he meant *they* ought to see the doctor, and she'd said, Freudian slip. And then they'd had a silence, broken by her saying it was probably just a matter of time, and he'd pointed out that she didn't have unlimited time and again she'd demanded what did he mean *she* didn't? Then he had started to shout: damn it, it wasn't his fault that men could go on fathering children till they were ninety but usually only by women who weren't too far the wrong side of thirty-five; he was prepared to take personal responsibility for every other form of unfairness suffered by women but *not that* and now he was going to sleep. His display of doing so with his back turned gave Lynn the giggles because she remembered the speech the best man had made at their wedding, all about how the point of married couples sleeping together was not the maximisation of sex but the minimisation of high dudgeon because it took a very pompous person indeed to remain umbraged while rubbing bottoms with the offending party. And they'd kissed and made up but Lynn stayed awake for a long time, realising that by confiding in anbyody (let alone going to some damn infertility clinic) she would leave behind forever the no-woman's-land of *I'd quite like a baby but I don't really mind* . . .

She woke early, meaning to spend all day writing, but she couldn't concentrate so she wandered down to Collindeane. And there she learned that a bruised and silent Judy had come crawling to the door in the small hours, alone, terrorised and unbudgeable from her assertion that she had not got and never had had a baby. And this time even Lynn could not change Judy's mind. Apart from the anxiety, this hurt.

'Who hurt you, Judy? Was it an accident?'

You could almost see hysteria boil behind the film of her eyes; her lips were locked but she would nod and shake her head, glaring at the goddess-mural with its muscular Virgin Mary and its Boadicea.

No it was not an accident. Yes she had been hit. Yes by a man. Yes a man she knew. Yes a man she lived with. And where was the baby? What baby? There was no baby. There was no baby.

Lynn said to Marsha, 'I'm worried. Do you think David could help?'

'David? He's the last thing she needs. He'll give her a lecture on accepting her responsibilities.'

'But Jim.'

'Yes, we ought to find Jim.'

They found that Jim was in care. There was no information about Judy, but David promised to keep them posted.

Lynn said to Derek, 'You know the Archers.'

'Not an everyday story of country folk?'

'Yes.'

'Good heavens. I thought I was joking. I thought you were

talking about someone we knew.'

'No, but you remember they had a character who couldn't get pregnant – '

'Daisy the cow as I recall.'

'Shut up. They tried and they tried, but – '

'Lynn, dearest, what are you saying? The Archers don't fuck.'

'No, but in the end they gave up and adopted, and lo and behold all her tensions disappeared and she got pregnant.'

'So instead of one baby they had two.'

'That wasn't quite – '

'What's brought this on? Is that what you want to do?'

'I thought we might foster.'

'Hm. Do you know anything about it?'

'Marsha's bloke's a social worker, he'd be able to tell us.'

Derek said, 'I thought you had to be a pillar of the community to foster.'

'That's why I thought we'd be so suitable. No, I gather they're pretty desperate.'

The quarrel of the night before seemed forgotten. When they went to bed, Derek said, 'We'll keep trying for our own, though, won't we?' and Lynn chucked him under the chin.

'Don't look so anxious. You're getting to quite like it, aren't you?'

'It's not too bad.'

'I wonder if I'll be able to stop you when we don't have to do it any more.'

'You may well find you can't,' said Derek.

'I think I've found out what happened,' said David Laing grimly.

He was sitting behind his desk in the Social Services department and Lynn was sitting opposite him with Marsha, trying to work out why Marsha liked him and whether she herself did. He was in his twenties but managed to seem both older and younger; his manner of speaking was anxious and dogmatic, and the thick upper rims of his glasses only added to his appearance of constant worry. His hair was quite short but didn't look right that way; he might have been to the barber's to please his mother. He sipped compulsively at a plastic mug of cheap machine coffee; he had not offered Lynn or Marsha any, but this seemed to be preoccupation rather than rudeness. Lynn remembered being told he was addicted to the stuff.

It was a great high-ceilinged hall of an office in a converted mansion; the hall was divided off into territories by shoulder-high movable screens. Bells shrilled constantly; it took a while to realise they were not a burglar alarm but telephones out of sync. David had his off the hook, but even while he was speaking people kept bustling round his screen and saying things like 'when you've got a minute, Dave' as they dumped piles of photocopied sheets into his in-tray.

Judy, it seemed, was known to the Social Services. 'A classic case of multiple deprivation and inadequacy,' Dave called her.

'You mean black and a woman' said Marsha quickly.

'May I do this?'

'Course, sorry, go on.'

'Father unemployed, mother feckless, history of mental disturbance and so forth. Threw her out when they found she was pregnant – GP no help with abortion, told her she had a real live baby in there and did she want to see it chopped up in a pedal-bin. Sent her along to us. She saw a colleague of mine who was not of the same persuasion as the doctor, denied the chopped-up babies story and said she'd try and arrange things. Only Judy was a bit confused by then, understood her to be saying there wasn't a baby at all and just wandered off. By the time we saw her again, of course, it was much too late.'

'So she had the baby, right, but why is he in care?'

'The social security found she was living with a man.'

'What, the father?'

'White guy, could be. She'd only just moved in too. She'd had a bedsitter of her own, been managing quite well apparently, only she took up with him and went to his place. Well, of course, they don't pay social security money in those circumstances, if the woman's living with a bloke he's got to support her. They're a lot of insensitive buggers. They went barging in late at night, caught them in bed together, took away Judy's order book and said they might prosecute. She flipped. Made them take the baby away, kept shrieking that he wasn't hers, there wasn't a baby and she wouldn't be any man's prisoner.' His grimace was half sad, half cynical. 'She's obviously picked up something in that tower of yours. Strictly speaking, it's not the social security's province, taking away people's babies, that's our job, but they were sufficiently disturbed by her behaviour to bring him to us.'

'And the bruises?'

'Two versions. The man in the case says she threw a fit of hysterics and fell down the stairs. Someone else in the house says he heard an argument to the effect that if he was going to have to keep her and her brat she could damn well clean the place up, and then the guy hit her. I don't suppose we'll ever know.'

'What happens now?'

'Judy's caseworker thinks she ought to go into hospital for a bit.'

'And Jim?'

'We'll find him some foster parents and hope it won't be too long.'

Lynn said, 'I'd like to foster him.'

'Oh.' David looked startled, then pleased. 'Yes, well, you know him quite well, don't you?'

'I know both of them.'

'On the face of it, it sounds like a good idea. You'd have to talk to the caseworker, be interviewed and so forth, and many hundreds of pieces of paper will have to be moved around desks before such an obvious and humane solution can be implemented, but time will be on your side really because everyone knows what a bad thing it is to leave a child motherless.' By means of some gesture, which Lynn could not remember afterwards, he indicated that the interview was at an end. As she went away, she wished he were not quite so indiscriminate in his use of irony; it made it hard to spot.

The Collindeane women worried and felt guilty about Judy going into a psychiatric hospital, and vowed to visit her and offer her a home when she came out. But once inside she refused to see anyone; she relapsed into depression, was violent with the nurses even under sedation and would not speak except to deny, viciously and emphatically, that she was a mother. At any mention of Jim, she turned her face to the wall. And one evening, when there were no staff to supervise her, she walked out of the hospital and disappeared.

Lynn worried for a few days that she would turn up at the house and claim Jim, and then for a few more days that she would not turn up at all; then she dismissed worry and guilt as self-indulgence and got on with the business of loving and enjoying him. He was amazing. He was all fun and no trouble. He slept through the night, and even in the daytime seemed to have got the idea that the clatter of her typewriter meant that he should lay low

and say as little as possible; and that if he complied, all his
physical and emotional needs would be attended to by a calm and
cheery woman who would sometimes take him to a cold but
curious place where there were colours on the walls and hordes of
women whose only apparent purpose in life was to pay him attention. And Lynn was finding that the pressure of his needs
didn't mean she worked less, just more efficiently.

The Social Services department gave her good support. In fact
she sometimes felt tempted to remind them that it was only a baby
to whom she was giving houseroom, not some adolescent vandal.
The caseworker phoned at least once a week to ask if there were
any problems. There were group meetings for foster-parents, if
she cared to attend. And she received a tax-free non-means-tested
index-linked fostering allowance of nearly ten pounds a week. Judy
had received just three pounds from the social security to cover
Jim's needs, and that only before she moved in with a man. Lynn
was also entitled to extra payments to buy Jim's birthday presents,
and help with her telephone bill.

She seethed for several months, then confronted David.

He seemed surprised. 'It's our normal rate for fostering babies.
When he gets older, it'll be more; if he turns into a juvenile
delinquent, there's a modest living to be made.'

'But I'm treated so much better than Judy was!'

'Different departments,' said David, his face hidden by a sheaf
of papers.

Lynn was well into her next burst of indignation before she
realised he was joking. At least – not joking. It wasn't humour that
lit his eyes when he lowered the papers, it was bitterness and
something else, even inspiration.

'My dear Lynn. Sit down.'

She didn't like being called his dear, but she sat.

'What you must understand is that the guiding principle on
which the social services of this country are based is to reward,
support and compensate those who make a mess of their lives or
renege on their responsibilities at the expense of those who do not.
I am one example of this principle in action; I do not, for instance, spend very much time patting young children on the back
for never having been through the courts, or helping industrious
breadwinners to get a pay-rise. Another is the man who can
get – '

' – more on social security than he can working, come on

David, you can do better than that, you know that's only because wages are low.'

'May I continue?'

'Go on.'

'You have come across the principle at work in a rather more exquisite form: the fact that we will give you money that, had we given it to Judy in the first place, she might never have abandoned her son at all. Then, of course, you have to take into account the additional costs that we shall no doubt run into in a few years when Judy turns up again and wants him back – '

'I won't fight,' said Lynn, 'if that's what you mean.'

'Possibly, but we may. The best interests of the child are paramount, you see – which interests are best served, apparently, by first of all insisting that the child is born, then persecuting the mother until she flips and then handing the child over to you. You understand?'

'No.'

'Neither do I. I want some coffee. Do you?'

'No thanks.'

He pushed some pennies towards her. 'The machine's over there. I take it black with no sugar.' The absent-minded command was so astonishing that she could only obey. She pressed the coins into the machine and a plastic cup appeared in a doorway to be rained upon by acrid brown granules and warm water.

David said, 'Have you got children of your own?'

'No.'

'Pity.'

'Yes, it is, isn't it?'

'You see, just supposing I wanted to commit suicide in the career structure and make a name for myself as a radical critic of social policy – just supposing – there's a wonderful game we could play.'

'Oh?' said Lynn coldly.

'Little dream of mine. Judy comes back, wants Jim. We oppose it on the grounds that she hasn't the resources to look after him as well as you can. Meanwhile you give up your own kid, put it into care. Guess who is appointed foster-moster – complete with tax-free index-linked non-means-tested fostering allowance, payable whether she lives with one man or ten or is just boringly married. So there you'd have it – two kids, two mothers – who looked after which would be your business – and two fostering allowances. We wouldn't get away with it for long, but it would make the point, eh?'

'Very funny, David.'

'It isn't.'

'No, it isn't.'

She got up to leave. 'Meanwhile Jim stays with me?' She was cold and shaking. 'You will let me know if she turns up again won't you? And I'll be sure and try very hard to make a baby for you to play political games with.'

A day later he phoned after talking to Marsha and was full of apologies. He hadn't realised, he said, that she was actually trying for a baby and he was sorry if he'd put his foot in it. Lynn tried to be gracious but the seal was set on her dislike of him. And something similar seemed to have happened in Marsha's mind too becasue she broke with him and shortly afterwards went away with Posy who had itchy feet. Lynn was surprised at how much their departure disturbed her. She wasn't seriously tempted by the prospect of taking off on a feminist odyssey, travelling the world and bonding with a woman (especially one like Posy); but it seemed very enterprising and youthful and made Lynn feel dull and uncommitted. Also she missed Marsha. Her combination of cautious commitment and kindness, her childlike incomprehension in the face of jargon or pomposity, had lent intense pleasure to their conversations together.

Repeatedly in the first weeks Lynn sat down to write letters to Marsha, often getting to the end before remembering she had no address.

PART TWO

3

The Wrong Rats

Nineteen eighty four came and went, but the discussion continued: had Orwell been right? Public opinion was divided. On a literal level, clearly he had not been. The nation had its problems, but the inborn good sense of its people had saved it from the excesses he foresaw. The country did not lie in thrall to an autocracy of left or of right; government was sluggish and pragmatic; proportional representation ensured frequent changes of party in power, but rare changes of policy. Outside parliament, of course, the fascist right kicked and spat at the Marxist left, but these factions cancelled each other out, proving if anything that freedom of political thought still existed. Inside parliament, individual MPs kept up their outward allegiance to the parties for which they had been elected, but in effect it was government by pact and coalition. For whatever their differences, the major parties were united in their perplexity as to why the coming of North Sea oil had not brought economic recovery on anything like the scale promised by their now-retired colleagues, and in their anxiety over what was to be done to appease their restive neighbours in the European community. No – the prospect of a one-party tyranny or a single-minded big brother overseeing every act and thought of the people, and bending them to his nefarious aims, was the least of Britain's worries.

It mightn't even be such a bad idea, some thought. He would at least do something about the bushfire of sexual permissiveness that was wrecking national morale. Hairy rubber cunts were sold in supermarkets (alongside the Feminine Aids counters which specialised in frothy nightgowns and books of poetry) and pornography publishers produced education supplements that could be torn out and given to children. Newspapers that had once dared to the limit by printing naked girls with erect nipples now had couples copulating in the 'position of the week' – usually they were heterosexual adults, but lesbian scenes were popular too, particularly if they involved children. With all the sex that was going on (and rape seemed to be on the increase, though it was impossible to be sure now that it was classified as ordinary assault) a boom in the birth-rate might be expected; but it was down, down, down on projections. Laws still theoretically controlled the availability of contraceptives and abortion, but the free market overrode these; what you wanted, you could buy. The ecology lobby that might once have been heard applauding such developments was now silent; and voices were raised pointing out that even such babies as were being born were coming mainly to immigrant stock, lower-class whites, single mothers and – not to put too fine a point on it – the stupid and inept. The reason being (well, one of them) that recent revelations about injuries and long-term damage caused by pills and intra-uterine devices had scared such women off using them, without giving them the intelligence to use other methods or the money to afford abortions.

And eugenicists who commented darkly on this phenomenon noted that it mirrored the situation worldwide; the population of the Third World was still exploding, the West was ageing and on the decline.

Still, this was what came of free choice. There was no tyranny, either in private or public life. And yet there were those who saw uncanny fulfilment of Orwell's prophecies. Here, for example, were the misnamed bureaucracies: ministries for law and order, health and welfare, that had ceased to dispense either; organisations for 'racial harmony' whose main function was to encourage blacks to accept voluntary repatriation; and all-male committees to promote sex equality. Here were the promises to keep the people together: *when the oil is flowing everything will be fine* had had to be replaced with *when the oil is flowing more abundantly . . .* or *when the oil that belongs to us, as distinct from that which was mortgaged to foreign bankers to shore up governments in the seventies . . . when the Arabs stop fooling around with world prices . . . when we've brought inflation under control . . .* then you can have your jobs back, and your hospital beds and your housing and all these other state bounties which you cannot believe are not your right.

And the dying welfare state brought its own newspeak as well: governments' failure to link child benefit, unemployment pay and so on to the cost of living was *the fight against inflation*; putting children on half-time schooling was referred to as *giving parents a free hand*; closing hospitals and dumping dying patients on the doorsteps of unwarned and distant relatives was *community care*; and a new political movement that saw remedies to the whole predicament, if only the nation's women would buckle down to traditional role and biological destiny, was known quite simply as FAMILY.

FAMILY's enemies (and it had many, most notably among feminists) were fond of equating its origins with movements of the seventies such as the anti-abortion campaigns, the racialist right and the pro-censorship lobby, and certainly it had drawn members from all these. But it was not the same as any of them, and could not seriously be dismissed as anti-black or anti-woman by anyone who took the trouble to find out the facts; after all, as FAMILY was fond of pointing out, one of its founders was a woman of Pakistani origin!

Rashida Patel was not its chief publicist, however. That task fell to the strictly British Mrs Isabel Travers, who never needed any encouragement to explain how FAMILY was born. 'We were chatting in Sainsbury's, Mrs Patel and I, rather more years ago than I care to remember. I do remember saying that these Asian women had a lot to teach us about family life. She replied that that might be so, but maybe in her community women didn't stand up for themselves quite as much as they should.' Mrs Travers seemed to think that said it all. Alan Travers had risen to prominence in his wife's organisation and was now one of the Family Party's two members of parliament.

The other MP, David Laing, was a younger man, around forty, with a passionate hatred of feminists. He shared this with many other members of the party, but not Isabel Travers. In fact, she was fond of saying that FAMILY and the women's liberation movement were both on the same side if they did but know it.

'How can you say that, Mrs Travers?' interviewers liked to ask. Mrs Travers was a delight to interview. Always blonde and cool and pretty and respectful. Always informal and chatty but never waffly. She tempered her approach to each medium like a professional: for newspaper journalists she spoke slowly in short, simple generalities; on television she smiled a lot and complimented her opponents on the intelligence of their remarks; on radio she allowed herself to be profound, even vulnerable. Yet in essence what she said was always the same.

'I say that because the true liberation of women will never come about until proper respect and value is placed upon their role as nurturers.'

Mrs Travers and Mrs Patel had shown flair for public relations from the beginning; and the beginning for them had been shortly after the famed conversation in Sainsbury's, when they organised a summer procession in honour of family values in a South London borough particularly hard hit by both government spending cuts and feminists insisting that 'family values' were a euphemism for women doing the housework. When she wasn't explaining that she and the libbers were on the same side really, Mrs Travers took pains to point out that FAMILY had no quarrel with the poor or socially inadequate; it was just that she wanted to pay tribute to the unsung millions of women (and men) who lived normal lives, did not swap roles, get divorces or abortions, become homeless or batter their children (or their wives); people who faced misfortune with resourcefulness and courage and without recourse to public funds. When a national newspaper first published Mrs Travers' views, the response was so great that a whole page had to be given over to readers' letters.

'My fiancée and I have a simple answer for homeless families. We won't be getting married until we've saved enough for our deposit. And we're old-fashioned enough to believe that children come after marriage, not before.'

'So sickness benefit is going up again! I have kept myself fit all my life, avoiding infections, abstaining from drink, tobacco and hazardous pursuits. Now, it seems, I am to be out of pocket . . .'

'Very nice to be an unmarried mother and live on social security. As a mere wife, I live on what my husband chooses to give me . . .'

The newspaper became embarrassed; so much so that they ran a follow-up feature called 'Lest We Forget.' Amid all the tales of scroungers, it said, let us not forget the deserving poor; and its journalists located hardship cases with impeccable credentials. The single mother who was a rape victim (*you have no excuse whatever*, the judge had told the culprit); the family whose home was struck by lightning the day after their insurers went broke; the legless man who packed cosmetics at home because he liked to feel he was paying his way.

'These are difficult times for all of us,' thundered the editorial, 'and will continue to be so until we are reaping the full benefits of North Sea oil. But let us not forget the reputation for compassion in which Britain still leads the world . . .'

Mrs Travers made one of her television appearances. 'Is it not remarkable,' she said, her pretty brows arched in bewilderment, 'that an organisation set up in support of the family is thereby assumed to be against the welfare state? Are the two incompatible? I hope not.'

Even the weather collaborated on the day of that first FAMILY procession. Sun shone through a gentle breeze. Crowds waited outside the town hall for three o'clock. A clash of cymbals struck the hour, trumpets and trombones burst into 'The British Grenadiers', the gates opened and the procession began.

Musical families from all over the borough formed the brass band. Their instruments gleamed with polish and sunshine. The players – men, women, children – were spotless in their white shirts and jeans. They sweated and marched, played and smiled. Their banner proclaimed, 'Families in Harmony.'

Cars followed. The mayor, the mayoress and an obscure royal rode in the first sleek open limousine. It was not an official visit by royalty. But it was rumoured that the Palace was enchanted by what it had heard of the planned event and wished to make a noncommittal gesture of support while not embroiling itself in politics. The mayor, who had a reputation for trendiness, wore a pale yellow suit under his chain of office; his lady was in pink flowers and a wide-brimmed white straw hat; the royal relative was orange from head to foot. The three dignitaries waved stiffly.

The second car carried Mrs Travers and Mrs Patel, respectively clothed in pale and deep green. There was no awkwardness in their greeting to the crowd; Mrs Travers' arm, pale and silk-gloved to the elbow, waved like the sail of a windmill, while Mrs Patel, shyly confident, gave little intimate grins and shook her wrist in short bursts. Watchers assumed they were film-stars or monarchs, but looked in their programmes and found each woman self-labelled as an ordinary housewife.

After the cars came representatives of the caring professions and local charities. There were few official delegations, but small contingents were present from most groups. 'Family Doctors for Family Life' handed out information on how mothers could treat colds at home without medical supervision. A few middle-aged social workers walked together with prim pride, while younger colleagues had leaflets: 'Lack of proper funding is making our job more difficult. But we're here to help families, and we'll help you all we can.' Nuns and priests had organised a float whose theme was the Holy Family.

Then came the families themselves. The Tynes, perched in their multitudes on the hand-carved cart that had lain cherished and unused in their garage. The cart, the programme explained, had been in the Tyne family for generations. Carpenters since the sixteenth century, the Tyne males now sat benignly sawing wood while the women and children did intricate carvings and played with sawdust. Then a family of writers: father published thick texts on the future of man, mother contributed to magazines, and the tall, serious children persistently took prizes in essay contests. Mr Meat the butcher (it actually was his name) with a pig's head on a tray, garlanded with strings of sausages carried by his wife and two sons. An income tax inspector (anonymous) on a rather flippant float, looking grimly into the crowd and singling out strangers. 'I want *your* money,' he roared, while his wife brought him piles of paper and the children sat at his feet counting money into a piggy bank.

Fairytale characters mingled with the children in the crowd, giving them toys and bits of fruit: Mary Poppins, Mother Hubbard, the Old Woman who Lived in a Shoe. Then came the International Section: an Indian family on the back of a lorry with a stove, the mother cooking real curry that you could smell in the air; an Irish group, parents with bagpipes and children dressed as leprechauns; a steel band from Trinidad.

Suddenly the section of the audience that was laughing at Italian children flinging spaghetti realised that everyone else had fallen silent. Their shouts died in mid-air; the procession had changed.

Discussing it afterwards, many people said it was too abrupt, but Mrs Travers and Mrs Patel defended it. These were just as much a part of family life as the healthy, celebrating adults and children earlier in the procession.

The afflicted families. Fathers pushing wheelchairs containing smart, vacant-eyed teenagers. Mothers with odd, floppy babies. Senile old folk in the passenger seats of cars, their younger relatives smiling bravely.

The spectators lowered their eyes and consulted their programmes.

'Mr and Mrs J's son Alex was born with spina bifida. "We were offered a special school" says Mrs J, "but it was so far away, we just couldn't." At thirteen Alex is very intelligent; he reads avidly (the Famous Five are a special favourite!) and is always cheerful.

COPING AWARD: a local laundry has offered Mrs J vouchers to cover fifty per cent of the cost of washing bed-linen over the next six months.'

The spectators swallowed hard and stood very still.

'The W. family have just welcomed their son home from Borstal. He is determined to make good and they are determined to help him. COPING AWARD: A local supermarket will give him a month's trial as a shelf-filler. After the month, he will be paid. The supermarket prefers to remain anonymous.

'Miss Joanna G. is one of hundreds of single women in the borough who have sacrificed career and marriage to care for elderly parents at home. Says Miss G: "Mother and I get on very well. I don't regard it as a sacrifice." COPING AWARD: Twelve double tickets for matinees at any local cinema.'

The sun beat down on the discomfort of the watchers, wondering if they were meant to clap or what.

The procession wound through the town, heralded by music and laughter, leaving perplexity and sadness in its wake. Only from the windows of a derelict tower block squatted by women was there any deliberately hostile response.

Each of the wide windows facing the road had been blocked with a sheet of paper. And each of these placards bore a stark message, white on black or black on white.

'Stop the cuts.'
'More hospitals.'
'More home helps.'
'More nurseries.'
'Better schools.'
'Women can't do it all.'
'Women won't do it all.'

And so the lines had been drawn for the battle that still raged, feminists and FAMILY glaring balefully at each other over the dying body of the welfare state. Each held its demonstrations, its counter-demonstrations; each established its model communities. It was a new dichotomy, to confuse and criss-cross the older ones of class and party. 'The state is responsible,' asserted the feminists from their squatted communes, their women-only states-within-a-state, when truant children ran wild and delinquent, and old folk died neglected; 'No, we women are responsible,' crooned the green-uniformed women stewards of FAMILY, running courses in domestic skills and home nursing, and publishing books called

Play His Game in the Marriage Bed and *You Promised to Obey*.
The feminists had marched in thousands when David Laing MP,
in his maiden speech, urged married women to give up their jobs
because 'there is so much to do at home'; they sabotaged a cricket-
pitch (cricket being 'male idleness elevated into religion') etching
into the grass with acid their crudest symbol: a round-cornered diamond to represent a vulva, with a large clitoris and no opening.

They ran health centres (offering a mixture of self-help,
herbalism, old wives' tales and orthodox medicine) for women
finding to their cost that FAMILY had a stronghold in the dwindling
official health services; they dug up neglected laws on sex equality
and fought hopelessly to get them obeyed. Women on the way to
FAMILY's housework classes would be stopped by feminists and
asked if they would like to do karate or woodwork instead; new
fiancées would receive congratulatory cards in the post, en-
closing leaflets outlining the legal rights of wives, while their
startled boyfriends got anonymous warnings to behave. And at
mid-day on Sundays, when streets in which FAMILY had worked to
re-establish the day of domestic togetherness were fragrant with
the smell of cheap meat roasting, shrill voices would be heard
through letter-boxes: 'When's Mum's day off, then?' (And it was
not unknown, FAMILY learned to its regret, for the woman in the
kitchen, hearing this, to respond: 'Good question,' and abandon
her pans.)

Unemployment was at a record high, particularly among men.
Heavy industry was quailing before foreign competition, but the
decline in traditional female areas of work was less steep. Women
were cheaper, some firms preferred them. North European
businesses found it satisfactory to farm out big clerical jobs to
London agencies, and international corporations making
domestic appliances found the nimble-fingered women of the
North and Midlands surprisingly to their taste. FAMILY knew of
whole streets where women went out to work and men stayed at
home and neglected the children.

FAMILY's anxiety was shared by industry. Today's children were
tomorrow's workers. Besides, women workers might be cheaper,
but too many depressed breadwinners could damage national
morale, and morale needed to be high for what was coming. The
country had been the sick man of Europe for too long, and Europe
suspected hypochondria. What was needed was nothing less than
a new industrial revolution.

The suspension of all social security payments was only to be temporary, part of a national effort to restore confidence in the pound.

The fact was, the beleaguered prime minister explained to a restive House of Commons, that when it came to income maintenance, history had turned the welfare state on its head.

He made moving reference to its founding philosophy. It was, he recalled, that people should first and foremost fend for themselves. Merciful provision must be made for those who failed to do so, but the failures must never be better off than the successes. Unfortunately, years of inflation, pay curbs and good intentions had taken their toll; and social security payments were outgrowing wages.

'In our mad pursuit of fairness, we have forgotten equity. Our British sense of fair play has recoiled from the prospect of anyone starving or suffering, even through his own fault – but where is the fair play when hospitals must close to put money in the pockets of the workshy? Where is equity when the idle are better off than the diligent? There have to be further cuts – on that we have no choice. But this we *can* choose: either to break faith with millions of decent, proud, hardworking citizens, or to look with more realism on the others: the tramps, the ne'er-do-wells, the offenders, the improvident – '

The Commons ceased to be merely restive, and erupted. House procedures used once to be compared by class-conscious critics to a public school debating chamber; these days it was more like breaktime in a comprehensive. No longer did MPs defer to the Speaker, grant courtesy titles or bow when they left; these days it was the loudest voice that got a hearing.

A socialist youth was on his feet, roaring with all the force and outrage of his years. The working class were not going to fall for this one, and neither were their wives. It was quite obvious what was going on. Foreign industry saw unemployment pay – meagre as it was – as the last obstacle before this country became a handy offshore pool of cheap labour. It wasn't a question of social security payments being too high, it was a question of wages being lower than even government estimates of subsistence! Offer jobs to the unemployed; then the prime minister would see who was workshy and who was not. If people lived mean, dirty, anti-social lives it was their mean environments, made by dirty, anti-social government policies, that made them so. There had to be cuts, did there? Then cut profits, cut arms spending, abolish the monarchy.

He was howled down by monarchists of right and left, and the house switched its attention to another speaker. David Laing did not have a loud voice; but newness was on his side, the novelty value of the Family Party. His appearance compelled the kind of attention a mouse gives a snake: in his late thirties, he looked shrivelled and ageless, anxious and ill. He was unmarried, lived alone, and, it was said, ate rarely and eccentrically, needing much of his salary to feed his addiction to coffee. The world shortage and price rises had made it a rare delicacy for ordinary citizens, but David Laing liked to sip and swig constantly. A beaker and a flask steamed on the bench beside him as he spoke.

All around, honourable members lounged on benches in shirts, slacks and occasional frocks of Olex, the new, cheap, crepey material being manufactured in the Far East out of North Sea Oil by-products. It came in two colours, medium brown or medium grey; it shone with a slightly oily sheen. Laing made it clear that he despised his fellow MPs for affecting the common touch and wearing Olex; he himself never appeared in the house without a worsted suit and a carnation. His hair was very short, the back of his neck shaven and stubbly. He wore thin-rimmed spectacles.

His narrow tongue flicked once across each dry lip. He glared at the prime minister.

'May I remind you that one of the largest groups receiving social security are receiving it not because they are neglecting their duty, but because they are doing it? I refer, of course, to unsupported mothers, women who have neither shirked their obligation to have children, nor left them to seek jobs, nor abandoned them to the tender mercies of the social services –'

The house sighed, wishing it had not let him start. The trouble with pressure-group MPs was that they were bores. Fanatics. They brought their favourite subject into every damn debate, relevant or not. With Laing it was mothers. Single mothers, married mothers, he didn't care. Just women who had babies and looked after them properly. Funny bloke. Unmarried, but didn't look queer. A Sunday newspaper had once revealed that he'd wanted to marry a feminist and she'd run off with a lesbian, which was why he had it in for both. That was before he became an MP. He'd been a social worker, then a deputy director of social services – he'd been fired after the famous 'babyswap' scandal, but that was how he came to be taken up by FAMILY. Some woman journalist friend of his had a handicapped daughter and found she was entitled to virtually no help looking after her, whereas if she fostered someone else's kid she got any number of handouts. Laing had worked some fiddle and hadn't minded being caught; he said he'd proved that the state only acknowledged the work of mothers when they didn't do it . . .

The prime minister was smiling indulgently.

'As I have said, the suspension of payments will be only temporary, and when the social security system has been overhauled, special consideration will be given to deserving groups. But in any case . . .' The prime minister's smile spread even further in the slightly crooked way it had when he thought he had an opponent hoist with his own petard. 'There are ways, are there not, of avoiding becoming an unsupported mother, just as there are ways of avoiding becoming unemployed? The Family Party above all would not wish us to place a premium on unorthodox styles of living . . .'

Alan Travers, the other FP member, took over from David. He was past fifty, tall and straight, lean-faced, with large handsome features. He dressed more casually, in a green suit; he liked to play the calm paternal figure to David's impetuous youth.

'Isn't this the point we're always making? We fail so utterly to reward responsible married women that if we give anything at all to single mothers we appear to be placing a premium – '

Something seemed to explode behind Alan Travers. David Laing had leapt to his feet again, spraying his neighbours with cold coffee. He seemed to be having some kind of fit. His eyes stared, his mouth spat.

'Yes!' he cried, 'Yes! Exactly! The prime minister dares – *dares* – to talk about unorthodox styles of living in a society that actually penalises motherhood, so much so that virtually the only women who'll take it up are those capable of nothing else! Who's having all the big families today? Social classes four and five, the filth, the dregs, the dross of society. The better females are too busy working, or seeking work, or fighting for their rights – and who in honesty can blame them? Who can blame a liberated woman for not settling for slavery? So they leave it to the ones who don't recognise degradation when they see it – I've been a social worker, I know about these people – women too stupid and disorganised to – '

Alan Travers grabbed his arm. 'Sit down, Laing.' David wrenched free and went on furiously: 'Those women whose homes are sties, whose habits are bestial, who couldn't raise a guinea-pig never mind a child – ' he drew a deep, shuddering breath to steady himself, then continued more slowly. 'Do you remember – it seems a century ago – we used to worry about being overrun by blacks? Send 'em home, some of us said, stop 'em breeding. Who but the lunatic fringe thinks colour is the issue now – as we look at the decaying bones of our great compassionate nation, gnawed by whining, idle, dirty, anti-social *rats* of all colours . . .' His voice had sunk to a piercing whisper. 'The wrong rats are breeding. Maybe we can't stop that,' he hissed, 'but we'd better make maternity a better deal for the others, or we're going to be overrun.'

The house dissolved in uproar. Police had to be brought in to protect Laing from the outraged violence of some of his hearers. But when he made his appearance in the members' bar a few hours later, there were others happy to shake him by the hand and talk with him far into the night.

The debate was resumed. The house would not approve the prime minister's plans for scrapping the social security system. The pound fell and fell on the foreign exchange markets. The government lost a vote of confidence. A general election was called. It was late summer.

The flags were out in Seyer Street. From every window of the double row of terraces, the FAMILY emblem hung: a gold hand, stitched to an oily green backcloth. It was a female hand with neat nails and a wedding-ring; in the better reproductions it was full of character. It had wrinkles, tiny muscles, even hints of honest dirt. It was a working hand. It was a hand that could be tender, it could beckon or admonish, make love or smack. No one knew who the model was for the patterns that FAMILY Headquarters sent out in thousands to its sewing circles; but FAMILY hands appeared as badges, on mugs, tee-shirts and posters; they were flyposted on walls and scrawled in public lavatories. They had even been poached by manufacturers of washing powders until FAMILY clamped down with a writ.

Most of the Seyer Street houses were on their last legs. Tiles were off, walls split, and there were open wounds in some of the roofs (covered in winter by sheets of plastic) where chimneys had fallen in. Some of the proud banners hid gaping window-holes, the frames too rotten to hold glass. Everything shone in the sun, silent and still, as Isabel Travers stepped forward to greet the knot of journalists who had accepted the invitation to visit. Her skin was soft and white; she wore a pale green frock of Family Fabric (a better grade of Olex that the organisation imported in bulk for its members). She was flanked by her husband, by Mrs Patel in a dark green robe, and by David Laing.

'Welcome to the press preview of the Seyer Street exhibition. It is one of fifty such displays being mounted over the next few days around the country. It is, of course, pure coincidence, that they are happening a week before the election. They were planned a year ago to replace our processions, which were becoming, in some ways, too successful.'

The only woman in the party of reporters, early middle-aged with red hair, said, 'You mean the time the youth contingent went berserk and stoned a claimant's home?'

Mrs Travers twinkled. 'If you have any proof of that allegation, may I advise you to lay it before the police? What I was referring to was our tendency to stop traffic the length and breadth of the land. Why, it's Mrs Byers . . . isn't it?'

'Yes.'

'And which publication are you representing, my dear?'

'I'm freelance.'

'Of course . . . and you're just here, what do you call it, "on spec." Well, I admire that. And I admire the way you find the time to keep on working, especially with your poor little daughter needing so much of your care. How is she?'

All the spirit seemed to drain from Lynn Byers' face. She flushed and mumbled, 'All right, thanks.' The other reporters looked at her curiously. Most were young enough to be her sons, pink cub reporters from local papers. This was a straightforward public-relations job, an easy assignment for beginners. It wasn't done to say anything contentious about FAMILY.

Mrs Travers led the party down the street, feet clattering over its broken stone surface. She stopped outside one of the more solid-looking houses. A sign proclaimed, 'Photograph Exhibition.'

Mrs Patel ventured to speak. 'You all have background information sheets, but Mrs Travers will make a few comments about the history of Seyer Street before you go in.'

The reporters glanced briefly through the sheets, each individually typed by a girl in a YFT (Young Families of Tomorrow) typing class. They told of how Seyer Street had been a poor but spirited community in the nineteenth century, but malaise had set in with the coming of the twentieth. Mrs Patel's contribution appeared complete; Mrs Travers resumed.

'By some anomaly of planning law,' she explained, 'Seyer Street missed two waves of slum clearance and is now something of a museum piece. Technically it is a slum.' She seemed to have developed a tic in her neck. 'And by rights and by conventional wisdom, it ought to have been flattened long ago, and replaced . . .' Mrs Travers' head was twitching as if it was being pulled in a direction it did not want to go, 'replaced by something like *that*.' And she turned to glare at Collindeane Tower, leaning towards her, crumbling (it seemed) before her very eyes, gashed down the side by a great meandering crack with tributaries and estuaries and deltas that reached every corner. The slogan in the windows made clear what it was (if anyone did not know): a two-generation community of feminists, some of the early settlers now having had children. The large letters in the windows spelled out: 'FAMILY ENSLAVES WOMEN.'

Mrs Travers stared, smiled sadly, shook her head, began to say something, stopped herself, turned, and led the party into the photograph exhibition. The interior was dark after the bright sunlight, and smelled damp. The rooms were painted green and the gold hand emblem gleamed in each one. Photographs plastered every surface.

'Seyer Street at the turn of the century.' Browning pictures of girls in smocks, boys with huge caps, sheepishly grinning with hoops, kites and marbles. 'Seyer Street in victory.' A forlorn youth in battle dress turns the corner into a street full of women waving flags. 'Hard times in Seyer Street.' A gaunt thirties mother feeds soup to her children. 'Seyer Street reconstructs.' Bare-handed men, women and children repair bomb damage.

And then a change of tone.

'Seyer Street and the "welfare" state.' Depressed men queueing for dole. 'Seyer Street never has it so good.' An old woman staggers with a crutch and a bursting plastic shopping bag. 'Seyer Street women's liberation.' Toddlers crawl in the street; a car approaches.

'Just a minute.'

'Mrs Byers?'

'Are those pictures genuine?'

'One or two are reconstructions.' Mrs Travers gave a pained smile to the pink cubs. 'How sceptical you are, Mrs Byers! Perhaps a word or two from the – shall we say – horse's mouth, will resolve the doubts you so transparently feel?' Like a conjuror she produced a girl of about thirteen with her finger in her mouth. Her floppy frock was clean and her plaits stretched the skin on her forehead. She was flushed with nerves over her ill-fed pallor, and she had the red scrubbed hands of a lifetime of domestic work. Despite the scrubbing she looked grubby, and dead-eyed, and malleable.

'This is Patsy Hindley,' said Mrs Travers, pushing the child forward with a deft shove to her shoulders, after which she discreetly wiped her fingers on a lace hanky.

'I am Patsy Hindley and I have lived here all my life.' The child's voice was husky with shyness. 'My mum and dad would be honoured if you would visit us.'

The Hindley house was the worst in the street. Holes in the walls showed daylight and not a window was intact. Doors hung drunkenly on their hinges, hardly coinciding at all with the shapes of the frames; and the press party walked gingerly over the rotten, creaking, uneven floorboards, trying not to take advantage of the views afforded of the house's uncertain foundations.

The smell of paint that hung in the air did not quite mask the rot, and the glossy greens and greys had not fully covered the great swamps of damp on the insides of walls worn away by water from broken drains.

But the Hindleys seemed determined to prove that family life could thrive under the most arduous conditions.

In the only soft armchair in the cramped front room sat Mr Hindley, serious in his role as paterfamilias. A squat, bald, plump man, he looked so clean that if you ran your finger over him he would surely squeak. His face was pink and grazed with close shaving. His hand was poised halfway to his mouth with an empty pipe.

At his feet, five-year-old twins were playing a game with toy oil-tankers.

Opposite him sat his wife, awkward in her hard-back chair, as if she were unused to sitting. Her pasty face was smeared with orange make-up, and she clutched a grubby hanky and a needle that had lost its thread. She was quite slim, but her skin hung loose and grey, as if she had shed weight by having it sheared off her.

Hindley children in their multitudes were arranged round the room, neatly and symmetrically by size, posed stiffly in attitudes of sibling conversation. If they moved as their home filled up with spectators, it was only to flick a fly or control a sheepish grin.

Patsy said, 'We are a large and happy family. My mum is a very motherly woman. My mum regards, thinks, looking after her family is the height of a woman's voc- voc- vocation, and she teaches us daughters the same. Don't you, mum? *Don't you, mum?*' At the second asking, Mrs Hindley's head nodded up and down, up and down, till Mrs Travers gave her a prod. 'My dad has no skilled trade and he used to get more on social security than going to work, but you was . . . were . . . demoralised, wasn't you, dad? But FAMILY found him a job, and now at least he has his self-respect.'

'Yeah,' said Mr Hindley, 'that I do have.'

'What work do you do, sir?' a pink cub asked deferentially.

'I measure washing machines.'

'He means the wires,' said Mrs Hindley.

'They mustn't be too long, see,' said Mr Hindley.

'It's for exports,' Patsy explained.

'And Mrs Hindley,' Mrs Travers intervened in the silence, 'You're finding it easier to keep a nice home now, aren't you? We had to be a bit hard on you at first – our people coming in morning, noon and night.'

'Morning, noon and night.'

'And they helped you with your slimming?'

'Helped me with my slimming, ooh I hate food now.'

'And got Mr Hindley his vasectomy?'

'Yeh, they got him done.'

'And we still pop round, don't we?'

'Oh yes.' The trace of a sigh escaped from the sagging, orange face.

'And now,' said Mrs Travers to the reporters, seeming satisfied, 'I'm going to show you our little school. Those of you who are parents – ' she looked straight at Lynn ' – will not be surprised to know that in recent years the parents of Seyer Street had simply stopped sending their children to school, so horrified were they by the subversion and immorality taught there. Is it any wonder that the parents of Seyer Street thought "why bother?" But it is FAMILY's

job to bother.' They crossed the road into a stuffy prefab on the
site of a Seyer Street house that had faced reality and fallen down.
Flies buzzed. Children sat motionless on benches, their hair
combed, their fingernails spotless. They sprang to attention.
'Good afternoon, ladies and gentlemen.' Around the walls, bright
posters showed men in fields and factories, women at home.

Mrs Travers' fingers touched a little girl's cheek.

'And what are we studying today?'

'Family values!'

'Indeed! And what are the values that make for happy family
life?'

'Self-sacrifice, and authority, and – and – '

'Whose authority?'

'The man, the head of the house.'

'Goodness. That seems a bit hard on the wife.'

'The true woman has her own authority.'

And again Mrs Travers' eyes met and held those of Lynn Byers.
She moved on to the next child.

'Self-reliance!' it piped.

'Self-reliance,' exclaimed Mrs Travers, 'Does that mean we all
look out for number one?'

'No!' cried the class in delight, 'it means we all look out for each
other in the family and don't expect to be spoonfed by the
government!'

Then the party saw a four-roomed house where eight old
women lived, all of them discharged recently from hospitals that
were closing. There was nothing much wrong with them, Mrs
Travers explained, apart from a general slowing up of bodily
functions which one could expect with old age. The Seyer Street
wives took turns to clean them and feed them and watch over the
ones that went for walks. Today the old women sat in the disin-
fectant-smelling rooms, each room equipped only with two beds
and two boxes of possessions, and smiled at the visitors.

The party was taken to look at a plump pink-cheeked mother
and her two similar sons. She sat in a bare, steamy cellar and
threaded wires into plugs. She was very quick and expert but her
fingernails were worn away. Mrs Travers explained that the girl
used to be a prostitute. Lynn Byers glanced at the wires and plugs.
'What do you get for doing that?'

The girl told her.

'Not much, is it?' said Lynn.

'But at least I have my self-respect.'

Finally, in the open street, Mrs Travers asked the reporters if there was anything further she could tell them. One of them turned even pinker and asked apologetically, 'Some people might say – er, what would your answer be to the accusation, not that I'm making it myself, that you're using these people – '

'Were any of them manacled to the floor, that you noticed?'

The cub's question subsided as quickly as it had come. Lynn Byers took it up.

'What would you say to a suggestion that you are a women's auxiliary for the far right?'

Mrs Travers patted Mrs Patel's shoulder. 'You can see we're not racialist.'

'That wasn't what I asked.'

'Oh Mrs Byers! Right wing, left wing – *you* know that women belong to all wings and none! If it is right wing to want to reward effort, we are right wing. If it is left wing to want the poor uplifted, we are left wing.'

'But is it true that you support government plans to abolish unemployment pay?'

'Let me say this about that. It would make no difference whatever to this street because *nobody* is drawing any.'

Looking slightly hurt, David Laing stepped forward to appropriate the question. 'Only as part of a package – ' he began.

A controlled but angry Asian voice said, 'There is not complete agreement on this within the organisation.' Mrs Patel held herself erect, trembling slightly.

'Close ranks, Mrs Patel,' whispered Mrs Travers, before explaining, 'There is ongoing discussion within the party as to the extent that there should be financial and other disincentives to anti-social behaviour.'

'Other disincentives?' Lynn queried.

'I beg your pardon?'

'I want to know how you did this. I know this street. I used to live here. Your tale of the thriving community that went to the bad isn't quite the whole truth, is it?' she lifted her voice for the cubs to hear, 'this street was a dumping ground for people whose problems were too expensive for the social services to solve, and you know that as well as I do, David, pardon me, Mr Laing MP. So what did you do with the ones who wouldn't fall into line?'

'It's not a question of falling into line, Mrs Byers. By a process of education and support – '

'And was there no one – no one at all – who would not accept your education and support?'

Mrs Travers began a reply, but Mrs Patel cut in again. 'It would be ridiculous to pretend that there were no difficulties. There were two young men squatting in one of the empty houses. They were living in an unnatural manner. The street decided they should leave.'

'It was one of their first collective decisions,' said Mrs Travers.

Polling day was uneventful, a bit of an anticlimax after FAMILY's marches and festivals and the midnight rally that swamped the West End in torchlight; not to mention the less photogenic efforts of the primmer but somewhat rattled major parties. With the results there followed a week of confusion, of thick newspapers and extended bulletins. Grey men with graphs explained that the new voting system had produced a very interesting left-right deadlock situation, with the meteoric Family Party's thirty members holding the balance and refusing, for the moment, to make a pact with either side. Blurred film showed furtive car-dashes to Buckingham Palace, and at last the Government of National Regeneration was formed, a coalition of patriots that would set aside party dogma and lead the nation towards the winking mirage of the technological paradise that the third millenium – now just ten years away – promised to be.

Fears that the Family Party might abuse its position were assuaged after the brief row over the Home Secretaryship. It emerged that what had happened was this. During the few days when it seemed no government could be formed, MPs from left and right had met with David Laing and Alan Travers and heard that the price of their joining an all-party group was that Travers got the Home Office and Laing a new welfare ministry.

This seemed a lot for an upstart party to ask; on the other hand, no one else seemed particularly keen to take on welfare. Travers' ambitions earned him suspicion and were sacrificed; Laing obtained his new ministry, which he named the Department for Family Welfare.

'Let us build a generation worthy of the world it will inherit,' he exhorted in his victory oration. His appointment had been controversial within FAMILY. His 'Wrong Rats' speech had raised heckles in immigrant groups, and Rashida Patel in particular took a lot of convincing that no racial slur was intended. She made him say it in public: 'We are in the business of rewarding responsible motherhood, not selective breeding based on arbitrary and outdated notions of race.' And when the details of Benefit were announced, it was there, plain enough.

All mothers, regardless of race, marital state or domestic competence would be eligible for the weekly payment, so long as they stayed at home and looked after children under 16. In calling the payment simply Benefit, no risk was run of confusing it with other benefits, for these were all abolished. They were un-necessary. The explosion of job opportunities that would result from the economic upturn and women leaving work, would ensure that no man need be unemployed; Benefit mothers would not need social security or income supplements; and, as for sickness and old age, people who wished to be insured could make private arrangements. Motherhood, on the other hand, was not a misfortune to be insured against; it was a national service to be paid for.

'We considered calling it a wage,' said Laing, 'but we realised that whatever the level it was fixed at – and naturally we hope to improve this – it would be an insult. We also considered calling it an allowance – but that sounded like pocket-money, to be withdrawn at will.' He smiled. He seemed to be growing more confident on television, exhilarated by the lights and the thick snaky wires. 'We decided to call it Benefit,' he said, 'because that is what we are all going to do.'

4

Marsha

The early years of the Benefit scheme in Britain were watched with interest all round the world: by economists, social policy planners, churchmen, mothers, demographers – and particularly by two middle-aged feminists who, after fifteen years of travelling the world, spreading the message of women's liberation and earning tidy sums of money from freelance article-writing and television appearances, had now settled in Sydney, Australia, to write a book.

At least – it was Posy, the Australian, the elder of the two, who felt settled and was writing the book. It was misnomer to talk of the women's movement in the singular; feminists in different countries responded to their different conditions, often appearing to contradict each other, which annoyed her. But Posy felt she had an overview. She knew there must be a unifying factor, something that would bring together the middle-class career women of the United States who wanted to share their husbands' privileges, and the peasant women of the Third World who gave national liberation higher priority than sexism, and show them they were all on the same side. Posy wasn't quite sure what this unifying factor was; she saw the business of discovering it and putting it in her book as her life's work – that, and offering herself as leader of the mass movement to overthrow patriarchy that would surely result. The fact that feminists in the countries she'd visited had unanimously rejected her pretensions (seeing her variously as a Western plot, an Eastern plot or a male plot to split the movement) did not bother her overmuch. She had Marsha – who, although she argued a bit and grumbled a lot, still stuck with her, kept her going.

The sun hung high over the Sydney beach. The skin of both women was tanned deep brown and leathery by their years of travel. Bronzed men surfed into the shore on curling waves; pretty women lifeguards perched on high look out points scanning the sea for shark-fins, a job more decorative than dangerous now that the worlds' fisheries had virtually destroyed the species. The high buildings of the city crept closer and closer to the shore; and in the parts of the beach not marked and patrolled for leisure use by the rich, shanty-towns were spreading.

Posy was a big, impressive woman. A rigorous life of physical self-sufficiency and roughing it and fitness training had prevented her muscle from running to fat, even now in her fifties. She wore a swimsuit that she had knitted for herself out of brown string, and two pairs of sunglasses, one over her eyes and one spare pair nestling in her grey bush of hair. She lay flat on a sturdy beach-bed, surrounded by beer-cans, sandwiches, books, recording equipment and litter. Her head was propped on a pile of newspapers. A second pile pressed down on her stomach; as she scanned each one she either marked an article with a slash of red pen and handed it to Marsha to cut, or placed it, muttering, behind her head, which thus rose higher and higher, doubling and trebling her chin.

She turned to Marsha who was fiddling with the long grey hair that framed her face like curtains. Marsha sat very flat on the hard beach, her bony legs sticking straight out in front of her. All her life she'd had the nail-biting, face-rubbing, hair-twiddling gestures of an anxious adolescent. The papers she was meant to be cutting piled up untouched. The notebook in which she was supposed to be writing down Posy's ideas was closed on her lap. She was staring out to sea in one of what Posy liked to mock as her stocktaking moods. Marsha's mind was always years behind her body. She was only just used to being out of her twenties (to not feeling included when people talked about 'the younger generation') and here she was, forty-three! 'Save your stocktaking till you're *my* age,' Posy would say sometimes, adding silently, 'and until you've done everything I've done.' Marsha wondered why she let Posy bully her so much, but she knew really. She wondered why she always had to be her assistant, and she knew that too. It was because Posy had saved her; when she'd been young and rich and made gloomy by her uselessness, and panicking over the hideousness of the only two roles that the future appeared to offer a girl in her position (housewife, or hard, peculiar career-lady) Posy had hauled the women's movement into her life, and shown her that you didn't have to accept anyone's view of yourself but your sisters' and your own.

And that wasn't all; Posy had saved her from the oddly compelling relationship with David Laing which, had she pursued it, would now have her as the behatted, multiparous wife of a cabinet minister who had become a reactionary of the most terrifying kind. Posy had saved her. And even if they slept together more for company than love-making (which was still hedged about with embarrassment, inhibition and good manners, probably because they never discussed it) it was better than David. Posy was a reassuring bulwark in the bed, and it was good to have someone who stayed with you, someone with whom you felt useful.

'Marsha, have you heard a word I've said?'

'Er, sorry, probably, remind me.'

'Er sorry probably remind me. You don't have to help me but please say if you're not otherwise I assume you are and get let down. I've been giving you things to cut, and I've been letting my thoughts come at random on the assumption that you were writing them down. You're good at writing notes on my thoughts, Marsh. You have this knack of spotting nuggets in the dross.'

'What's it about? I probably heard.'

'If you had, you'd be jumping up and down with indignation. Those new birth-control hormones – you know, the ones that work so nicely in the brains of rats and black women – now turn out to be, guess what, carcinogens. Nine countries repealed their anti-discrimination laws last year, and another nine decided to let women be conscripted on the same terms as men. Oh, and the pope's made another of those speeches on clitoridectomy.'

'Must respect the practices of cultures different from our own?'

'Got it in one.' Posy gave her a friendly hit with a newspaper.

'That's awful.'

'You sound as if it's awful, you really do sound as if you think it's awful,' Posy grumbled. 'I think we ought to do Britain now.'

Marsha stretched lecherously. 'Lucky old Britain.'

'What have we got on the feminist response to Benefit over the past four years?'

'Here, now, in the middle of the beach, nothing.'

'At home in the file.'

Marsha screwed up her face, trying to help. 'According to the British newspapers there hasn't been one and everyone thinks Benefit is wonderful. According to such feminist stuff as reaches us, the movement hasn't quite made up its mind what it thinks.'

Posy groaned. 'Get something on it, would you?'

'What, now? I'd rather have a swim.'

'The sharks'll get you.'

'There aren't any.'

'The ones on surfboards. Make yourself useful, for heaven's sake.'

That did it. Marsha scowled and lay back. *Make yourself useful, Marsha* had been a refrain from her childhood. The aunt who had brought her up on the death of her parents was an inexorably useful woman – taking in an orphaned niece was only the tip of the iceberg. The house rattled with collecting tins, burgeoned with jumble, echoed with coffee-mornings. The causes varied with the week and blurred into one in Marsha's memory – blind cats, lepers, nuclear disarmament, the promotion of good things and the destruction of bad. Marsha might have respected her aunt if she'd been less compulsive about it all – if she'd seemed to enjoy, or even believe. In the early consciousness-raising sessions in Collindeane Tower, she'd had fun mimicking the aunt's smug exhortations, but it always hid a little hurt. Posy knew this, and knew she wasn't allowed to say *make yourself useful, Marsha* other than in situations of perfect peace and harmony, and then only in unambiguously joky tones.

Marsha shut her eyes against the dazzling sun. She tried to imagine London. It would be winter. She tried to feel rain and dusty mist on her skin. What on earth was it like there, with David Laing now empowered to impose on a nation of women the ideas he had once sought to impose on her?

'If I apologise,' said Posy, looming through the gold light behind Marsha's eyelids, 'will you please help me write my book?' Marsha peered at her and she winked. Marsha couldn't stop laughing.

'Posy, there are few more ridiculous sights in the world than you flirting.' She hadn't meant to hurt but Posy flinched so she supposed they were quits. 'Okay,' she said, 'What can I do?' *And thus are all our arguments settled. What a ratty old couple we are. We might as well be married.*

'I think I'd like to interview you.'

'Me?'

'Well, you do have what we might call a unique insight on David Laing.'

'I've told you – I mean, I don't have to – it's embarrassing – '

'Come along, now, Marsha, the personal is political.'

Marsha wished she'd stuck to the quarrel.

No one had understood what she saw in Dave. They didn't see him when his ineffectiveness made him desperate, when vulnerability tempered his bitterness. 'My casework is the kiss of death, Marsha. A quiet talk from me to a juvenile pilferer and he turns into a bank-robber. And if I offer what's laughingly known as support to a family with a mad granny at home, the next thing I know, the family's done a bunk and granny's dead of hypothermia.' He would rage about Seyer Street, the drunken fathers, the slovenly mothers, the prostitutes, the frightened gays. 'These people live like animals, but why should they change? By my very existence, I'm saying, there there, it's not your fault, not your responsibility. And people like you chime in with the chorus: it's society's fault! Blame it on the social services, you all cry, which is a wonderful formula, isn't it? The social services. In other words – not me! No fear! I'm not going next door to tell that woman to stop beating hell out of her kid! That's the social worker's job! I don't need to do anything now and what's even better I don't need to feel one iota of guilt when the kid's in its coffin because it's society's fault! Marsha, there's a girl we're going to put into a brand new flat because she's got a baby and another on the way! And meanwhile married couples who're waiting to be housed before they start their families carry on waiting! How can I tell that girl she ought to control herself? And how can I not?'

He would rant like this till she reached a climax of hating him, and then, sensing this, he would seem to turn. 'I remember a lecturer when I was at college. Just one lecture stuck in my mind. The village idiot. It sounds like a joke. We all laughed. But the village idiot is what it all ought to be about. The village could accommodate a mentally handicapped person. He was as much a part of the community as the doctor or the parish priest. He had his hovel. He had his job, he gleaned corn and tolled the bell at funerals. He wandered about, people looked out for him, nothing really bad could happen. It's different now. He can't roam the streets as he roamed the village green, a bus'll have him. Even if he is in a village, he can't help with the harvest – the threshing machine'll take his arm off. He's intolerable in a tenth floor flat. There's no room . . . he must be put away . . . yes, I know what you're thinking, romantic rubbish, and you're right too. The village idiot raped young virgins beneath the harvest moon, and for every one that made it in society ten were dropped down the well at birth. Do you think I like thinking like this? I just can't see any way out, and I won't think in slogans . . .'

He would shake his head, sip his coffee, talk more gently; and she would get glimpses of his kindness. 'I sat with him till he calmed down,' might mean he had spent a night in a slum with a drunk, unpaid; 'I lent her a few pence,' could mean anything; and his cry, 'What else could I have done?' seemed to come from somewhere deeper than the heart.

His voice faded. Posy was interviewing her.

'David Laing, as I remember him, was something of an idealist.'

Posy made an exploding sound with her nose.

'Anyway,' Marsha ventured, 'If we want to know what's going on in Britain, there is one way to find out.'

'We've been into that,' said Posy briskly.

'Posy, it's been years, and it's my *home*.'

'I thought you'd made your home with me.'

'Yes, but – '

'There's no yes but. I said when I left England that the women's movement there would never achieve anything because they wouldn't structure the thing and have effective leadership, and nothing I've heard since has convinced me any different. I'll go back when they invite me, and not before.'

'Posy – we're ridiculous.'

'Speak for yourself.'

But the idea of going home, just for a visit perhaps, grew in Marsha and spread like a germ; just to see – oh, the white cliffs of Dover and Buckingham Palace, the black waters of the Thames at night, never mind the more personal things. It worried at her. She said nothing to Posy, allowed her to think the subject had been dropped. She turned to her researches with a will and, as part of the work on Britain, wrote to Lynn Byers.

The reply when it came was happy to have heard from Marsha, but listless.

It seemed that Lynn, who had been trying to get pregnant when Marsha and Posy left, now had a twelve-year-old daughter. The daughter's name was Jane, and she suffered from a hereditary illness called cystic fibrosis. Lynn's tone was brisk. Both she and Derek must have been carriers. The disease primarily affected Jane's lungs and she needed a lot of care at home if she were to lead a normal life. It meant that Lynn hadn't been able to combine career with motherhood to quite the extent she had hoped. Nevertheless, Jane was as well as could be expected, intelligent and pretty. Derek was well. And so was Lynn. Jim, their foster-son, had gone back to his mother.

It was as if Lynn kept a tight rein on herself while she wrote about personal things. Her tone relaxed as she moved on.

'You ask about the women's movement. I don't see much evidence of it, quite honestly, but then I don't go out of my way to look. All the old splits have hardened. The socialists are more socialist. The moderates joined we're-all-on-the-same-side FAMILY. (Well, I didn't, but some did.) The radicals and the lesbians and the separatists just moved out. They say FAMILY's an attack on lifestyles, and lifestyles are where the struggle's at. Well. You can believe that, or you can think it sounds a nice excuse for getting the hell out of boring old politics and going to a commune and raising hens. (They raise them to the tenth floor in Collindeane Tower, I kid you not.) What's funny is that they say Benefit (which oh yes is what you asked about) is a bribe, but they're happy to take it. A lot of them have children now and their Benefit's a handy income for the 'moneyless' economy of the women's communes. Pardon me if I sound cynical . . .

'What else do you want to know? Oh, there's lots, birth-rate figures (going up, surprise surprise), texts of speeches (you heard about you-know-who and the Wrong Rats) sociological surveys, but I can't get it together, I only do occasional dull local paper stuff, all the old skills and ambitions are gone, but best not to think of that; I have new ones, like keeping my daughter alive to adulthood, physiotherapy to help her breathing . . . I am not sorry for myself, I love her and it's okay. Derek is lovely and a professor and famous, or so he keeps telling me. Why don't you come home and see, for heaven's sake? I thought you'd vanished, except I kept reading silly things about you in the papers. I was over the moon to get your letter. I've written so many to you, in my head and on paper but I couldn't ever send them because I never knew where you were . . .'

'That poor little girl. I think I'll go back,' said Marsha.

'Goodbye then.' Posy was reading the letter and didn't look up. 'Call herself a journalist? There's nothing here, nothing.'

'Come with me, we'll find out, get involved.'

'I'll come when I'm asked.'

'I'm asking you.'

Posy found this beneath consideration. They stopped discussing it. Posy changed the subject every time it was raised. She worked on all the sections of her book except the British. She bullied Marsha as much as usual and several months passed before Marsha screwed up her courage and said, 'One berth or two?' Posy refused to reply and Marsha went and booked a single and made sure Posy knew.

'Of course you realise it's classic,' said Posy.

'What is?'

'Lured away from your political commitment by an appeal to your maternal feelings.'

'Ridiculous!'

'Ridiculous, is it? Maybe it's something else, then? Which one, I wonder? Lynn or David? Fancy being the politician's wife after all, do you? You always did like to pick and choose.'

It was Marsha's turn to ignore Posy, but Posy warmed to her theme, kept calling her Mrs Laing. They were still quarrelling when their last night came. Ostensibly Marsha was still trying to persuade Posy to change her mind, but she was also growing weary of her. She was leaving to get away from her, and she guessed Posy knew, maybe was glad. But they had had some good times. Marsha tried to put all the good times into their last lovemaking.

Posy lay inert. Marsha said, 'You don't seriously think David would enjoy being married to me, do you?' and Posy said, 'He may be all kinds of pervert for all I know.'

Marsha woke very early to a sound she had not heard before. Great sobs racked Posy's body like an earthquake.

'You can't leave me high and dry, Marsha.'

'Come with me.'

'We've got so much to do here.'

'*You* have. I've got to find something for myself. I've got to stop being your bloody wife.'

Posy sat up fiercely and dashed a single tear from her eye. 'I might have known,' she said, 'not to expect constancy from a lesbian.'

The remark was so stunning that Marsha fell back to sleep, but it troubled her dreams and she woke again and demanded to know what Posy had meant.

'Nothing.'

'Of course.'

'You want a cup of tea or what?'

'I want to know what you meant.'

'Well.' Posy swung her legs out of the bed and fumbled with the day's clothes. 'You made me into a lesbian and now you're leaving me.'

'*I* – '

'Come on, you'll miss your boat.'

'Posy, you can't just say – I mean, I was the one – I mean, I always assumed – '

Posy stood up and turned on her. Her hair was standing on end and the rims of her eyes were encrusted with sleep. Her massive flesh drooped and there were stains under the arms of the nightshirt she had made out of an old sheet.

'You assumed. Yes. Everyone always assumed I was because of how I looked. Big bossy butch bitch. Must be gay. Of course.'

'Posy, I've got an hour before I leave and you say this to me.'

'I've been saving it.'

'Why?'

'Because I don't want to hear you apologising, Marsha. Your apologies bore me. You don't have to apologise to me. You didn't insult me by assuming I was a lesbian, you insulted lesbians, you insulted yourself!'

'Me! But I'm not – I mean, I wasn't – until – '

'I'll carry your suitcase.'

As they neared the harbour, Marsha said in a low voice, 'There's so much I want to know.'

'Forget it.'

'Just one thing.'

'*Forget it*.'

'When we first started going to bed together, I always felt it was, you know, you who knew what to do and I was sort of following.'

Posy shrugged. 'You made it clear what you liked.'

'Didn't you like it?'

'Oh, sure. But there was nothing I couldn't do for myself. Better if you want to know.' She looked around the morning wharf. 'Is this where the prostitutes go? I might get myself a man.'

Marsha shrugged. 'It's a woman's right to choose.' Anger rose in her. 'What a bitch you are. Giving me all this to think about. I don't even know if I believe you.' It was time to board the ship. She put her arms round Posy and kissed her several times. It was always a surprise how soft and sweet-tasting her lips were. She said, 'I may be back, you know.'

'Yeah, well, I may be here.'

'Send me an address if you move.'

'What will *your* address be, Marsha?'

'Care of . . . I don't know.'

'House of Commons?'

'Lynn's.'

The sleek ship slid from the harbour. *Called ourselves lovers*, Marsha thought wildly, *and I still don't even know whether she said all that to hurt me or because it was true. Still, there's lots of time to work it out*.

The ship steamed up to Darwin and lit out to the open sea. Marsha had a berth and a table with three other single ladies. She hinted at a bereavement so they would not press her to talk.

She remembered the early time at Collindeane Tower when she went every day to help the women build and paint, but kept her own flat. Posy had always sought her out even then; she'd felt like the new girl favoured by the head prefect. 'I don't know why you don't come and live here like the rest of us,' Posy had said one day when they were scraping rust from window frames, adding, 'at least, I do really. It's that boyfriend of yours.' And Marsha had been so relieved that Posy had not discerned the real reason, which was that she liked being private and comfortable in her own place, that she'd nodded and pulled sheepishly at her hair: 'Yes, I suppose David would have blue fit if I moved into a squatted commune of women.' 'Women *only*,' Posy had leered, 'wouldn't get his oats then, eh?' 'He's not getting them now,' Marsha had retorted, thinking, *she's jealous*, (only now she added, *but of whom?*).

David hadn't got his oats for some time; but in the end her curiosity and mild desire overcame the reluctance that his insistence inspired – it seemed a little enough thing if he wanted it so much . . . the discovery that he actually wanted to hurt her took her breath away. 'David, for heaven's sake!'

'I'm sorry, you must have a tough hymen, it's inevitable.'

'What do you mean, it's not hurting *you*, is it?' He sighed, withdrew, explained: 'It's an evolutionary mechanism to prevent young girls embarking on sex with a man they don't love – well, trust – enough to let him hurt them a little.' 'Great. Thanks very much.' She permitted him to proceed, but it got worse, he became masterful and tender, the reluctant inflictor of cosmic pleasure-pain, a role to which he was so grossly unsuited that her physical discomfort melted into embarrassment. Posy had been utterly unsympathetic when she heard about it (*jealous*? Marsha had wondered again) – 'Should've broken your own hymen. Do it in the bath, quite painless.' Now Marsha wondered: had Posy ever been with a man? Did she want to? Had her sex life been a succession of women seeking gentle love and political correctness when what she really wanted was a man to enter through her self-ruptured hymen, all evolutionary mechanisms forestalled?

Crossing the equator. Fun and ceremonies for the youngsters. (Youngsters, twenty and thirty! She was not much more, surely – she caught a glimpse of herself, gaunt, grey and witchlike in the sunlit waters of the swimming pool.) She remembered leaving England. After the performance in bed, David had seemed obsessed with a need that she should know he would not abandon her. His offer of marriage was so fervent that she felt trapped. When she told him she was going away with Posy he said bitterly, 'I always knew she'd take you away from me.' (You see? He'd assumed it too . . .)

The African coast, the canals, the coasts of Southern Europe. The uniform tall, white buildings creeping to shorelines all over the world, across desert sands or lush vegetation, as technology and the press of human bodies advanced. From the ship they looked celestial, clean, white and misty; you could not see the conditions inside, or the people who scratched a living from the alleys that separated them, like dirt between toes. What would England be like? Would anyone remember her? Did she want to be remembered? Some caustic things had been written about 'media stars ripping off the women's movement' and Marsha had recently become suspicious of the ease with which Posy obtained television or newspaper coverage. Media men seemed to think that by giving space to a quotable, eccentric, hilariously photogenic middle-aged lady who was prepared (unlike most feminists) to call herself leader and speak on behalf of the female world, they did their duty to women, and the tired topics of equality and birth-control could be given a rest. And if Posy noticed the increasing tendency to put her on gossip pages and comedy shows, she did not seem to mind overmuch.

The ship was in European waters. The same waters they'd passed through in the packet-boat when they'd first left. The night crossing. Posy laying down the law about how they would go to Paris, stay with feminist sisters there (of course they'd be welcome), Marsha terrified, wondering if they were both mad. Swigging whisky in the saloon to put off going to bed in the tiny cramped cabin Posy had booked. Posy urging, 'Come on, you'll feel awful in the morning.' Going to bed, separately, nothing happening. Getting to Paris, nothing happening. Marsha, frustrated, frightened, humiliated, adrift, picking up a man; Posy scornful (scornful she'd seemed, but now, for the hundredth time, Marsha wondered: *jealous*?) 'Like it did you?' 'Yes.' 'Experienced, was he?' 'I would say so.' 'Makes a change from Laing. Hope he didn't give you the clap.' But it was a good quarrel because later in the night Marsha wanted to make it up without waking the other women sleeping in the big communal room, so she crept over to Posy's bedside and crawled in beside her to keep warm while they talked, and fell asleep; and woke in the morning to Posy's big relieved grin and her voice saying, 'Well, that's solved that one!'

Now as she reached London's docks, Marsha tried to put aside all remembering, tried to leave everything in the churning wake behind the ship. She was glad she'd come gently by sea. She couldn't have tolerated the brutal metamorphosis of air travel.

She leaned on the ship's rail. It was December. Summer in Sydney. The air was wintry, her coat was thin. She shivered as the dim wharf got closer. Little knots of cold people huddled together, waiting. Were any of them for her? It was impossible. No one knew she was coming. If she had written to Lynn it would have closed the option of changing her mind, it would have meant spelling out what she was going for.

She approached the immigration desk. The officer peered closely at where her passport said she had right of abode. He rubbed the ink with his finger and checked her face against the photograph. A security man wandered over with a gun at his belt – but she was waved through.

Disappointed? Did she want to be sent back?

She felt her nose go red with cold, she pressed her warm hair close to her cheeks. She looked for a taxi. (Where to? Lynn had said *why don't you come home*? but that wasn't necessarily an invitation.) There was no sign of the old style box-shaped London cabs, but maybe they were new now, different. A green car whispered to a halt in front of her, polished and bright. A shiny-uniformed chauffeur stared straight ahead. The back door with its smoked-glass window opened a few inches and she was shocked to recognise David Laing. He looked smart and tense. He had aged. He no longer wore those thick anxious spectacles; now his gimlet eyes blinked at her from behind tiny ones with round gold rims, thin as the wrinkles on his brow.

'David.'

'Welcome home, Marsha. Would you like to get in?'

He was trying to look formal. He was pretending to be a cabinet minister.

'How did you know?'

'Get *in* Marsha.' She recoiled from the savagery in his voice. He toned it down with a watery smile. 'Or – or don't. I can't hang around.'

She got in. They were partitioned off from the chauffeur by the thick glass.

'Well – '

'How – '

'Who – '

'When – '

Marsha shrugged. 'Did you just happen to be passing in your chariot?'

'I knew you were landing today.'

'How?'

He let himself smile. 'Cabinet ministers know these things.'

'I don't like that. Where are we going?'

'Nowhere in particular, till you say where you want to go. We can stop any time and let you out. I'm not planning to intrude on whatever's brought you back – I just thought you might feel a bit bleak landing alone a day like this.'

'You knew I was alone as well?'

'No. If you hadn't been, you wouldn't have seen me.'

'I'm alone.' She shut her eyes in alarm against the onrush of the first tears since leaving Australia. She felt his hand pat hers, inept and tender.

'Don't,' she said.

'Okay,' he said, 'I won't.'

She felt mean. 'It makes it worse,' she explained.

'No one can see you, just sit there.' The oily plastic seating was uncomfortable, even through her trousers; there was a sweetish smell, vaguely reminiscent of coffee. 'Anyway, we're all alone when it comes to it.'

He could have meant anything, except perhaps what she meant. The surge of tears died away. 'Well, Minister. How's Family Welfare?'

She opened her eyes. He was looking at her in a way she pretended not to recognise. 'I think I know why you've come back,' he said.

'Oh, no doubt.'

'Britain's been chosen as the flashpoint, yes?'

'Sorry?'

'For the world revolution of women?'

If it was sarcasm it was subtle. He seemed embarrassed by her incomprehension, but deadly serious. 'I read that you and Posy –'

'Oh, you follow feminist news, then?'

'It's part of my job. Have I misunderstood?'

'A bit, yes.'

He was silent for a while. She realised she ought to be alone soon, find out what was happening before she said something foolish or lost some advantage. He said, 'What about . . . Posy?'

'What about her?'

'She's not here.'

'That's right.'

'What an idiot I am,' said Dave dully, 'Do you know what I thought when I heard you were coming back? I thought – if you were alone and could perhaps – well – feel differently now we're both a bit older – I thought we might, well, get married.'

She didn't want to believe him mad, but his eyes were wild and his voice shook. Her adrenalin coursed, clearing her grief and confusion like detergent chasing oil; she was alert to him. He was talking now as if she wasn't there. 'It's obscene. Reducing such things to politics . . .'

'What are you *talking* about?'

'It could be a symbol, couldn't it? If we got together – an alliance of moderates –'

'David.'

'Do you remember how you used to keep a rein on me?'

'I did?'

'I used to get so brutal. I couldn't stand the pain of people who wouldn't be helped. You always said it wasn't their fault –'

'I didn't know you listened.'

'I listened. I've missed you. How much do you know of what's going on here?'

'Not much. Sexual politics don't make the international editions, you know. Trivial, fashion-page stuff. Oh, I know about your famous Benefit.'

'You know we pay it indiscriminately?'

Marsha stared. 'I thought that was the idea.'

'We may not be able to go on with it. Things are getting out of hand.'

'Things! You mean women?'

'Marsha, stop it and listen. Who's going to hold me back? I couldn't believe it when I heard you were coming. There are pressures. Hounds snapping round my heels. Youngsters in the party after my job with their modern ideas. Benefit's expensive, Marsha, and the great oil miracle hasn't been a miracle at all. Foreign bankers . . .' he shrugged, lost for words. 'Read the papers.'

'They want you to scrap Benefit?'

'Oh, I should shut up. But I never talk to anyone, Marsha. I never have, since you went. I just argue and make speeches.'

'Will you ask your driver to stop the car and let me out?'

'Yes of course I will, if you want me to. Can I say this first, though?' He poised his knuckle to attrack the driver's attention, but waited for Marsha's nod of permission to talk a bit more first. She gave it. 'It was silly to say that about marriage, why on earth should you? Why on earth should I? I get carried away – I'd like you to be my friend. My . . . adviser, though no one would have to know. Well, you wouldn't want them to either. It's frightening, being a politician. It's like a drug. I manipulated my way into it, it was sport, I won. It's more frightening than being a social worker, you've only got individuals then. In politics, it's masses, millions. Theory and reality come together. You've got to get the theory right and then you've got to be ready to hang on when reality picks it up and runs with it, otherwise you're sunk.'

'Interesting mix of metaphors,' she murmured, and wished she hadn't.

'Sometimes I wake in the night to the sound of my voice saying the things I've said in public, and they're unbearable, unhearable. Once I made a speech about people being rats. The wrong rats. I got elected.'

'Yes, I heard about that.'

'But if you'd been here you'd only have had to say "you can't call people rats, David" in that way of yours, and I'd – '

'Hadn't you better stop crying, Minister?'

'I believe the things I've said – sometimes – I have believed them, some of them, but things come out wrong. I don't believe people are rats, of course I don't, but I do believe some people are better than others and you believe it too if you're honest, and so does everyone but most people aren't required to say anything or act on the belief, so it never gets embarrassing for them, they can stay pious, keep their hands clean.'

'What do you mean, exactly,' she asked, 'by some people being better than others?'

'Better.' He hunted despairingly for different words. 'Better, better, better. That's all I can say. If you don't know what I mean, maybe we can't talk any more, but I think you do, I think we all know, but you leave it to people you can then call fascists to work out what you mean and what to do about it. What I'm trying to say is . . . you sort of saved me from that. Your ideas were always as ludicrous as mine but we sort of . . . anchored each other. Stopped each other from getting washed away.'

'And now?'

'And now I think I'm going to need the anchor a bit more.'

'I have this feeling I'm being threatened.'

'It could be. It could be that the most important thing you could do for women would be to be my . . . friend. Everyone says I'm anti-feminist. I'm not. But how can I know what feminists even want –'

'Are you going to tell me what this is all about?'

'I can't.'

'So why say anything?'

'Work it out.'

'Have you decided how you're going to do it?'

'Do what?'

'Promote the "better" people? Eliminate the others? That's what you're saying, isn't it? Keep women in their place without Benefit?'

David stared at her and smiled ironically. 'You understand every word I say.'

'Of course.'

'And you see why I need you?'

'Of course.'

'It's yes, then?'

She listened to the purr of the car, looked out into the murky streets. An icy sleet was beginning to fall. She had nowhere to go.

'At least spend Christmas with me,' he coaxed, 'and let me tell you –'

'Christmas. Is it?'

'Nearly. Is it yes?'

'No, David, it isn't. You can keep your guilt all to yourself and we'll fight you. May I get out now, please?'

Obediently David tapped on the glass partition and the car stopped. Marsha stepped out quickly and the car was gone in seconds.

There was one position, just half way up Seyer Street, from which Collindeane Tower was invisible. The houses blocked it; then if you walked on, it sprang into view again, dark against the chill racing clouds.

The street looked derelict; some of the houses were no more than ruins, but here and there a light flickered or a shiny green curtain twitched as Marsha edged by. She raised her eyes to look at the tower. It was terraced with window boxes from which foliage and twigs spilled, as if the whole place had been taken over by giant creepers. It seemed amazing that the block stood at all; it tilted, and cracks wound up the wall showing light or boards or curtains damming out the cold from inside. More windows were blocked with paper or wood than glazed; the grass patch was ploughed up; and the courtyard looked like a scene from the first world war, coil upon coil of wire, barbed with rusty spikes. As she looked closely, Marsha could make out a possible pathway through the wire, like the parting of the Red Sea, wide enough for a slim, careful person. But a metal gate cut the path in half, and behind the gate there stood a woman with a thick coat, a club and a large dog on a leash. The sign that had once proclaimed 'All Women Welcome' was gone.

Fear, pride and loneliness choked her. She approached the guard through the gap in the wire. She shivered, but she hardly felt the cold. The battered old tower was ablaze with lights, winking from behind makeshift curtains and through cracks in the wall. Wisps of noise reached her: a few notes of music, the wail of a baby. She looked into the guard's face and felt reassured; the glance was strong and steady in its challenge, but not un-friendly. The girl was so young. She was of strong build, but had the skin and features of a teenager. Young for such responsibility.

She met Marsha at the gate. The dog lowered her head. Marsha searched her mind for a greeting that would forestall the girl crying 'Halt.' None came.

The guard said, 'Would you stop, please? Who are you?'

Marsha gave her name and the woman frowned. 'Haven't I heard of you?'

'You might have heard of my friend Posy –'

The girl said, 'I think you should understand that we accept no leadership.'

'I know, I know, it's not – ' Marsha stopped. She was being goaded into denouncing and mocking Posy. Well, Posy had her faults, but who was to say that if the women's movement had listened to her it would still be skulking in a high-rise fortified slum, guarded by children with dogs, while people like David Laing . . . 'Posy and I helped set this place up,' she said, adding without thinking, 'I put a lot of money into it.'

The girl's glance made Marsha shudder; she'd seen it before, directed at Posy: indulgence for an eccentric older sister grown too big for her boots. The dog sniffed at Marsha's bags. The guard pulled her away.

'What's the dog called?' Marsha asked miserably.

'Germaine.'

'Can I come in?'

'To check up on your investment?'

'I'm sorry,' said Marsha, 'I just got back from abroad. It's been a long time, and this seemed the obvious place to come.'

'I didn't realise.' The girl's name was Pam. She was the daughter of one of the early squatters in the tower, though Marsha did not remember her. She had lived there all her life.

Marsha flinched for the slipping away of time that she would feel when she lifted her foot over the threshold of the tower. But time did not slip; instead it seemed to pile in on her, past, present and future shattered and whirling around her like a window-pane grabbed by wind. The tower was timelessly old and modern, the guard at her side was a child, she was every age and none. The dust smelt the same as ever. Women scrubbed and mopped to hold back the tide of dirt; that was timeless. But there was a futuristic weirdness about the place too, it was almost supernatural, the upward stretching coils of staircase, the disrepair, the dim light, the hum, heaven and hell in one place.

'What's that noise?'

'I don't hear anything,' Pam said.

Soon Marsha didn't hear it either; it was the noise of people in the building, living with their doors open.

Pam showed her round. There were rooms where walls parted and windows did not fit and damp fungus grew. The floors were covered with mattresses, some with women asleep. There were bruises, wounds and bandages. It was like a refugee camp.

'It is,' said Pam, 'one thing about family values, it brings a lot of rape.'

'Organized?'

'We think so. We call them Family Men.'

'Just in London?'

'No, Everywhere.'

'And are there places like this . . . everywhere?'

'We think so.'

'You think so?'

'Somehow there's always something more urgent to do,' said Pam, 'than send out a newsletter.'

'But you have lists . . .'

'It's safer not to be on lists.'

'Is that why . . . the barbed wire?'

'Yes. Do you want to stay the night here?'

'No, it's all right.'

'Please,' said Pam, 'I'm sorry I was so crass out there.'

Marsha smiled.

Pam showed her the floor where they stored food; sacks and boxes and tins lined the walls of four flats. Some of the food was grown on the premises – winter greens on the roof and in the window boxes, potatoes in the ploughed-up surround of the tower, and an ingenious range of indoor cultivation: mushrooms in bags in dark cupboards, herbs, beans – even Lynn's account of chickens running free on the upper floors was true. Other food was bought by women who drew Benefit or had jobs, or was stolen – 'But we don't talk about that.'

There was a cooking floor – rows of rickety little cookers and spirit stoves and tables. Marsha found this oddly disappointing – she had expected canteen-size vats and large, comforting, brown earthenware pots. Pam read her mind. 'We can't afford to make a big production out of it,' she said, 'everyone ate too much. Now you eat when you're hungry, and not always then.' There was a medical floor, spotless and staffed by a couple of doctors who trained the women to become specialists in one skill apiece: early abortion, for example, or chest infections, or so-called old-fashioned methods of contraception involving rubber, or sponges and herbs and bodily rhythms. These, Pam said, turned out to be at least as reliable and far safer medically than techniques involving chemicals and male supervision.

Each flight of stairs led to a tier of flats more dilapidated than the last. Rich tapestries billowed over holes in the walls, but the women bustling about in light clothes (nodding to Pam, smiling to Marsha) seemed not to notice the cold gusts that made Marsha shiver. There were rooms for babies and young children to play; rooms for exercise and training, old women and young girls practising unarmed combat together, laughing and deadly serious. And everywhere the cleaning and the mending and the maintenance went on, as if the tower were the Forth Bridge upended.

'What about men?' said Marsha.

'What about them?'

'Do they come here?'

'No. Some of the sisters are hostile or frightened, and with reason. Sons are a problem. We haven't agreed a policy on when they become men, and of course many of the women would leave if we didn't allow sons. So they have a special floor.'

'This may sound like a silly question, but how do the women conceive?'

Pam smiled. 'Some still go for the traditional manner. Some prefer AID, and we can fix that. Some are raped.'

'What's at the top?'

'The woom.'

'Pardon?'

Pam spelled it out. 'A little girl called it that and the name stuck. It's a sort of chapel. Some of the women are into things spiritual. I'm not. It dissipates energy. It's Judy mainly – hey, you may know her. She's been her since the beginning. She's . . . well, not always calm or happy. She says there's a goddess who talks with her and watches over the tower and keeps it safe and who are we to argue? Women can do anything here, believe anything, as long as they understand, no men and no leaders. Now. Do you want to stay?'

Marsha longed for the anonymity of a hotel room. Today had been going on for years. 'I must go,' she said.

'There's one thing I didn't show you,' said Pam.

It was a quiet, clean room with a wide bed and cushions and pictures of flowers on the walls. It was as near as anything in the tower got to luxury.

'There's always someone who wants to be alone. You won't be disturbed.'

At the sight of the bed, Marsha's legs gave. Pam helped her lie down, loosened her clothes, pulled covers over her. The bed swayed with the motion of the ship. Dim thumps came from above and below. She must have fallen asleep immediately because she woke to find a mug of some kind of herbal drink, just the right heat to swallow. She did not remember Pam bringing it, or lighting the candle that flickered by the bed or drawing back the curtains so that she could gaze out into the cold, blue night with its scattering of stars, its few wide clouds and its thin slice of moon.

She didn't know how many days she stayed in that room, thinking, sleeping, relieved to find herself not wanting to eat much. She met some more women and helped with odd jobs. She was disconcerted to find that Judy Matthews (for it was the same Judy, wild-eyed, dreamy, volatile as ever, and still obsessively wearing red) not only recognised her but kept falling to her knees in front of her, seeing her as some manifestation of her goddess, come from a far-off place.

'Must've been reading the papers,' Pam said slyly, digging Marsha in the ribs, and Marsha dug back.

'I must go and see Lynn at least,' Marsha thought. She was so comfortable in the tower and the atmosphere was so free of any hint that she should leave or even make herself useful that she was starting to feel unwanted.

'At least stay for Christmas,' Pam urged.

'Do you have it?'

'Not as such. The birth of a male who thinks he's god isn't such a rare event. But Judy says there are earlier origins of a midwinter festival – it used to be the birth of the *sun* s-u-n, to the goddess, and the goddess-worshippers in places like ancient Egypt used to have lovely female ceremonies.'

'I thought you weren't into things spiritual,' said Marsha.

'Well.' Pam turned up her nose. 'It's only once a year. And it's very beautiful.'

It was. Marsha watched from the end of the street. She felt she had no right to be part of it. It was dark early morning. She pulled her coat close round her shoulders. Seyer Street seemed to decay before her eyes despite the beautifying effect of the snow that had begun to fall. The tower was in complete darkness, leaning slightly in the barbed wire field, stark against the lightening sky.

Marsha strained her eyes; a dark figure on the roof swam into view and out again. Snow crystals stuck to her eyelids.

She moved her feet up and down. They sounded like pistol-shots on the hard ground. The tower bisected the elusive pale line of dawn.

A clear tone cut the silence. A steady, high, wailing note that was unlike human or animal but pulsated with triumph. A dot of light glowed on the roof, in the hand of a robed woman. And then the tone turned to words, miraculously clear in the stillness: 'The Virgin has brought forth! The light is waxing!' And the figure turned towards the sunrise, a tiny silhouette with uplifted arms. Collindeane blazed with light, and shouts and songs came from the women who appeared with lamps at the windows. In ones and twos the lamps winked and burned the shape of a diamond down the side of the tower, and near the top of the diamond where the lights were closer together, they picked out a smaller round shape, winking like a jewel turning in firelight.

5

Lynn

Feminists had been pushing leaflets through letter-boxes urging women to ignore Christmas. If they were not taking part in female festivals they should stay in bed on December 25, go for long walks together, or do political work. Christmas was a myth. Christmas had never been a holiday for women. Christmas was when families came together in greed and discord, and women slaved in kitchens. Christmas was in celebration of the male god of a brutally masculist religion, it was about a misogynist fantasy, a woman who was maternal but not sexual – the reverse of the truth more often than not.

One such leaflet had flopped through the front door of the Byers' house just as Lynn was embarking on her thrice-daily battle to persuade Jane, red-faced and sulky, to swallow the enzyme tablets that would supplement the failings of her own digestive system; and an embarrassed Derek was trying to explain politely that he needed his meal *now* as he had a departmental meeting to go to. Lynn stamped exasperated to the front door and read the badly-printed bit of paper.

'Great,' she said, 'Christmas is off this year.'

If only Derek had laughed or argued the moment would have passed; but he just said, 'All right, dear,' (playing the henpecked husband; was he asking for it?) and that appeared to be settled. And when a woman came round from the Neighbours' Association (a FAMILY front which Lynn had refused to join) to ask if anyone from the Byers household would care to join the estate's Christmas party, Jane had piped up, 'Ooh yes, because mummy says we can't have Christmas this year.' And Derek had said, 'Er, yes, that is kind, my wife has been rather tired of late,' and the bearer of the invitation (mother of six, who also housed her husband's elderly parents) had given Lynn an expressive glance and said, 'Excellent. I'll expect the three of you then.' And Lynn had growled, 'Two.'

So now she was all alone on Christmas afternoon. It was still early, but midwinter gloom was gathering. She went to the front door and peered out at the neat estate with its festive lights beaming smugly through curtains on to the vegetable allotments. (The Neighbours' Association had agonised long over whether to permit allotments; cheap food versus the tone of the neighbourhood; cheap food won). Lynn yearned for Seyer Street. Of course it was no place to raise a child with lungs so vulnerable to infection that a common cold could kill her; the houses on the estate were clean, centrally heated, with indoor loos; but she detested the rise in their station in life, the professorial couple. And the way the houses were built, the open-plan ground floor with no door to slam between herself and the rising tide of debris that being a full-time housewife somehow created; and the upstairs, the trendy brainwave of 'accommodating a family's needs at different stages in the life-cycle' by having not rooms but adjustable partitions. Thus the newly-married couple were expected to frolic freely in the open space, like rats in a garage; the first baby could be closeted off in a corner; and each additional toddler or teenager could have its own territory, ceded by parents who by now probably didn't need that big a bedroom anyway. And in time, of course, when the children moved out, the·elderly grandparents could move in. 'Homes built for a lifetime of caring,' crooned the builders' blurb.

It was disconcerting to have won the battle over Christmas so easily, to be by herself as requested. (*Where has it gone, that old exultation in being alone? Died the death probably – and a merciful release. I am never alone.*) What should she do? Read something? A bit feeble. Write something? Ah, but either it would work or it wouldn't, and either way it would hurt because she'd never get it finished. Drink something? Nothing in the house. She giggled. How sacrilegious could you be? How low could a mother sink, how much more could a husband tolerate? A gust of wind blew burning powdery snow in her face. She slammed the door, put the radio on for company.

We take you now into the candlelit chapel at King's College for the Festival of Nine Lessons and Carols –

She caught her breath. Even in the Christmases of her most rebellious, anti-religious youth she had loved this, braving teasing to listen to it. She'd missed it, the past few Christmases, too busy with the parties Jane always wanted. She didn't even know they still had it. Now she could listen alone. Was that all right? Was it all right for a wife-and-mother who'd gone on strike against domestic chores to listen to the carol service from Cambridge?

Once in royal David's city
stood a lowly cattle shed

Tears pricked the backs of her eyes. Lovely pain surged in her. As the note rose she waited for the falter, the flaw that was never there.

And his shelter was a stable
and his cradle was a stall

The Benefit babies weren't being sheltered in stables or cradled in stalls, she thought suddenly; adding fiercely, *not quite*. Her mind wandered to the women she'd read about, unable to find jobs or weary of depending on oafish husbands, who were increasing their families as the only way of increasing their incomes. Market forces! You want babies, you pay for 'em! Lynn laughed. The poor little things shot from their startled mothers under the ministrations of the new vacuum-operated labour-aids in the great state maternity wards which were virtually all that remained of the National Health. Yes, birth was moving forwards to the twenty-first century, but what about the other technological miracles so breathlessly promised in the colour supplements up until a few years ago?

It was not that you necessarily wanted a robot to do your housework, or computerised shopping or supersonic underground trains or a meal-in-a-pill, as they had (one was told) in the more advanced Western countries; it was just that it was oddly embarrassing to be cooking and cleaning as you always had as the century of progress limped towards its end, or queueing for a slow, seatless bus to the hypermarket, or popping round to the corner store with a plastic bag to see if they had any rotten potatoes. No, there was no doubt. As far as the housewife was concerned, the technological revolution appeared to have been postponed.

> *And through all his wondrous childhood*
> *he would honour and obey*
> *love and watch the lowly maiden*
> *in whose gentle arms he lay*

Lynn's thoughts wandered to Jane. (*Love and watch! Honour and obey! I should be so lucky!*) Poor kid. She was bright, that was one thing; she lost little by not being able to go to school regularly. She loved to read, anything she could lay her hands on, science, philosophy, novels, history, comics, and her brain arranged the information more effectively than any syllabus could. It was the one concession she made to pleasing her mother; or maybe she did not realise how happy it made Lynn, or she would have given it up immediately and become a gawping moron.

Lynn had always fought to dispel her own depression about Jane's illness by reminding herself how much worse it could have been (Jane's case was fairly mild, and she seemed to have good resistence to infection. With proper care there was no reason why she shouldn't survive into healthy adulthood.) But Jane could hardly be expected to see it from that point of view. All she knew was that she had deep, unpleasant coughs, difficult bowel movements and regular, hated physiotherapy sessions in which she was lain over cushions in five different positions, three times a day for half-an-hour, while her mother thumped her chest. And that she was forbidden to eat fried food or anything with fat, and coaxed constantly to down more proteins than the family could afford. She was bullied to take exercise but forbidden to get cold or wet. She swallowed pills till she rattled. And she couldn't go out for whole days because her mother didn't trust anyone to look after her properly.

The one thing Jane didn't know yet was that it was all her mother's fault. Well, and her father's. The thing was hereditary, they had given it to her. Once she discovered that, Lynn thought, the final seal would be set on Jane's hatred and rebellion.

Was it that, though? Weren't all thirteen-year-olds difficult? Especially only children, loved invalids? Jane was so innocently deft in directing her venom. The precocious questioning: 'Why haven't I got any brothers or sisters?' 'Were you ever a *famous* writer, mummy?' 'Why don't we ever see Jim nowadays?' like darts to the heart from that sweet, clever face, those cloudless eyes; the instinctive interest in anything her mother disliked, the insistence, for example, on listening this morning to the monarch's Christmas message.

The usual stuff. Happy to think of you all together at this family time. Not much can go wrong with a nation that reveres its families. Etcetera.

The royal women were breeding like rabbits – *and drawing Benefit too, you bet your life*. Set a good example. Was everyone mad? The world groaned and choked with population, yet some European nations were uneasy about their own falling birth-rates. Finding a work-force might one day be a problem; and they had grown tired of immigrants, who brought discord, not to mention dependants. Besides, who could say that their countries' cartels might not shut off supplies of labour power one day, as nations in the past had shut off oil or coffee, as a means of blackmail? The British birth boom was of some interest.

Lynn went close to her radio as the voices of the carollers blended and soared and faded back into murmured prayer – every one of them, from the piping choirboys to the sonorous bass, from the Eton scholar reading the lesson to the extension of themselves to which they all prayed – every one of them male.

Our Father –

Some feminists were into goddess religions. Lynn considered it all irrelevant. Nevertheless – how different would it sound – would it feel – would it be – if it was Our Mother? If it was (she tested as the service moved on) *for unto us a daughter is given, and the government shall be upon her shoulder, and her name shall be called wonderful, counsellor, the mighty goddess, the everlasting mother, the princess of peace –*

It sounded like a different person, but what did it matter?

> *frosty winds made moan*
> *earth stood hard as iron*
> *water like a stone*

And dossers thronged, she knew, through the corridors of the abandoned building at a road junction just south of the Thames that had once been the headquarters of the nation's social security system, and they probably thronged in the churches of Cambridge too, when they weren't turfed out for a service; and pensionless old folk knocked on doors for money, or grudging relatives crammed them into tiny flats and houses; and FAMILY had organised a Christmas procession through the centre of town, featuring pregnant women, and mothers with babies in their arms, and prostitutes whose banners proclaimed them reformed.

> *And to Adam he said, because thou hast hearkened to the voice of thy wife, and hath eaten of the tree, of which I commanded thee, saying, Thou shalt not eat of it; cursed is the ground for thy sake –*

Christmas had always been a boom time for broken marriages, and whatever Benefit had done for the birth-rate, it had done little for marital harmony, shifting the balance of financial control and uncovering new tensions. As usual, battered women would go streaming to feminist havens like Collindeane for comfort, treatment (for weren't doctors entitled to a holiday?) or permanent shelter; they would tell of rows ('you're paid, aren't you? damn well keep the place clean!') and blows struck as the twelve days of unpaid compulsory vacation succeeded each other and the walls of the home closed in, and husbands grew bored but would not pick up a broom, and the cheap liquor that made their heads ache ran out, and children cried for things they could not have. All this was known by anyone who cared to read the more honest newspapers, or to listen properly to themselves or their next-door neighbours, but the myth persisted, the slush and the tinsel, and the bloody damn beautiful carol music continued . . .

> *Nay had the apple taken been, the apple taken been, then never Our Lady crowned heavenly queen* –

Another story: almost incredible: men grew primitive when denied food. Women would tell of how they had to stock up for twelve days (for weren't shop assistants entitled to a holiday?) and stand guard as their families' boredom and hunger threatened the stocks . . . women had their eyes blacked for reminding adult men that tins of beans devoured today would not be available tomorrow. (If it came to court, magistrates put it down to the time of year.)

Now a dignatory of the city of Cambridge, his voice resplendent in velvet and fur, was intoning, *Behold the handmaid of the lord, be it unto me according to thy word.* And Lynn gave an involuntary shout of laughter as the vision snapped into her mind of a golden FAMILY hand, which emblem she never saw without wishing to paint a chain round the pretty wrist. Factory after factory had fired its married women: you're not suitable, they said, and besides you do not need to work. Often the policy cost them money; men had to be paid more; but there was male morale to be taken into account, and once the women were gone, male wages could fall. Childless men were told – you do not need so much, with only yourself to support. Fathers were told – you do not need so much, your wife is drawing Benefit. To this the unions responded with the meek suggestion that when a man was unemployed he ought at least to be the one to draw the family's Benefit, for reasons of morale; but the government said – no way. If a man wants the status of breadwinner, let him earn it.

Glory to God in the highest, and on earth, peace, goodwill towards – Lynn turned the radio off. The silence beat in her ears. And a soft tap at the front door broke it.

She froze. The wind? Or Jim, fleeing from some fresh eccentricity of his mother's, or of the tower where she made him live? Or the heavy mob come to beat up renegade mothers? There it was again.

At first she did not recognise Marsha. Marsha from the past! Marsha trying to look like a middle-aged lady but failing utterly, being still skinny and gauche with long hair that looked fiddled-with, and snow on her nose.

They stared at each other.

Lynn was feeling increasingly uncomfortable; it took time to realise it was because she was forgetting to breathe. She let air out of her lungs and felt better. The cloud of her breath spread and vanished, a magic mist that would spirit Marsha away as oddly as she had come. 'Well,' she said, 'it's you.'

'Happy Christmas.'

'Oh. Well. Yes.'

'Can I come in?'

'Er, sure. Of course.'

Marsha came in, her coat dripping on the carpet. She looked rounded in alarm at the emptiness. 'I thought you'd be, you know all together. I thought I could visit.' Still Lynn couldn't find any words for her. 'What are you staring at, for heaven's sake?' Marsha seemed very distressed now. 'What's happened, where is everyone, what are you staring at?'

'Your nose. You've got snow on it.'

They laughed and embraced and would not let go of each other.

'What are you *doing*?' Lynn cried.

'You invited me. "Why don't you come home and see, for heaven's sake?" you said.'

'But why didn't you tell me? I mean – when did you arrive? And where have you been? Oh Marsha, how do we even start to talk?'

They giggled and punched each other and had another hug. Lynn brought Marsha a hot drink.

'Good God. What's this?'

'Koffee with a k, from the industrial heart of Europea.'

'The industrial heart of what?'

'Europea. Oh some new broom's bright idea for a new version of the Common Market, more exclusive than the last. Haven't you heard of it, you colonials? *Well*. You obviously aren't going to be asked to join.'

'Don't want to join.' Marsha sipped her drink and flinched. 'Got punch, this, eh? Gets you in the gut. What's it made of?'

'Plutonium.'

'Ha ha.'

'Maybe not, but our rich partners don't half sell us a lot of waste.'

'Does Dave have to drink this stuff, or do ministers get the real thing?'

'What makes you ask that?'

'He used to go a bit mad if he didn't get enough coffee.'

'Have you seen him? How long have you been back? Where have you been?'

'Collindeane.'

'Did you see Jim?' Lynn's face was eager.

'I don't know . . . there are some boys, but they don't sort of mix . . .'

'But Judy's still there?'

'Oh yes.'

'Then he must be.' Lynn clenched and unclenched her fists. 'He's devoted to his mother.'

'When did he go back to her?'

'When she found she could claim Benefit for him.'

Marsha tried to break the silence by describing the birth-of-the-sun ceremony. 'It was beautiful, but I got a bit sentimental. Odd, isn't it? I thought, today is Christmas day, and what I need is a family.' She paused, seeing the hard thin line of Lynn's mouth. 'I've said the wrong thing, haven't I?'

Lynn laughed. 'It's a knack you have.'

With time and talk they relaxed a bit. Marsha gave a vivid account of her travels and adventures, but her silence on Posy and herself screamed aloud. Lynn presumed that the thing with Posy (whatever it was) had ended sadly, and she would learn about it when Marsha felt ready. Lynn's inhibitions melted. It was a long time, she realised, since she had had a good honest talk with a woman friend, one of those talks in which politics and jokes and emotions just interwove at will and conclusions emerged only to be shattered into pieces, each one of which contained as much truth as the original.

'So this is the future,' Marsha sighed, after Lynn's account of the fall in living standards, the inexorable creep of poverty. 'Whatever happened to the oil-bonanza?'

Lynn frowned. 'There was one . . . I think. Or maybe we're still in it. A lot of factories got built and there's less unemployment now and rich people went abroad to escape the taxes. It didn't penetrate very far to the, you know, lower echelons. Well, we owed a lot of money anyway, didn't we – to Arabs and people. And the Third World countries started getting uppity about their commodity prices, and Europe practically dictating trading terms to us . . . whoever thought the oil was going to solve everything? I didn't, for one. The government could have asked me.'

Marsha wasn't laughing. 'Would you like that? I mean, to be a sort of government adviser, or civil servant or something?'

'You're tactfully asking me if I don't wish I had a job. I've got a job. I look after a little girl who'd be dead if I didn't. Okay? Anyway, no one employs women now, and if you earn anything at all you lose your Benefit.'

'Yes.'

'We can't afford this house for a start. But we had to move, for Jane. Her things are expensive too – quite apart from the pills, she's supposed to eat three high-protein meals a day. Who in the world can afford three high-protein meals a day? And Derek's on half-salary. He's in one of these very democratic departments where they share jobs instead of making people redundant. What it means in practice is that he does twice the work for half the money, you get the idea? Behind the picturesque frontage, we're dirt poor. I work, of course. I type and edit and index stuff for Derek's mates, and there are agencies that specialise in finding home-work for intellectual Benefit mums on the quiet, but you can guess how they pay.'

'Do you mind very much?'

'I mind. No, not very much. There have been times – you'll laugh.'

'I won't.'

'I've pretended to go out on stories. I've gone along to some event and pretended to be from a paper that doesn't exist. I don't know why.'

The conversation retreated, rallied, regrouped, advanced over dangerous ground. Marsha wanted to know why, really, Lynn was so tied. Lynn explained sharply about Jane needing constant care. Marsha persisted. Couldn't Derek, neighbours, schoolteachers, learn how to look after her? No, said Lynn, because she fusses and cries and becomes so piteous that it takes a mother's love to cut through all that and hurt her for her own good. 'Maybe you could teach me,' said Marsha hesitantly, and Lynn snapped back, 'Why? Are you planning to live here?' She didn't feel as hostile as she sounded; she would quite like to have Marsha around, even for a long time; she'd just had a flash of anger at being taken for granted, of being intruded upon, of yet another free person using her home as a base from which to sally forth and take over the world.

Marsha said shortly, 'I'm going to live at Collindeane. You could get involved there if you wanted. And bring Jane.'

'I'm a FAMILY woman myself,' said Lynn.

'You?'

'No, of course not. They're smug and revolting, but they have emotional appeal, a thing the women's movement is a bit short on for someone in my position. FAMILY tells me I'm a valid, glorious noble person and gives me money of my own. It doesn't tell me I'm a sucker wasting my time, it doesn't tell me I should be on the streets demanding institutions to put Jane in so that I can go out and fulfil myself, unquote.'

'Lynn, it isn't like that.'

'Isn't it? It's just coincidence, is it, that the majority of those women are either childless or selfish bitches like Judy Matthews who only want their children because of the income they bring in –'

'That isn't even true.'

'I know. Have you seen this?' Lynn tossed over a glossy, colourful booklet entitled *Family Care in these Difficult Times*. Marsha thumbed through the laborious hints for saving money: getting the best from cheap meat, high-rise horticulture, mend your own shoes. 'I have been known,' Lynn was saying, 'to sneak out on dark nights to the perimeters of hypermarkets and forage in the gutters. You'd be surprised what you find. You'd be surprised who you run into as well – the nicest class of person. This is the new style professional poverty, you know. No rags, no begging. Just a bloody load of work.'

'For women.'

Lynn shrugged. Marsha said, 'You do talk well. I wish I'd been making notes.' She explained about Posy's book. Lynn said, 'What's this then, a fact-finding mission?'

'That, and to see you. Hey, maybe you can help?'

'Oh? How much are you paying? It's all right, it's all right, just a joke. It's just this assumption that boring housewives are always just dying to help people write their books. Don't you think I'd be writing my own if –'

'Lynn I'm sorry and you couldn't ever be boring.'

Lynn stuck out her tongue. 'I know.'

They talked and drank koffee and Marsha glanced round the room, bare of decorations, and declared it the best Christmas day she'd ever spent. The snow was swirling thickly outside, and the night sky had a greenish tinge. At about seven the front door opened and Derek and Jane came in; Derek was pink with slight tipsiness but trying to hide it by being very solemn, crumpling a gold foil hat into his pocket; Jane was giggling as she came in the door, but immediately took on a pale, pained expression as she caught sight of her mother and her visitor.

Derek didn't recognise Marsha at first, but was enthusiastic and welcoming when he did; Jane, however, made it clear that she did not want third parties intruding on her relationship with her mother. She had a normal build for a thirteen-year-old, skinny with the faint beginnings of breasts, but very adult features. Her hair was flaming red, her skin white and her eyes penetrating and resentful. She seemed to lack any sense of play; she spoke in short, economical sentences and sat about in adult poses, only deigning to behave like a child when her mother ventured to announce that it was time for her physiotherapy. A painful scene ensued. Marsha was torn three ways. She felt pity, of course, for the child. But as a visiting aunty she must not, by so much as a flicker of her face, show any emotion that might be taken as interference. Overriding this dilemma, however, was the murderous anger she felt against the brat whose struggles and howls as Lynn coaxed her upstairs seemed timed with the precision of a ballerina, and deadly accurate in their power to hurt.

When she was alone with Derek, he said, 'What do you think of her?'

Marsha had always liked Derek. He had struck her as the sort of man who, if there were more of him, would make feminism unnecessary. That was how he used to seem, at least; things might be different now, with his daughter, his homebound wife and his professorship. Still – it was touching, the air of apology that hung round him like a halo, this naked request for admiration of his obnoxious, unfortunate daughter.

'I think she's lovely,' Marsha stammered out, 'Can she live a fairly normal life?'

Derek smiled. 'You knew I meant Lynn?'

'Oh. No. Lynn seems tired.'

'She is tired,' he said.

'How has she adjusted to – you know –'

'The only way Lynn would adjust. By being obsessive and conscientious and not letting herself think about how it needn't have happened –'

'I'm sure she doesn't expect you to take the blame. Not more than half, anyway. If it is blame, which I doubt.'

'She seemed to decide to have a child very suddenly,' he said, 'in the middle of being very anti it. I was glad it took us such a long time. It meant it wasn't just an impulse. I still can't help feeling I pushed her into it.'

'Does she say that?'

'Of course not.'

'Well then.'

'Are you staying long?'

'Not here,' she said touchily, 'I'm going to get involved in things at Collindeane tower – you remember?'

'Do I remember? I'm always telling Lynn she ought to go up there.'

'Hm. Interesting dilemma, when a man tells his wife she ought to be more feminist.'

'No!' He spread his hands in anxious apology, 'No, that isn't what I meant at all, it's just –'

'Derek, it's all right, I'm only teasing.'

Their invitation to Marsha to stay for the rest of the holiday seemed sincere enough, so she did. She kept off the subject of Collindeane, trying instead to make friends with Jane and learn to look after her. The two proved mutually exclusive. The only role in which Jane would accept Marsha was as an ally against Lynn. But even this seemed exploitable. 'Mummy always hurts me,' Jane would whine. 'Maybe I could learn to do it so that it won't hurt you,' Marsha coaxed. 'I don't want it done at all,' Jane would say, though on the few occasions when Lynn left the treatment late, Jane became edgy in spite of herself. Marsha managed to interest her in the possibility of proving mummy wrong in her theory that nobody else could thump Jane's chest in the correct manner; and Lynn got a few days out with Derek and some uninterrupted reading.

At night, Marsha slept in a partitioned-off corner upstairs; she had a collapsible bed with uncomfortable sheets which seemed clean to the eye but felt shiny and sticky. The central heating imparted a uniform airless warmth through the place and could not be controlled. It was hard to imagine this being good for anyone's respiration, but Lynn insisted it worked wonders for Jane. Some nights Marsha's body felt the motion of the sea, and odd dreams came: she was on a ship that was a block of flats with Posy at the top of the steps saying, 'Marry me, Marsha, and we'll make ourselves useful', but the ship sailed on and it wasn't going anywhere. She awoke, wet with hot-and-cold sweat, hearing Jane's rasping breath through the partition, thinking, *I must help with –* but unable to remember whom she had to help. She went back to sleep fretting, *I'm not welcome, I must leave here*, and then she was in David's house, in his bed for heaven's sake, and he was explaining very gravely that he had to hurt her for her own good.

Lynn stood over her with a steaming cup and an old radio with David's voice coming out of it.

Marsha hoisted herself up in bed.

'What time is it?'

'Nearly mid-day.'

'You should've got me up –'

'Why?' Lynn handed her the cup. 'Last day of the Christmas hols. All the politicians are back at work.' She turned up the volume on the radio. 'Thought you might like to hear your friend.'

Marsha sipped. There was something about this koffee for getting you up in the morning. It grabbed you by the throat like a ferret, shook you into wakefulness. It sharpened up her hearing for Dave, who didn't sound at all like himself, and it wasn't just because of the rather old transistor.

'. . . certain necessary modifications in the administration of Benefit, owing to the need to concentrate national resources on preparing industry for . . .'

Marsha yawned. 'Wait for it,' Lynn said.

'. . . until now has been paid indiscriminately. We are now introducing an element of selectivity . . .'

Marsha put her cup down. She was wide awake.

'. . . linked to a programme of education for motherhood, necessitated by a decline in standards which is a cause of grave national concern . . .'

Another voice cut in, a silvery, resonant, younger man's voice. 'This is not simply a matter of economics.' He himself was interrupted then, for commercials. It gave Marsha a chance to ask Lynn who he was.

'Peel,' said Lynn, 'a frightening young man in a hurry. Whizz kid, coming up fast under Laing. his approach to social policy has a pleasing simplicity. It's just another branch of industry. He is of the opinion that Benefit is a matter of investment, pure and simple. Paying mothers produces good workers and hence is cost-effective. He made a wonderful speech the other day, against the re-introduction of old age pensions. Point one, old people are useless. Point two, they only need pensions because they have lived improvident lives and haven't kept in with their families. Therefore they don't deserve pensions. They say he's descended from the original Sir Robert. Of whom it was said his smile was like the silver plate on a coffin.'

'There's something pretty coffin-like about this guy's voice,' said Marsha, 'when I really listen.'

Peel was speaking again. 'The Family Party remains a party of principle. Our founding principle was to reverse the discrimination that our society practised against dutiful mothers. We were the first party ever to assert that such women ought not to be in complete financial subjection to their husbands. Yet women in absurd numbers and on the flimsiest of pretexts have been exploiting the independence we have given them. They walk out on husband and home; they raise children unnaturally in all-female communities. Standards of moral and physical hygiene defy belief. With the aid of male dupes or perverted science, fatherless infants are conceived. Daughters are raised to hate men, sons to hate themselves. The women blaspheme, rewrite history, pervert nature, are greedy and immodest. They attack the state, yet draw money from it. They abandon the old and the sick. Families should be the cement of the nation; women should be the cement of families – the importance of which role we have acknowledged in the only way that counts. But the nation is falling apart. We must change our brand of cement.'

The magical voice paused and David's came back.

'It will be open to any woman who has her Benefit withdrawn to present herself at her local FAMILY branch for rehabilitation and training. On satisfactory completion, payment may be restored.'

And then the men moved on to talk about something else.

'Is that how it works?' Marsha asked with wonder, 'Don't they put things through parliament any more?'

'Oh sure. They'll do it one night when there's a football match on. Mrs Patel will say something against it – she's the Family Party's bleeding conscience – but no one'll be interested, Marsha. These are *women's* issues.'

Later in the day they listened to government announcements

detailing how the new scheme would work. Women could assume that their Benefit would continue unless they heard to the contrary. Anyone wishing to make a complaint against a specific mother could do so anonymously.

Lynn said, 'One thing. This'll bring a lot of women together.'

'Yes . . .' said Marsha cautiously, not wanting to forestall whatever was coming next.

'It'll prove what one lot said all along. That the whole point of Benefit was to control us.'

'And at the same time,' said Marsha, 'we'll fight to the death to prevent it being taken away.'

'It's what they call feminine logic.'

After they'd laughed together, Marsha ventured, 'We're going to be there, aren't we Lynn?'

'Yes,' she said, and there was no hesitation, 'Oh yes.'

Marsha wrote to Posy.

'You must come. No, *not* to lead. It may exasperate you (it does me) the way everything is so untogether but at least there is something now on which we can all agree. All feminists, that is; and some others too – already some women from FAMILY have come over to us in disgust and asked us what we plan to do. The reception they get varies – the ones who go on about the government undermining women's sacred vocation to motherhood tend to get short shrift, and some have flounced out in disgust at their first sight of lesbians kissing! Others find our leisurely style of decision-making every bit as infuriating as you would, my dear. But still . . . Isabel Travers always used to say we were all on the same side! She's the grandame of the party, she never stood for parliament, thinking it more womanly to manipulate from the rear – she's given a sort of grudging endorsement to the idea of selectivity, but it sounds as if it's more in the interests of party unity than anything else . . . Mrs Patel, her chum, now turned radical (all things are relative) has been deafeningly silent. Of course, for every renegade, FAMILY's acquiring new friends, nastier and further right than before, but still . . .

'Now we wait on tenterhooks to find out who will be the first to have her Benefit withdrawn, and what the famous rehabilitation and training will consist of. It's assumed that women in the feminist communities will be first for the chop, so Collindeane is trying to increase its self-sufficiency. You would be surprised at the farming that can be done in a block of flats and a patch of land. And of course no one sees anything wrong with shoplifting or burglary from the rich. And we have skills here which we never have to buy – plumbing, (your legacy, I like to think), making clothes, doctoring, etc. And while it's necessary, some of us can still work for pay.

'Posy I miss you, and you would love it here. Please come.'

Some women fled from Collindeane. They felt that by severing their links they could safeguard their money. Judy Matthews was one who went, taking her son Jim. This saddened Lynn. The chance of making peace with Judy and re-establishing contact with the boy she still thought of as hers had been a factor in bringing her to the tower with Marsha.

An official letter came to a woman who lived there with her three babies. She'd come to escape the bullying of her violent husband, and was now getting hesitantly into an affair with Pam, the girl Marsha had first met on sentry duty. The woman opened the letter and read it, but everyone knew what it would say.

'I'm an unfit mother.'

'I should hope so,' said Pam, 'living here.'

'My husband has complained.'

'Good.'

'What am I going to do?' Her flippancy dropped. She was scared.

The women said, 'It's okay, you know. If we starve, we starve together.'

'But it's not fair if I stay here and can't contribute.'

'You can contribute. We need to know what goes on at these rehabilitation joints.'

Pam interrupted. 'Hey, wait a minute.' The unfit mother said, 'It's true. I'll go.'

When they turned up at the office marked REHABILITATION, the green-uniformed clerk looked at the six of them and said, 'All of you?'

'All of us,' they said in unison, but the unfit mother said, 'No, just me.'

'This way. The rest of you can go home.'

'We're waiting.'

'You wait outside them.'

They stood for four hours in the bitter cold outside the olive-painted office that had once belonged to the Department of Health and Social Security. Strange women walked through and up to the green door. They were forlorn or frightened or stiff-faced with defiance but they did not stop to talk and none of them came out. Snow was making patterns against a black sky when the unfit mother at last returned. She was laughing but unnerved.

'They're mad.'

Pam cuddled her. 'Come home, love, and tell us.'

'No, I have to decide, there's something I have to decide now.'

'Tell us.'

They formed a ring to keep her warm.

'They asked me lots of questions. Where did I live, why did I leave my husband, what sort of eduction were the children getting, why hadn't I brought them with me. I didn't know I had to, I said, all wide-eyed.'

'That's the trouble with you unfit mothers,' said Pam, 'you don't read so good.'

'They said, "You do realise, don't you, that having your Benefit withdrawn is a very serious matter?" As if it was something *I'd* done. They said I had a choice. I could walk right out – "you're not a prisoner, you know, Mrs er-um," they kept saying. Or I could go home to you-know-who, which act would immediately reinstate my fitness and restore my money. Or, if I refused to see sense and do that, I'd have to prove my willingness to get fit. "How do I do that?" I said –'

'Wide-eyed?'

'Wide-eyed, quite. They said, "how d'you fancy a few months on the continent?" "What?" I said. "We've found this nice family for you," they said, "diplomatic service, three children of their own, they need a bit of help. In return for that, they'll help you and train you in the best ways of mothering your own."' The unfit mother looked round with grim satisfaction at her friends' astonishment. 'I said to them, I said, "I knew we were doing the shit-work for their industries. I didn't know we were cleaning the shit out of their lavatories as well."'

'Great. What did they say?'

'Well, we argued a bit, and then I said I'd go. To play along, you know. They said I had to see a doctor first. "It's all right, thank you," I said, "I'm quite well." But they gave me to this loony doctor. The first thing he said to me was, "Lie down.." "No,"

I said. "But this is for birth control," he said, as if he expected me to say, oh, *birth control*, I *see*, that's all right then. And then I saw it. He didn't mean me to, not then, but he lifted the wrong cloth. It was like a small glass crab, full of green fluid, and it had spikes. "It's very modern," he said. "I can see that," I said. "It's not like something you've got to remember," he said, "once it's in, it's in." I was looking at the spikes. He was going on. "After all, we don't want you having more babies till you know how to look after the ones you've got, do we? And it's quite safe, we've tested it on gorillas." "You keep that thing to decorate your Christmas tree," I said, "I'm gay."

'Then the shit really hit the fan. It appears there's a special rehabilitation place for lesbians, and this wasn't it.'

Pam put protective arms round her. 'Wherever it is, you aren't going.'

'It's somewhere out in the fens. And I am.'

'But what if it works?' Pam wailed.

A mother living in Seyer Street had her Benefit withdrawn. She was told it was because of her morals. But it was years since she'd been on the game. She'd given up all that when FAMILY moved in to make the street a showcase of their methods. Someone must have been spreading scandal.

Now she went to FAMILY and asked what she had to do to get her Benefit back. She should know, they said. Was she being a good mother? She had better give up boyfriends and let them fit her with a Pellet. The Pellet was filled with stuff that would be gradually released to stop her getting pregnant, if she were to slip up on her vow to give up boyfriends. No, they didn't think there was anything to be gained by letting her see it.

Would she get her Benefit back now, she enquired woozily through the fading anaesthetic? Well, they said, they would see.

Back home, her children screamed and punched her, demanding food. She went out and quaked on a street corner. It was stupid to be frightened of being grabbed by a stranger when that was your line of business.

It wasn't long before a man came by and asked, 'Do you fuck for money?' Moonlight winked on a flash of gold on his shoulder. She couldn't take him home because of corrupting the children. She led him behind an empty house. The proceedings were short and peremptory. He didn't want any clothing removed. He didn't want to talk either, which embarrassed her; in the old days even the most silent customer usually said *something*, if only an obscenity, or his false name, or hers. In her awkwardness she chattered, and let fall the fact that she came from Seyer Street.

'Seyer Street? Then you had every chance to reform.' His whole weight was behind the fist that smashed her face. She stood her ground, thinking, *right mate, that doubles the fee*. Every chance to reform! Bending metal for fancy gadgets for rich foreigners, doing it at dead of night for fear of losing Benefit – and losing it anyway in the end! Wicked, sharp metal that fought you and gashed your fingers – 'You are a bad girl,' the man was saying, 'and I shall have to punish you.' *Oh God, one of them*. He had a stick – a club, a plank. He had picked it up on the derelict land. He hit her head and her legs and her back, over and over till it didn't even hurt. 'And don't ask for money,' were his parting words, 'You liked it.'

Women from Collindeane found her crawling up the street, dumb, weeping and covered in blood. They took her in.

'We know you're not ready to talk, but can you understand? Tap once for yes, twice for no.'

The woman's hand tapped.

'You were raped?'

She hesitated before tapping once, yes.

'And beaten up?'

Tap.

'We can give you some injections, in case he has given you a disease. Is that all right?'

Tap

'And we can do a minor operation to clear your womb in case he made you pregnant.' She shuddered and clutched herself. 'Do you want that?'

Tap, tap, tap, tap, no, no.

'All right. Is that because you would want to be pregnant?'

No.

'Then it's because you know you can't be? Because you've got something inside you?'

She stayed at Collindeane, in the quiet room, and became calmer. She was not badly injured, but she couldn't speak. Through signs she communicated that she wanted the women to go and find her children, but when they tried, the house was empty. This sent her into deeper silence.

A neat lady came to the tower in an Olex suit and home-made shoes.

'I wouldn't normally come,' she said, 'to a place like this.'

'But your Benefit's been taken away?'

'You're the only people. My husband said I should come.'

'What did they say?'

'They didn't. They say it might be a mistake in the computer. They're looking into it.' She started to sob. 'I've been in FAMILY since it started.

The women exchanged glances. 'I'm sure they'll find it was a mistake,' they soothed.

'But in the meantime – '

'You're short of money?'

'Good gracious no!'

'Then – ?'

'I can't face my friends.'

The unfit lesbian mother who had gone to the fens for rehabilitation escaped back to Collindeane. She told of a honeycomb of little white cells in the middle of a marsh. Rehabilitation meant being put in one of the cells and making it into a home. You were supposed to paint it and keep it clean and furnish it tastefully from a catalogue. When you had done one cell satisfactorily, they removed one wall and hooked up a second, and so on until you had made a beautiful home. At which point your children could be sent for, and your husband (or surrogates, if these were not available). You would then learn to look after them.

As far as sex was concerned, the unfit mother had been given to a pleasant-mannered man who did not hold with the notion that it was necessary to inject anaesthetic into the clitoris of a lesbian or frigid woman in order to relocate her sexuality where it belonged; he felt sure that he could rely on his technique.

'And could he?' Pam demanded.

A dreamy look came into the unfit mother's eyes. 'He was certainly nice.'

'There,' stormed Pam, 'I said she shouldn't go.'

The unfit mother hugged her. 'Only kidding.'

'Well, don't,' Pam grumbled.

'Did you finish the course? I mean, are you now fit?'

'No,' said the woman, 'I ran away.' She looked round at her

lover and her friends and the battered walls of the tower. 'I got lonely.'

Sometimes after stories like this, Lynn spotted mild smugness in Marsha's eyes.

'The point is taken,' Lynn said archly, 'It's good that there are places like this.' She was spending three or four days a week at Collindeane now, helping newcomers or cultivating window-boxes or writing things. Jane came with her, and as Lynn relaxed, she relaxed too. She helped in the creche, finding delight in children, the younger the better. Both felt nervous about the prospect of Jane being looked after by the women in the tower, but the ones learning medical skills were keen to discover all they could about her. When Jane found herself authorised to deliver lectures on her illness she went to it with a will, and although she retained her slightly hurt and supercilious air (keeping in reserve the possibility of being a bitch again at some future date, Marsha speculated) she enjoyed her times in the tower, even to the extent of occasionally coming by herself, and taking her treatments from strangers without a murmur.

Marsha moved in and lived at the tower. The women invited her, and Lynn had not suggested staying indefinitely with her and Derek. Lynn's stayed as her mailing address, though, and whenever she saw Lynn she asked anxiously if there was anything from Australia. She tried to hide her feelings when there wasn't.

One night Marsha was taking her turn as sentry with Germaine the dog. It was quiet and mild and peaceful; the only movement was the constant flicker of curtains in the street, whose occupants remained fascinated by goings-on at the tower. Suddenly Marsha heard what sounded like a fight between a man and a woman. She tensed, prepared to call help, till she realised that the woman seemed to be getting the better of it. She peered through the gloom. It wasn't a physical fight anyway. The figures approaching the tower were an adult woman and a tall, sullen boy. The woman kept yelling at the boy to go away, leave her alone; she was angry rather than afraid. He was following her forlornly, like a huge beaten puppy. The woman's red clothing registered, and Marsha realised it was Judy Matthews with Jim.

Judy seemed physically well but her mind was all over the place. She muttered of goddesses and moons and starvation and monsters. She'd run away to safeguard her Benefit, she said, but they'd taken it from her anyway. No, she didn't know why; no, it wasn't because she was black or because she'd lived with feminists or because she'd once tried for an abortion; she didn't think so; she thought it was because she was holy; they were frightened because she was holy and magic.

'You'd better come in,' Marsha said.

Judy barred Jim's way. 'This man cannot come into the women's tower.'

'You know we make an exception for sons.'

'You think I would not know,' Judy said haughtily, 'If I had a son?'

By this time more women had come out, attracted by the commotion; Marsha waited till they had taken Judy away to be cared for, then quietly signed for Jim to come in too. She asked another woman to replace her as sentry, and found him some bread and a few mushrooms. He was big, dark and morose. He said please and thank you as if demonstrating manners. He flinched each time she spoke to him. He seemed to cry out to be touched but she knew she couldn't.

'What have you been living on, Jim?'

He shrugged. 'This and that.' The food was gone and there was no more.

'Do you know why they cut off her money?'

'Of course. I'm eighteen.'

Of course, he must be.

'And now,' he growled, 'she says I'm not her son. She says she never had a son.'

Marsha sighed. 'She isn't well, Jim. She's had a hard struggle.'

'It's been hard for me too. I am her son, aren't I?'

'Of course . . .'

'I'm not staying here,' he said fiercely, 'She's told me I'm not wanted one time too many. This is a bloody madhouse. I'll get work abroad.'

'Stay here for tonight. Tomorrow we'll see.'

She found him a corner and some cushions and rugs; he kept saying he wouldn't stay, but fell asleep in the middle of saying it. It was still very dark. The tower settled down again to finish its broken night. Marsha resumed her watch, Germaine at her feet. She relaxed. One incident per night was the norm. She dozed.

A scream tore the air. This time it was inside the tower. More screams followed, and shrieks and running feet. By the time

Marsha found the source of the noise it had been calmed. It was
the ex-prostitute who'd been raped and beaten. She had broken
her silence. She had been shocked into screaming by the appearance in her room of an intruder, a black man come to assault her.

Enquiries were made, the mystery was solved. There was no
intruder. Jim Matthews had been wandering about, half asleep,
looking for his mother to make her admit she was his mother. He
had wandered into the room of the terrorised woman. He
mumbled his apologies. She accepted them, even made a few
trembly jokes about how the shock had helped her find her voice.
She even thanked him shyly and patted his arm. But Judy's rage
was terrible.

'It *proves* he is not my son. No son of mine is a rapist.'

She wouldn't listen to anyone. She insisted that Jim must leave
or she would throw him from the top of the tower. Other women
came bleary-eyed to join the argument. It moved from Jim in
particular to the whole issue of having sons in the tower at all.

'You see!' one woman cried, in the middle of all the early-
morning acrimony and chaos, 'they divide us by their very
presence!'

Marsha withdrew from the argument to find Jim getting his
things together.

'Would you like to go to Lynn's?'

He didn't answer. He just started to cry.

Cold fury closed in on Lynn's face as she heard the tale, sitting in
her dressing gown while the sun came up. After a happy, confused
reunion with Jim, she had given him a bed. Now she sat with
Marsha, drinking bitter koffee.

'What you seem to be saying is that Judy no longer wishes to
care for Jim now that she can't make money out of it.'

'That's not –'

'What about the other sons living at Collindeane?'

'The women are deciding.'

'Oh they're deciding, are they? Send them all along here, why
don't you? Bloody home for waifs and strays, this is!'

Marsha looked at the floor. 'I'm sorry. I assumed you'd want
Jim.'

'Of course I want Jim.'

'Look, Lynn, it's all very well, but he scared the life out of a
woman who'd been raped!'

'Deliberately, of course.'

Marsha sighed, stood up. 'Judy'll feel different when she's had some sleep and some food. She'll have him back.'

'Over my dead body,' said Lynn.

'I guess I'd better go. Will you be coming in later –?'

'No,' said Lynn, 'I won't.'

PART THREE

6

Foreign Policies

The 'Towards 2001' conference was held in the conference centre in Europea City. The centre, round as a tennis-ball, white as the moon, gleamed over the city on impossibly thin legs. To Derek Byers (seconded by his college as part of the international organising team) there was something optimistic but unnerving about the way the building, which could not possibly stand, stood; symbolic, perhaps, of the way it was to be the nerve-centre of the new superstate which, superseding the old economic communities, would unite parts of the world that had never been united, solve problems that had never been solved.

Now it was the year two thousand; just months away from another year made famous before its time by fantasy fiction. Memories of films about space odysseys made Derek smile; it wasn't going to be quite like that, it appeared. Survival on this planet took precedence over voyages to others.

At the feet of the sphere lay the city: an unpleasant ticky-tacky fabrication, rows and clusters of pastel-coloured boxes, pink and lilac and pale gold, homes for planners and builders and civil servants. Derek didn't like the sphere or the city or, if he was honest, the notion of Europea. Partly, he assumed, it was his age. He was nearly sixty and Europea was a young man's dream. And his heritage of jingoism, the shameful uneasiness of an Englishman throwing in his lot with foreigners. This sort of thinking had to stop. Sentimentality and chauvinism were equally inane. The twenty-first century would be no time to go it alone. And it would be no time to be marooned on the outer fringes of trading blocs either – your consumers prey to foreign price agreements, your population to demands for migrant labour, your markets to dumping. The Europea standard of living seemed to promise great things: even the pale, clean buildings smirked – our air is clean, we have machines to wash it.

Once inside the sphere for your conference, you had no need to leave, nor did the guards expect you to. Meeting halls, restaurants, shops, gyms, saunas, telecommunications, entertainment, were all enclosed in the huge glistening ball. You could talk back to your boss or your wife in your home country on a telescreen; you could board the high-speed monorail car in the base of the sphere when it was time to go home. And there were brothels too, where the discreet girls wore blindfolds.

Floors moved, you did not have to walk. Open escalators crisscrossed and radiated in a circle. Glass-walled lifts rose and fell with whispering speed. Wherever you looked, eminent men were being moved by strange forces to unknown destinations in the pale, white light, and the air was like mountain air, bracing and heady, but not cold.

Derek Byers was amused and irritated to notice the British contingent behaving in the sphere like children at a fair: playing with gadgets, gulping down free drink, making quite unnecessary trips on the moving floors, watched with condescension by foreigners to whom it was no novelty. There were many who thought that when it came to it, Britain would not be admitted to full membership of Europea; its economy was so rickety, it had so little to offer; and this sort of behaviour, Derek mused, did nothing to dispel that impression. He had been here several months, preparing, serving his country's apprenticeship along with other international tea-boys from aspiring members of Europea. The sphere made his head spin, made him feel slightly mad, as if he had lost touch with anything natural, as if he had to remember to draw breath or he would suffocate. He remembered conferences in the old days, at universities, staying in student halls of residence with tiny cold rooms and narrow beds and the faint smell of unwashed socks seeping from the locked cupboard.

He sniffed the white air of the sphere and dreamt of unwashed socks.

Wherever he looked, faces known to him from the dust-jackets of books sprang into life – and sometimes he caught strangers looking at him too, with puzzled or admiring recognition. The pulsing brain of a continent. A new continent. Not every state in the old Europe would be included in the new Europea, whereas some countries on the far side of the globe had been invited to join. The great sphere – and there would be answering hemispheres in the capital cities of all the member nations – was a symbol of the smallness of the modern world; distance didn't matter. Race didn't matter either, nor did ideologies. What did matter was that those nations which had kept a grip on their affairs and weathered the economic storms of the last thirty years should join together and hold on to their means of survival (and defend themselves, Derek added when he felt cynical, from the jealous whinings of those who had not fared so well).

Power, food, population, world peace, trade, health, industry – these were the cornerstones of survival, and if agreement could be reached the oddest of enemies might become bedfellows. 'And talking of bedfellows,' a tipsy colleague had recently responded to Derek's strivings for conversation, 'there aren't any women here.' And he had warmed to his theme of the preferability of a woman who knew a thing or two.

It was an exaggeration to say there were no women at the conference, but only a minor one. It was the usual scene. A few tokens, lauded for their sex as much as for their specialities; two types: fussily dressed with clouds of perfume, or stern and austere, one of the lads. Apart from them it was a gathering of males, albeit black males, white males, yellow males, capitalist males, socialist males, political males, scientific males, humble males, puffed-up males, all convinced (in this year two thousand) that they represented humanity.

Derek was on call for organisational emergencies. A row of telescreens perched like squirrels on the edge of his desk; in each a tiny man waved his arms and mimed a speech. Press a button and you could hear what he said in one of twenty languages, tinny and computerised.

'Planning!' A video-recording of the introductory address by the President of Europea, an erratic quicksilver of a man whose mood changes were said to be the biggest single obstacle to Britain's entry. He had surrounded himself with advisers who predicted doom for the British economy and pointed out how little it had to offer; and on a purely personal level he affected to despise every Briton he met. There were plenty of colleagues to disagree with him, of course, and his powers were not autocratic; but the giant infant of the Europea bureaucracy would not be hard to control. Derek twiddled the knob and listened to him.

'Planning! Planning is the key! Let the twenty-first century go down in history as the century of planning! Let us see all the world's problems, which seemed so momentous in the world's infancy – for so the first twenty centuries AD will appear – let us see them rendered soluble by planning –'

You had to admire the aplomb with which the man delivered himself of his stream of clichés. Derek frowned and tuned into the Power seminar. Another white man in middle age. Talking about nuclear energy. Every home in the superstate lit by it, every vehicle powered. Early teething troubles no longer applied; present day technology far safer than oil. Problems of waste-disposal being overcome; deep in the earth in unpopulated areas . . . well, underpopulated. Shot into space. Rendered water-soluble, tests were hopeful.

World Peace. Best protection from war was obviously to range all militarily mighty nations on the same side – their interests might in any case prove to be the same . . .

Health. The long list of diseases that could be rendered obsolete. The organs that could be transplanted, substituted. The ages to which man might one day live!

Trade, Industry, Food. The earth had a vast population to support. Need to end wasteful competition, inefficient farming and processing. Europea to be of a size and variety to be self-sufficient. An interruption, not fully heard; the speaker replied: 'We nations have got together, organised ourselves. Nations outside Europea are free to do the same. Their problems are not our problems; we will not impose our ways on them.'

Population. Despite nearly a century of efforts by international agencies, still a headache. Increasing out of control in some places. Elsewhere – Europea, for instance – problems of imbalance. Large elderly populations supported by too small a workforce, too few caretakers. The product of a baby-boom followed by a slump. 'The fault is not with science,' explained the professor who ran the agency Europop, his tone slightly hurt; he looked unreal, badly-drawn, with the lines of late middle-age in his face but thick, youthfully-black chin-length hair. 'The technology of contraception is perfected. The problem is social –'

'I know what my wife would say to *you*, mate,' Derek thought, 'she'd say what you call a social problem is a woman's right to choose.' For a woman who felt so let down and exasperated by organised feminists, she adhered remarkably strongly to their principles and beliefs. She read a lot, of course, and Marsha was a frequent visitor (even to the point when Derek began incredulously to wonder whether he was being supplanted; but even if it were true, there was nothing reasonable he could do about it, so he tried to banish the thought); Lynn even did little jobs for the women in the tower, like sorting cuttings or tracking down articles for the medical groups or sending along some of the food she grew and could ill-afford, but she performed these tasks with a sort of resigned cynicism.

She had not set foot in the tower since Judy Matthews threw Jim out nearly four years ago. 'I know she's ill,' she said, 'and I know I ought to be nice to her. But it's better if I don't see her. That's all.' Jim, tall and taciturn, was a polite but irregular resident at the Byers house. He was trying to make a life for himself, was even into gently left-wing politics which pleased Lynn; but work was intermittent, he had joined the band of rootless unskilled labourers who got boat-trains in London to whichever foreign factory needed workers for a while. He found it hard to make friends, and Lynn swore he still bore the scars of the maternal rejections and changes of mind that had striped his childhood. Also, Jane didn't like him to stick around; she liked to be queen of the roost, trying her mother's patience to its limit, joining Young Families of Tomorrow and falling in love with a young patriarch called Martin.

The screen flickered. The Europop professor dwindled into a silver line. Derek switched to Power, to World Peace, getting perfect reception. Back to Population. Blank nothing. He thumped the screen. An answering thump came back pertly from the machine's innards. Nothing.

'And I know what she'd say to me, too. She'd say, get down there and find out what they're planning to do about this social problem of theirs.'

He hesitated. He was getting international rates for being here, he had a job to do, and attending the population seminar wasn't part of it. But then he didn't do much for Lynn these days, and this would interest her.

As if some airwave had beamed his thought to a higher power, a light flashed, a buzzer bleeped.

'Professor Byers.'

'Yes, sir.'

'We seem to have scheduled the president to be in two places at once.'

'Oh dear.'

'Sort it out, would you, old chap?'

Old chap? Was that what they taught them in these language schools? The line had gone dead. Derek sighed. It would not do to have the president incommoded. The population seminar would surely publish its papers? He ran his eye down the scheduling lists, but he knew it was no good. It was the questions and the interjections that were important at a meeting like that, not the polite pedantry of the papers.

Derek consigned the president of Europea to the wastepaper basket. (Chances were the mix-up was the old egotist's own fault anyway.) He stepped gingerly on to the moving corridor that flowed like a solid white stream outside the office door. Shop-windows showed the spherical bottles of Europerfume that could be bought in coy pink wrappings; that was for other men's wives, Derek thought stoutly; he would take a seminar report home to his.

'Press not allowed.'

'I am *not* press,' said Derek, as if no greater insult could be devised. He thrust his chest out, displaying his organiser's badge. 'I've come to check the relay system.'

'It's been turned off, sir.'

'I *know*. I've come to check.'

He slipped in. It was a small meeting. A panel of three sat round a table, an audience of a dozen listened. At Derek's entry a few heads turned. He returned the stares with the discreet smile of one who has just got back from the gents and regrets any disturbance caused.

The professor's voice was shrill and quick. ' – no point, no point at all, in planning our food industry to the last crumb, our power to the last atom, if population growth can fluctuate and bend on the wind of human whim, yes? Human beings, the most complex machines, the cleverest, most dangerous species, does it not offend the rational mind that they should be the result of the most random phenomenon in the world, productive coitus – ' (*Fancy a spot of random phenomenal coitus, Lynn baby?*) ' – yes the British experiment is interesting . . .'

Derek sat bolt upright.

A furious voice was saying, 'There is no experiment.' For one horrified moment Derek thought the voice was his own. With some relief he realised it had come from a stoop-shouldered man with a sharp white collar in the front row. He listened.

'You have completely misunderstood.' Derek knew the voice. He knew it well from the radio. David Laing, Secretary of State for Family Welfare. Derek had always loyally shared Lynn's suspicion and hatred of the man, but privately he found him rather pathetic, with his ubiquitous caffein tablets and his darting, birdlike eyes.

The professor shrugged. 'You pay women whom you wish to have babies. You sterilise those who are unsuitable.'

Next to Laing was a taller man, younger, with a silvery, hypnotic voice. Peel, Derek realised, Laing's second-in-command, a man with his eye on the stars. He sat very still and calm, happy for Laing to talk himself into a corner, awaiting his moment to contribute.

Peel said, 'That is correct. In essence.'

'It isn't an *experiment*,' Laing insisted.

Peel's whispered protest darted at the quailing Laing like the tongue of a snake, but Laing held his ground. 'We seek only to reverse the discrimination against dutiful mothers –'

'Mr Peel. Are mothers in your country receptive to the idea that having children is a public service like any other?'

The grin sounded in Peel's voice, Peel the man who never smiled. It was like the grin of a yobbo through chewing gum.

'We haven't had any complaints.'

'You have no, er – ' The lines in the professor's face writhed apologetically, 'er, *lib* movement?'

'We have a few misfits. *Outnumbered* misfits, I might add.'

'And does it work?' the professor was insisting.

'It's not a question of anything working!' Laing said, 'It's not an experiment! The point is, recognition –'

'It seems to be working,' said Peel, 'it's too early to say.'

The professor was speaking again. His face was surreal, all those wrinkles and that thick black hair. The rolling eyes, the fine mist of spray from the gabbling mouth. Hypnotic.

'If it can work – if a judicious mix of propaganda and payment and penalty can induce some women to bear children and others not – what an advance for the human condition!'

Derek cursed softly, wishing he could record this.

'These are dangerous doctrines, professor,' Laing muttered.

'No no no no no no no. Always this is what people say to me!' The professor flapped his hands. 'I am not talking about genocide. I am talking about making rational use of our human stock as we must of our other resources! I am talking about eliminating hereditary defects – maintaining the strong and the healthy, ceasing to bring lives into being that will merely be lives of suffering. The idea has been abused in the past. I will be the first to admit it. It has been so much abused that we do not see its possible benefits. What about this? A rational welfare state, based on a sufficient ratio of workers to dependants, yes? An end to unemployment – for we can predict labour requirements and ensure that no more babies are born than will grow up to fill them. An end to poverty – for the people we cannot feed will simply not be born! All this is far into the future, far beyond my lifetime and yours, there are many questions we cannot answer – but must we not at least ask them? Is it possible, for example, to identify those genetic strains that make a man happy and effective as a soldier or a doctor or a sweeper of the streets, and then produce for the needs of society? A dangerous doctrine, Mr Laing?'

'And this . . . selective breeding, we'll call it, to be polite . . . would it be voluntary?'

The professor sighed. 'Is it voluntary that the power workers must produce so much energy, or the farmers so much food? Planning is for the greater good – is that not what this conference is about? Why should women be different? Is that not what they are always saying – they want to be equal?' He panted with wet laughter. He looked around for answering smiles. Derek manufactured one.

'It'll never work,' said Laing.

The professor was so excited he looked as if he might rise into the air.

'Will it not? Who says it will not? We shall see! We must try! We have tried similar programmes in the underdeveloped world, but the women there were too unintelligent. No matter. Those countries are of no concern to Europea and may be left to their own devices. We need a modern industrial society – whose women respect themselves for the wealth of their contribution – where we can try! A geographically confined space – such as an island, Mr Laing, hm? – would be ideal!'

The meeting was ending. Derek realised he must either disappear or bluff it out. He remained in his seat, consulting his clipboard. People walked by him; he heard laughter and the words 'the man's mad' in several languages. Peel, Laing and the professor remained. Derek kept his head low, his ears strained.

Peel's voice was seductive. 'An admirable paper, professor.'

'Your colleague does not appear to think so. You must see, Mr

Laing, that population is the louse in the ointment of planning.'

'Fly,' said Laing sullenly.

'I beg your pardon?'

'The expression is, fly in the ointment.'

'Quite so. Would the British government be interested in a few tests?'

'What tests?'

'It would be useful to know how close one can get to total planning of population. In a manner acceptable to public opinion.'

'Oh, you do propose to take account of that?'

'Naturally.'

The three men were leaving. Derek stiffened. It seemed impossible that he would not be challenged. But they passed him, deep in conversation. Derek waited a minute, then left the room and stepped on to the moving corridor, several feet behind Laing and Peel, engrossed in his clipboard. The professor had gone his own way.

'What choice have we got?' Peel was raging, 'What else has the rundown country your generation has bequeathed us to offer Europea?' His voice had lost its charm. It nagged. 'We're finished if we don't join, and we can't join empty-handed. What does it matter to you at your age – ?'

Laing mumbled, 'It was never what we intended when –'

'The good old days! How sentimental you are about your precious ideas – be sentimental about the whole human race for a change!'

Laing stepped off the moving corridor, bound for a sign promising real coffee. Derek got off too. Peel stayed on, alone. The corridor seemed to accelerate.

'Let me get this straight,' said Lynn, tipping beans into a pan. They rattled stonily, then shifted, maggot-like, as the heat stirred the water. Jim had brought them. The story was that he'd found a job and been paid in kind. Lynn knew perfectly well that the beans were stolen, but had said nothing. He wanted to contribute to the household, and anyway she didn't want to see again the come-now-mother-dear look that came into his eyes when he informed her that *everybody* got bits and pieces under the counter these days. Nor for that matter did she wish to hear the prissy tones in which Jane would declare that her patriotism would not permit her to consume goods of dubious origin, and anyway she needed meat. At least the beans were real food (for all the hours they took to soften, and the thick, sour-tasting steam they emitted when boiled) – not like the substances in the garish tins that cost such a price at the hypermarket, highly scented and tasting of sponge and rubber and dough.

Derek had materialised through the steam, anxious and early home from his conference on another planet. He'd come with a lot to tell her.

'Let me get this straight, Derek. They want to plan population like they plan the production of – of steel girders.'

'Yes,' said Derek.

'Not just the old zero-population-growth idea.'

'A bit more sophisticated than that. Advancing on it, reversing it in some cases. They're worried that there are too few young people in Euopea, for example. And, by implication though it wasn't spelled out, too few European types in a world teeming with nasty niggers. They want to get the balance right.'

'Right for what?' She prodded at the contents of the pan.

'Right for . . .' Derek spread his hands. 'Right for balance.'

'But they didn't say what balance. That's my point, Derek – they didn't say what they meant by right.'

'It's not my fault.'

'No, no.' She shook the pan. 'I'm trying to work this out. Europea's the last ditch stand of the developed world, right, to support an ecologically disastrous style of living at the expense of everybody else. We're all to live in boxes with adjustable walls and have meetings in air-conditioned spheres and eat rotten beans and chemicals, and everything will be planned according to the whim of whatever power-crazed clique of males happen to be in office at the time – everything, right down to the last fuck –'

'The last *productive* fuck.'

'Oh, is that all? Well of course. Men will always want to fuck.' She was shaking.

Derek said, 'Are you sure you weren't there?'

'I didn't need to be there, did I? And women are to be baby-factories. Correction. Some women are to be baby-factories.' And she thought of all the women Marsha had told her about, who had had those crab-like pellets fitted as the price of continuing to receive Benefit, and how recalcitrant doctors were about removing them, however badly the women were suffering from back pains and odd hormone effects such as changes of voice-tone, depression, unexpected tufts of hair. The medical women at Collindeane were trying to learn how to remove the things, but warnings from the medical profession about dire and dangerous consequences made them reluctant to experiment.

Derek was saying something believable. She blinked at him.

'What did you say?'

He flinched.

'I . . . I just said, this could be your scoop.'

'Scoop?' She might never have heard the word.

'Maybe you could get back into journalism with it,' he said lamely, adding, 'it would help the women's movement too.'

She said, 'Yes. It's funny, Derek, I hadn't thought of it like that. You know? Really. No, don't be guilty. You're right, it could be a scoop, but we have to be cleverer than that.' Slowly, hypnotically, she prodded a bean with a fork, peered at it, offered it to Derek to taste.

'Could do with a bit longer,' he said mechanically, 'What are you going to do?' She didn't answer. 'Aren't you going to write about it?'

'*Write* about it?' She blinked. Her eyes were at once blazing and bewildered. Her face was damp with steam.

'Lynn, you look quite beautiful. What are you thinking?'

'It's the last thing they'll ever take from us. It's been their excuse, for years, for ever – their excuse for every kind of shit they've heaped on us: you have babies. You are the sacred mothers, the founts of life. You can't do this, you must do that, because you have this special role. You have babies. You're wonderful at it. It's important. We'll leave that to you, and you leave everything else to us. And now they've found they can't leave it to us. Not even that. The randomness, the – the wildness of it, won't fit into their planned century. How abstracted can they get? What's the planning for?'

'Lynn, I can't bear it when you seem to be blaming me.'

'You're a man aren't you? Sorry, I didn't mean that.'

'Well, thanks.' He forced a smile. He had never felt such a gulf between them. 'Population is the louse in the ointment of planning.'

'Fly,' Lynn growled.

7

International Relations

Mrs Rashida Patel shuffled slowly down Whitehall, leaning on her stick. From behind piles of rubbish, little knots of beggars made hopeful sorties, but, recognising her, gave up. MPs had taken a decision not to encourage beggars by responding to them in the vicinity of the House.

Soon, she thought, she would have to retire. Her limbs were weak, her hearing almost gone. It was hard to make speeches not knowing the sound of her voice, seeing only the little smiles passed like sweets among the few men who listened, not hearing their jokes and interjections.

She was the only woman in the House now, and she was black.

Alan Travers had gone into a self-satisfied retirement; Isabel, tyrannical and coquettish in her old age, issued statements on morals from their home. Rashida herself and David Laing were all that remained of the early Family Party members, the older generation; and Laing was coming increasingly under the sway of the new.

Politicians should be able to hold office for two hundred years, she thought. They should see the genesis of things, understand how they came to be – not take them as fixed, as given, as a jumping-off point for some grotesque flight of logic, which was how some of the youngsters these days seemed to be looking at Benefit.

'Mrs Patel. Madam. *Madam.*'

She turned at the sound of her name. A tiny, sunken-cheeked woman was looking at her, Asian by appearance but with a cockney voice. She threw her a coin.

'I'm *starving*. So are my children.'

'I've given you money. I'm not supposed – '

'My Benefit's been taken away.'

'I beg your pardon?'

'My *Benefit's* been – '

Mrs Patel sighed. They were so many. What was there to say?

'Then maybe you are not a good mother.'

'In my street it has been taken away from all the coloured women.'

Rashida limped on, pretending not to hear. But the woman's dark face haunted her. What were they doing here, the two of them, in this cold country? She went to Laing.

'I have had a complaint from a constituent,' she said, 'Benefit policy is not being equitably applied.'

Laing sipped koffee. 'There are anomalies which will be ironed out – ' he mumbled, his words lost in steam.

Peel was lurking in a corner of the room. His voice was contemptuously loud. 'You really must stop being so sensitive about your colour, Rashida.'

'I never mentioned colour, Mr Peel.'

It was a drab, never-ending afternoon, neither cold nor hot but thick-aired and still. Some sounds were clear. A fly buzzed manically as it flung itself at a glass pane, refusing to look upwards at an open window and a route to freedom. The ticking of the clock in Rashida's office seemed to get slower and louder. She looked for something to do, something she could be bothered to do. A message came up that a Mrs Lynn Byers would like to see her. She knew no one of that name. She wasn't even a constituent. Still – visits from strangers either raised the spirits or fuelled anger. Either was better than this lethargy.

The minute Mrs Byers came into the room, Rashida felt a link of trust between them. She felt she might have seen her once before – but she had met so many people. Still, there was this feeling of a reunion with an old friend.

'I'm a reporter.'

'Oh yes? For whom? And could you please speak up?'

'Freelance.'

'Would you like some tea, Mrs Byers?'

'No thank you.'

'We have the real thing. We are very privileged.'

'In that case . . . yes please. Thank you.'

Rashida made tea from her special store. Mrs Byers explained that she wanted to write profiles of the founders of the Family Party. She was particularly interested in Rashida as a radical, a dissenting voice. She was acute and surprising; Rashida had not realised her doubts were so apparent, she had always tried to toe the line in public . . . now she was speaking freely. Her voice sounded clear in her head. She kept reminding herself she was on the record, that this was just another shrewd and cynical reporter. Finally she heard herself telling Mrs Byers that she was going to retire. Mrs Byers showed no surprise, and asking why seemed a polite formality. Rashida said it was her age, and Mrs Byers said, 'That isn't true, is it?'

Rashida said, 'Why don't you put your notebook away?'

Lynn showed her the empty pages. 'I'm not really taking notes.'

'Oh?'

'I just wanted to talk to you. I wanted to tell you something. I know I'm taking a chance, but less of one than I thought when I first decided to come.'

'You are very cryptic,' Rashida said, and listened to what Lynn had to tell her. And when Lynn finished and said, 'You didn't know?' Rashida said, 'No, I didn't know.'

'But you're not surprised?'

'No, I'm not surprised.'

'What will you do?' said Lynn.

'What do you want me to do?'

'Me? Well, I – I don't know.'

Rashida shrugged. 'I don't know either.'

'You know what they say,' Marsha said, 'Three ways to spread news. Telegram, telephone, tell-a-woman.'

'What can Mrs Patel do for us?' asked Pam. All the Collindeane women were crammed together, excited and a little afraid. The meeting was different from any that had gone before. The feminist traditions of having no one in the chair and allowing no one to dominate were observed, but judiciously; Lynn was doing a lot of talking, a lot of organising, and somehow everyone felt it right to let her.

'We can have the names and addresses of every woman in FAMILY.'

'What will we do?'

'We have to make a definite plan,' said Lynn, 'and we have to take a chance. Two chances. First, that other feminists won't mind us taking a lead because there's no time to consult. Second, that when we talk to the FAMILY women, they'll be shocked enough to act with us.' She paused, flinching for the protest that would surely come, but it didn't. She ventured on. 'We'll have to phrase it in their terms. Yes, motherhood is women's sacred calling and that's *why* it mustn't be a bargaining counter in male power politics . . .'

'"We're all on the same side"' someone said, giving a passable imitation of Isabel Travers. The moment trembled between cynicism and laughter. The women laughed.

They talked for many hours, and there was no dissent.

Collindeane women would set off in twos and threes to hunt out feminist centres and FAMILY groups up and down the country and explain what was going on. Finding the feminists would be the hard part. Lynn would look through the crates of cuttings and newsletters that the tower had accumulated down the years to help locate them.

Meanwhile, the government announced the date of the state visit by the president of Europea and his entourage. They'd dot the i's and cross the t's on the agreement regarding Britain's entry and eat lunch with the royal family. The date was carefully noted by the women.

The withdrawal of many mothers from Collindeane, and the confiscation of the Benefit from those that remained, meant the tower was short of money. And for all the women's ingenuity and the surprising agricultural possibilities of the building, there were limits to how self-sufficient an urban commune could be. There were women in the country who might grow things for them, but transport was a problem and they had nothing to give in return. So more women had to do clerical work for Europea firms or take the dreadful risks involved in thieving, and living standards were lowered. Strict priority was agreed. Boys no longer lived in the tower. Baby girls came first, then pregnant or sick women. If food was short, the others went without. Getting food was the main priority. Repairs to the building were neglected.

So the building was cold and draughty and damp and dirty; and many women went hungry. Marsha rarely felt hungry but was fascinated by the shape of her bones that stood out more and more clearly under her thin flesh. She had eaten nothing but flower-pot grown beans for two days. She supposed her general state of health must be poor, which was why she kept getting thumping feverish colds like this one.

She was supposed to be on a visit up north, but the cold had felled her and she'd stayed behind in the nearly-empty tower.

Her head throbbed, and the effort of raising a handkerchief to her nose made her muscles ache till it seemed better just to lie with her head tipped right back. Except that it made her feel sick. It was a windy day, and the window-boxes were rattling. She'd gone staggering to the medical centre where the women had been sympathetic but brisk: 'There's no known cure for a cold, and any that you have heard of are placebos, meaning tricks that insult you. Keep warm, do whatever makes you comfortable, and it will pass.' 'You mean don't waste your time,' Marsha had grumbled, and they had said yes, they were rather busy; they had girls with measles and were keeping anxious eyes on two women whose birth control pellets they had at last found a way to remove.

So she'd found herself a draught-free corner to sit in and feel sorry for herself; but then Judy Matthews came upon her, and her solicitude was even worse than the medical women's good sense. She informed Marsha that she, Marsha, was a favourite of the goddess, and thus she, Judy, had been empowered by Her to cure her. And not even Marsha's querulous enquiry as to why a favourite of the goddess should catch such an unpleasant cold in the first place would put her off. She brought pungent drinks down from her chapel in the roof and slapped hot herbal poultices on Marsha's neck and joints.

Marsha tried to locate her thoughts elsewhere. 'Women were always the healers,' Judy crooned, but Marsha longed for an authoritarian doctor to pump her full of antibiotics. Her mind moved on; Posy had been in her thoughts a lot; not one of her letters had been answered, but she retained the dream that she would turn up one day. She wasn't even sure that it would be a good idea, politically; a delicate efficiency was imposing itself on the anarchic women under pressure of the emergency, and Marsha could just imagine Posy blundering in and shattering it. But she missed her companionship and love. For all the general feelings of sisterhood and care in the tower, everyone seemed to be in a couple (best friends if not lovers). And Lynn – well, Lynn was married and cautious and a mother, and she came and went and they kissed each other in greeting and had long talks, but something remained unresolved between them and there was no way of getting at it to resolve it when neither of them could articulate what it was.

Just as there had been a time (it was probably still true) when a man and women couldn't just be loving friends without at least signifying their intention to become – or not become – more, so now, in the women's tower, question-marks hung over her relationship with Lynn. At least, in her mind they did.

How bloody silly it was! Why couldn't they just be friends who had grown together? Women would be buying each other wedding-rings next, demanding fidelity, taking each other's names!

Marsha's tolerance reached its limit when Judy started dancing round her, singing spells. Her throat was on fire. She practised words to say she felt better now, thank you, and Judy shouldn't overdo it because you couldn't be too careful with spells. One of the women on sentry duty saved her.

'There's someone for you downstairs, Marsha.'

It couldn't be. The timing! Marsha's throat was suddenly wet, soothed. She knew without asking that Posy had arrived, that if she enquired further the sentry would say, 'An Australian woman. Quite big.'

'An overseas woman,' said the sentry.

In she would stride, all grin and muscle and competence, and declare, '*Now* we can get it together, Marsh. I think we're old enough.'

'She's black,' the sentry went on, and Marsha's jaw dropped and her throat was dry again.

'I'm too ill to see anyone.' It was almost true. If her aches and pains had retreated as an organised force one minute ago, they were back now as guerillas. Pinpricks stabbed deep inside her ears; spasms shook her lungs and chest. 'I mean, it's not because she's black, it's –'

'I think she's come a long way.'

Judy shook wet twigs in her face. She turned away, coughing.

'Of course. D'you mind sending her up? And Judy, for pity's sake leave me *alone*!'

Judy shot a glare of uncomprehending hurt, followed by a smile of generous peace. 'I shall pray for you,' she said, 'in my chapel.'

The visitor was a short, wiry woman with glossy skin the colour of tree-bark. She looked clean and vigorous and efficient; her manner was hurried yet painstakingly courteous. A vivid multicoloured scarf hid every trace of her hair and fanned out into whorls and wisps like the flamboyant headdress of a bird; in contrast she wore an old-fashioned English raincoat, buttoned tight to her chin against the elements. Marsha made an awed decision not to mention her cold.

'I'm Marsha,' she said.

'I know.'

'How do you know?'

The woman dipped briskly into a pocket. 'I have a photograph.' Marsha looked at it and knew it came from Posy. The woman peered closely at her face. 'You are thinner. Are you ill?' It was the enquiry of an engineer who perceives that an important part of a machine is not working.

'It's nothing,' Marsha said, 'how is Posy?'

'Unfortunately I have to tell you that she is dead.' Unfortunately I have to tell you that the machine is beyond repair. Marsha gaped, wanting to hate the woman for her calm, informative stare, but drawing strength from it.

'How, why did she die?'

'She died in action.' The flicker of a smile on the blue-black lips was somewhere between mockery and compassion.

'Tell me please.'

The woman came from a country long deemed overpopulated by the West. Agencies had striven for years to persuade the women to limit their families in order to transform the society into a modern one that could produce healthy workers and afford consumer goods; but the women knew that their children were the only wealth they had, for who else would care for the homes and the farms when they and their husbands were too old? They had been politely unco-operative with a succession of birth controllers, but finally a team came from Europop with a special plan. They offered free cookers to pregnant women who would permit long silver needles to be driven (quite painlessly) into their wombs to ascertain the sex of the baby. The birth controllers then went to the husbands of the women found to be carrying girls, and offered them motorbikes if they would persuade their wives to abort.

Girls grew up to increase the numbers of mouths to feed after all, they explained, and they couldn't even help on the farm.

Individual women objected, argued, resisted, but they had no cookers to offer their sisters. And even when the gas cylinders that powered the cookers ran out and were not replaced, a wife with a cooker and a horde of sons remained an important status symbol for the men, and the promise of motorbikes kept up their interest. Some women became restive, but it never occured to them that anyone anywhere else in the world might be interested in their plight. Their village became known as the place where no daughters are born.

And then Posy came. She'd come winging into the country on a jet, then driven a jeep for five days through rock and desert to reach the village whose name she'd spotted in a footnote to a learned article on future strategies for birth control. She'd stopped only to push the jeep out of pot-holes, or trap small animals to eat. She'd roared to a halt in the centre of the village, and jumped to the ground, the only thing moving in the shimmering heat of mid-day. Arms akimbo, she'd looked round. And through the cracks in the walls of their huts the women had looked at her.

'How did she seem?' Marsha asked, trying to control her voice.

'Myself, I thought I had never seen such a powerful woman. She was almost like a goddess, or a rock of flesh. So much flesh!' The woman's voice warmed, though a gust of wind through a crack in the wall made her tighten her raincoat about her. 'Her arms and legs were bare. In our society it would be immodest, but Posy did not look immodest. She had a great red hat that made her look even taller; the sun glowed on it, it almost seemed to burn. She had dark glasses over her eyes, and more glasses – for spare? – over the hat. With the sun on them she seemed to have four eyes. Her legs and arms were as thick as trees, and everyone in the village could hear her voice. She spoke our language – not well, but she had tried to learn so we listened to her.'

'What did she do?'

She had summoned the women to hear her. Polite and curious, they had gone. The men went too. Posy said she would not speak if the men were there. The men objected and the women supported their protest, so Posy said in that case the men must sit at the back and keep quiet. The women laughed at such turning of the tables and the men obeyed. Secretly the women nudged each other and agreed that the white woman was mad, and what she said next convinced them further.

'There is a world conspiracy of men against women!' she shouted.

'There is a world conspiracy of white against black!' retorted one of the men, who was in touch with a national liberation movement. Posy was undaunted.

'What do they mean,' she demanded, 'by a "population problem?" They mean that they have built a world that cannot feed its own people!'

Everyone nodded. Posy had not specified who 'they' were.

'They say they can solve the problem by wiping out women! That's all they see you as – baby-trees to be chopped down when no more babies are required. Well. Which would you prefer? To exist in a world with a few problems, or not to exist in the sort of nightmare that an all-male society would be? Think about it! What would it be like?'

One woman said shyly, 'They would fight all the time.'

'Quite! All violence and pomposity!' She turned on the men. 'How can you trade your daughters for junk machinery that doesn't even work?'

'Yes,' said the women, 'how can you?'

The men sulked: they had meant no harm, and their wives had been pleased enough to accept the cookers. But there was no stopping Posy. 'The powerful Western nations, all of which are run by men, want to carve up your country. They want to eat the food that you produce, steal the goods that you make so that they can sell them back at twice the price, despoil the land that you have conserved. To do that they have to stop you having children who might also want a share of the food and the goods and the land. They want to run your lives to fit in with the way they want to run their lives, and the first thing they want to grab is the very source of your lives – your wombs!'

In time, the women began to think maybe she was not so mad after all; and some of the national liberation men nodded at her words too, when they were not directed against them. Next time the birth controllers showed their faces they were chased from the village, and the unborn girl-children remained intact.

Posy said she'd love to stay, but the women of the whole world needed her. The village women were secretly relieved but they asked her to stay for a holiday. She was tired. She huffed and puffed in the heat and refused to protect her skin from the sun, insisting that sunburn was thought attractive in her country. She strode about in shorts and raved of the world revolution of women that was coming, and whole families came from neighbouring villages to look at her.

They gave a farewell party for her the night before she was due to speed away in her jeep. The women put a garland round her neck and hoisted her on to their shoulders to carry her through the village. But she was heavier than they thought. They dropped her.

It seemed a short, soft fall, and everyone got ready to laugh. But Posy went pale and fought for breath. In less than five minutes she was dead from a heart attack.

The desire to laugh wildly put Marsha in a panic as she heard this. In a shaky voice she asked, 'Did she ever talk about me?'

'Oh yes, and about the great tower, taller than the highest trees where you were leading the women to revolution.'

'Posy always did exaggerate.'

The woman shrugged. 'She did not exaggerate about the height of your tower. It is remarkable. What was it built for, originally?'

'To keep people in.'

'I have brought you this. From the garland we buried her in.' And the woman gave Marsha a spray of dried twigs and leaves and berries. Despite the distance it had travelled, a faint, sweet, woody odour hung in the air. It cleared Marsha's head. She felt well.

The woman kept a respectful silence, as if Marsha might be praying. But she didn't move. Marsha said, 'There's another reason why you've come?'

'Yes.'

'What is it?'

'Resistance has grown in my country to the exploiters from Europea. We wish to have contact with other liberation struggles. The men laughed when I said I would contact you, but –' she dipped deep in her raincoat pocket again, like a housewife hunting for change. 'I have brought you something. I can get more.' She dropped a little yellow gun into Marsha's hand.

'It looks like a toy,' she said, fascinated.

'It's no toy.'

'A water pistol, then.'

'You can practise with water. This is better.' The woman's eyes were flinty as she handed Marsha a gold foil cylinder that felt full of jelly. It was heavier than it looked and had strange markings on it, unfamiliar lettering that Marsha seemed to know spelled out Danger, Caution.

'They are specially shaped for women's small hands and easy to use.'

'Where do you get them?'

'A friendly government.'

'How does it work?'

The woman took the gun and showed how the cylinder slotted into the barrel. She demonstrated pulling the trigger, at which point a pin would pierce the cylinder and jelly would squirt under pressure from the gun, ignited by a spark. 'Accurate and very long range. You can burn off a man's head while his feet are still in his boots. I can get you a crate.'

Marsha forced her brain to work. Some women were into non-violence and some would complain about the fire-hazard of storing the fuel and some would –

'Would we have to pay?' she fenced.

'The cost.'

'You see, we don't have much money.'

'What could you afford?'

'You see, it's earmarked – I couldn't – not without –'

The woman frowned. 'You are armed already?'

'No.'

'Then what is the difficulty?'

'You see, it isn't that kind –'

'It is serious, this revolution of yours?'

'Yes, but –'

'How can it be serious if you are not armed?'

'Can I contact you?'

'I leave today. I can get you a crate. Yes or no.'

Marsha said in despair, 'I'd need to ask the others and nobody's here. They're all off visiting other women's groups.'

'I thought it would be sufficient,' said the woman, 'to come to your headquarters.'

'This isn't a headquarters. We don't have headquarters.'

The woman got up to go. 'Our men were right to laugh at you.'

'Wait. Wait here.' Marsha's body felt feverish again, but she dragged herself to the top of the building and back down again to see who was around. Judy making spells in her chapel; medical women preoccupied with their patients, very unlikely to want to discuss flame-throwers, let alone give up the precious money earmarked for supplies to have them on the premises; child-minders. There were the sentries, of course, but even if they wanted arms they were not enough to make such a choice democratically. Marsha did not need to ask to know the answer: 'Wait till the next house meeting.'

The visitor left, radiating scorn.

Marsha went back to her chair and her cold. Wind blew straight on to her but she couldn't be bothered to move. Something yellow caught her eye; she realised the woman had left her gun. Deliberately? Marsha hid it. Then she pressed the little spray of twigs in her fist and stared at it till it dissolved in the mist of her eyes.

'Marsha?'

Not Judy, please, I won't be nice to her, I can't –

It was Lynn. 'They said you were ill.'

'I'm not ill, I'm crying.'

'Why?'

'Because Posy's dead.'

Lynn knelt and put her arms round her. 'How do you know?'

'I just got a message.'

Lynn's shoulder was bony and insubstantial. 'Come home with me?'

'No thanks. I don't want to intrude on your family.'

Lynn held her face, looked puzzled. 'What's brought this on?'

'Derek thinks I'm a lesbian,' Marsha wailed.

'But so do I. Aren't you?'

'I don't know!'

'I always assumed you and Posy –'

'Don't assume anything!' said Marsha fiercely, 'I'll tell you one day, one day I will.'

Lynn had come to return a box of papers she'd given up trying to sort. 'I wish women had always remembered to put addresses on things in the old days,' she said helplessly. Marsha kept on crying. Lynn had told Derek she wouldn't be long, but she leaned against the wall and closed her eyes. 'I'll stay a bit,' she said.

The long silence was broken only by the soft whistling of wind and Marsha trying to control her breathing. 'D'you know what she said once,' she blurted fiercely, 'she said there was nothing I could do for her that she couldn't do better for herself. In bed, I mean.'

'That was nice of her.'

'Don't –'

'No. But look. Are you doubting your whole sexual identity because you didn't live happily ever after? Heterosexual people don't do that.'

'You are, though.'

'What?'

'Living happily ever after, and Derek thinks I'm trying to break it up. Well, doesn't he? Doesn't he think there's something between you and me?'

Lynn shrugged. 'There is. I'm very fond of you.'

'Don't be naïve. I want more.'

'Why?'

Why? The only answer Marsha could think of was *to hold*

someone warm because Posy died, but Lynn was going ahead with the kind of pent-up fluency that made Marsha wonder if she had been waiting for an opportunity to say all this. 'Why? To prove something? It wouldn't prove anything. I mean, you might think it does and Derek might think it does and even I might think it does, but it doesn't. It's a great male idea, you know, that you pass some magical point of no return when you go to bed with someone, or when you touch some particular part of them, or tell them some important secret – it's all part of the great male mania for labelling things and classifying them and planning.'

Marsha smiled damply. 'You've got a lot to say on this, haven't you? Have you been thinking again?'

'Yes.'

'Why?'

'Rationalising the fact that I want to sleep with you or whatever the hell it's called between women.'

'Why?'

'Because it's my turn now.'

'And to see what it's like, hm?'

Lynn flushed. 'I suppose that would be no worse a motive than trying to get at my really-quite-nice husband.'

Marsha said, 'This conversation is getting embarrassing.'

'It is, isn't it? So not tonight Josephine. Come home though, Marsha, and let me make a fuss of you.'

'No, I'll stay here.'

Marsha dreamt so pleasantly that night that she woke unsure of whether she had actually slept with her arms round Lynn or not. Her cold was better, but depression re-descended. Posy was breathing down mighty contempt. *I arranged for the women's movement to be armed, Marsha, single-handed I arranged for the first great international gesture of women's solidarity with women – across the seas, across the borders of race and class, alone I did it, and at a crisis in history you turned away because you had not taken a collective decision! Ye gods and goddesses – was this why I died?* Sadness and guilt suffused her. She should have had courage, she shouldn't have flinched like that from the reality of physical conflict because it was going to come anyway, sooner or later, and then cowardice would be called by its name and no one would be fooled by special pleading of commitment to non-violence or collective decision-making! She could have been useful. She would never tell anyone, she decided, looking at the little yellow gun and the foil cylinder hidden away. After all, what use was there for feminists in a weapon that could burn off a man's head and leave his feet in his boots?

It was the day for the visit of the president of Europea. It was summer. The dawn sky was pale, the sun wreathed in mist. Not a leaf stirred. It was going to be hot.

The president's swift fleet would reach Dover around 10 a.m. He and his party of ministers and experts and wives and journalists would be whisked to London in bullet-proof cars. At a pre-arranged point they would transfer to open cars for a slow public drive to lunch with the prime minister, the cabinet and the royal family.

The president had had to be reassured. 'Of course open cars are safe. Of course the people want to see you. London has no civil disorder problem.' But the city's tramps and beggars had been rounded up and sent to suburban parks, just in case.

Policemen strapped guns to their waists and looked uneasily out of their windows as they got up in the morning. Sun made for a better spectacle, but rain meant smaller, more docile crowds.

'There'll be no problems,' their commissioners had assured them, 'Most of the crowd'll be FAMILY.'

But the policemen remained uneasy, and none more so than those with wives in FAMILY. Each thought it an individual worry and told no one. There was prestige in having a FAMILY wife, not to mention a comfortable home. So they didn't discuss how odd the wives had become of late, how quiet and preoccupied and even hostile; they didn't share their puzzlement over the number of times they'd come home to find their front rooms full of women and children planning urgently and angrily but switching the conversation to fabric or recipes the minute their husbands came in.

Mr Peel was uneasy too. David Laing had washed his hands of the Family Welfare aspects of the Europea agreement, told Peel to get on with it. Peel knew it was a sticky area and his own political future hung on it. He felt certain that the women would step into line when it came to it, particularly if the price and the penalties were right – but it would only take some insane performance by the women's libbers (who fortunately knew nothing) to undermine the image of the nation of public-spirited mothers just waiting for the chance to serve the human race and the new supercontinent.

The gleaming fleet of cars prepared to move off. The visitors found it quaint to be carried in Rolls Royces. They were going to the royal palace, a skyscraper on the corner of Tottenham Court Road and Oxford Street that had been built for offices but never occupied.

The monarch, the president and the prime minister climbed into the first car. The engine purred as it crept through the police cordon and into the main street. The second car carried VIP wives and the princess.

The crowds – women and children mainly, with flowers and flags – cheered. The police watched them. Plainclothes men pushed their way tensely along the pavements.

The third car. Mr Peel, David Laing and the professor with jet-black hair. Sun flashed on the car's mirrors and the hubcaps of the wheels. Sudden movement rippled through the crowds. Police hands shot to their belts . . . but it was nothing.

'Let the children through.' Just mothers pushing kids forward to see better. 'Let the children through.'

Mr Peel stood up in the car, his arms wide to acknowledge the cheers of the crowd. David Laing sat slumped, his hand over his mouth, his eyes downcast.

The professor's eyes, soft and avuncular, roamed over the cheering children at the front of the pavements. When the procession slowed, knots of little girls in green rushed forward under the policemen's stern eyes and gave flowers. The professor pinched their cheeks, chucked them under the chin.

It was a heart-warming spectacle, the VIP wives and the princess agreed in the second car, as the procession wound its way through the sunlit West End.

8

The Protection of Women

All along the route children were being pushed forward. It was a reassuring sight for the police who had feared that movements a good deal more sinister might come from this crowd. Not that there was any serious dissent over Britain going into Europea but international terrorism could threaten any visiting statesman. To-day, though, there were no bombs, no offensive yells; just the age-old appeal of mothers at a spectacle, passed up the line like some gentle army dispatch: let the children through, let the children through.

Had the police looked closely, they might have noticed something odd. They might have seen slight anguish suppressed in the eyes of the mothers who let them go. They might have seen a lingering kiss, a last whispered word, or they might have wondered why so many of the children carried coats on this warm day, or clutched books or teddy-bears as if they were being sent to bed. Police officers later chided their juniors for not spotting these clues, but, as they had to admit, this was not the kind of detail a policeman was trained to look for.

The last car vanished through the tall gates in front of the royal skyscraper. Lights winked, messages of relief buzzed between guards. The policemen relaxed and turned back to the crowd, which seemed suddenly thinner, and, now that the cheers and the excitement had died away, oddly quiet.

'All right, kiddywinks,' the policemen said, 'Back to mum now.'

The children gazed up into the policemen's faces and said nothing. The policemen looked over their heads into the blank space where their mothers had been. Like puppets from a story-book the policemen scratched their heads and bent from the waist to examine and reassure the children who surged silently around them, then glanced along the line to see their colleagues similarly surrounded, similarly perplexed, and not a mother in sight.

The prime minister peered at his drink. A paltry pool of cheap liquor, hardly worth dirtying the glass for. The mania for economy had struck even here. Glass chandeliers replaced by inelegant plastic. Reproduction old masters, stretch Olex covers on bursting armchairs. Not like the old days at Buckingham Palace.

He glanced at the Europea group, hoping that they at least had been given proper drinks. Their oafish president was quite capable of commenting on it if he didn't think he had been.

The royals hadn't put in an appearance yet. In deference to the president's sensitivities, they weren't following the usual procedure of guests being formally introduced and expected to bow. The president might refuse to bob at the critical moment, and then there would be the tedious search for the right response to the snub, at a time when the nation's diplomatic resources were already stretched to their limits. So the guests had been shown into the lounge for a pre-lunch drink, and the royals would filter in when the conversation was moving and the gathering relaxed.

Which wouldn't be yet, the prime minister thought grimly, glaring at the knots of people sizing each other up as if for a fight. Peel, sleek and slim in his shiny suit, was laying down the law to somebody's wife. David Laing stood alone, swigging the koffee he'd made difficulties by asking for, making no effort to mix.

The prime minister's toe fidgeted with a wrinkle in the carpet. They hadn't even bought new carpeting for the move from the palace, they'd had the old stuff refitted, badly. A gap by the wall corresponded to the wrinkle – maybe if he pushed – he sighed. The wrinkle reared up into a roller-coaster, stopped like a sand-dune. It would be on his nerves throughout the meal. Among other things. He wished it was over, wished the whole visit over. He thought of the country cottage he would flee to when all was signed and sealed. He hadn't had a proper night's sleep for a month. Always there was a delegation, a firm, a cobbled-together pressure-group to see, to reassure that their interests were being taken account of. And always, of course, that assurance could be given. Europea was good for everybody.

At least. There was one part of the agreement that troubled him, and that was the Europop project. He wasn't sure why. Politically it was feasible – birth control came low on anyone's agenda these days, and all that was needed was a photogenic expert who could blind people with science and wouldn't mind going on television in the middle of the night when nobody was watching. In practical terms it made sense; and morally . . . well, it was superstitious to feel uneasy, and superstition had no place in the third millenium anno domini. He sighed. He'd been won over. Public opinion could be too, when the time came to tell them about it, if it was couched in the right terms by the right man.

His eyes fell on Laing, hunched in a corner. He seemed to be trying to eat his cup. Curious fellow, not long for the political world, the prime minister guessed. All the heart seemed to have gone out of him. Never very much talent anyway – typical that he should have chosen a two-bit party like the FP in which to pursue his curious obsession. He'd never have got anywhere in the jungle of real politics. He held his job because nobody else wanted it.

A door opened; eyes swivelled, expecting royals. But it was a footman who informed the prime minister in a slightly contemptuous stage whisper that there was a call which the switchboard felt he ought to take personally. Embarrassed, the prime minister excused himself, avoiding the president's glance of questioning indignation.

'Who *is* that?' he demanded. The line crackled. He cursed as he fiddled with the volume control . . . damn gadgets . . . never had volume controls confusing the issue on a perfectly simple telephone in his day . . . the line screeched. He flinched. The screech became women's laughter.

'Who *is* that?'

Giggles. 'Who does it sound like?' Damn silly schoolgirl giggles. Had he been called away from a turning point in the nation's history for a practical joker? He'd have things to say to the switchboard, and their boss! 'It sounds like some damn fool women –'

'That's right.' A shadow fell across the phone and the prime minister looked up into the grave face of a police inspector. The shrill voice nagged on: 'That's right. This is the women. You have our children.'

'I haven't got any children,' said the prime minister.

'You have now,' said the woman.

The policeman was starting to talk in his ear. He silenced him impatiently. The woman went on: 'We've decided not to look after them any more, you see. We're having a day off.' The voice was pert, almost coquettish now. Giggle, giggle, giggle. 'Sorry, I should say we're on strike.'

'Damn kids – ' the inspector began.

'*Quiet!*'

'And don't think the children'll give you any excuse to take it out on them. They're all very obedient. FAMILY-reared.' The phone went dead. The prime minister's enraged hand twiddled the volume control till it fell off. He turned on the inspector who informed him, quietly and with respect, that the streets through which the Europea party would pass after lunch were now blocked, thronging with children, unsupervised, in their thousands.

'Arrest them!'

'Children?'

'Send them home!'

'They won't say where they live.'

'Aren't they vandalising or something?'

'No, sir. They're mainly playing. They're just a bit obtrusive.'

Equally obtrusive was the graffiti that had started to appear on walls along the route, the inspector continued. In places where it certainly had not been the night before when his men checked. What did it say? He consulted his notes. It said things like 'Benefits for all The Women.' 'The Women are on Strike.' 'The Women are not Test Tubes.' 'The Women are not Guinea Pigs.' 'No to Europop.' 'No to Europea.'

'But they didn't know!' the prime minister roared.

'Sir?'

'Change the route, dammit.'

'Sir, they're everywhere and we haven't got long.'

'Good god, you've handled worse crowds than a bunch of children, I should hope. Deal with it, give 'em sweets or tear gas or something –'

'Tear gas, sir?'

'Anything! Well, not tear gas, you know what I mean, use your discretion man, you're paid enough. Tear gas on children! You think the president wants to tour London on a carpet of dead infants?'

.'. . . quite accustomed to the idea of motherhood as a public service,' the princess was explaining to the president as they sat round a table that was slightly too long and shiny for the simple meal it carried. 'Why, they even get paid.'

The prime minister glanced at Laing, picking morosely at his salad. Somehow he had to speak to him.

'What was your message?' asked the president, chatty and imperious.

'Just a small matter.'

'What?'

The prime minister gave a short laugh. 'My mother-in-law's birthday present, as a matter of fact.'

The president enjoyed this and bellowed with laughter. 'A matter of state, that, eh?'

'Is your salad to your taste, Mr President?' the princess asked.

'Thank you. I am not fond of salad.'

A sealed envelope passed to the prime minister with his after-lunch cup of koffee revealed that when a Northern train pulled into Birmingham an hour ago, it was found to be full of unaccompanied children eating sandwiches. They would not give their surnames. Pupils at a school in Norfolk had refused to go home for their lunch, or, indeed, at all; and three big city cathedrals swarmed with youngsters. Graffiti was appearing everywhere, reports still poured in and all London's main streets were blocked.

The prime minister faked a cough and got up from the table. The cars were due in thirty-five minutes. He phoned Isabel Travers.

'But you know I am no longer active, prime minister. My health is delicate.'

'Isabel, this is an emergency.'

'I understand that.'

'You have stature. Go on television or something. Good God, you can't expect me to deal with this.'

Isabel's sigh was heartrending. 'I shall make some enquiries and call you back. Where are you?'

'The palace.'

'The *palace*?'

'Yes, the palace and we've got thirty-five minutes.'

Back in the drawing room the royal ladies were examining the pale yellow foam on their koffee while the professor harangued the silent room on the dangers to civilization of random productive coitus. The president's eyes bored into the returning prime minister.

'Something has happened, I think.'

'No, no.'

With ten minutes to spare, the prime minister learned that Isabel

Travers could do nothing. FAMILY, so disciplined and orderly and reassuring, was in disarray. Rashida Patel had taken leave of her senses and made unauthorised use of the mailing lists. Women's liberationists had spread panic in the ranks with a rumour that the government planned to forbid some women to have babies. Their reaction was only to be expected; the mass abandonment of children had been planned as a protest for months, with skill and precision. In time the misunderstanding over the government's plans would be cleared up, but for the moment it was not even clear who was loyal and who had gone over to the group who had rather arrogantly assumed to themselves the title of 'The Women.'

Isabel said, 'I am assuming that the misunderstanding *will* be cleared up.'

The prime minister scoffed to avoid answering

'I am assuming,' she continued, 'that there is no truth – because you are tampering with women's birthright if it is true, you know, and getting into dangerous areas.'

'Isabel, I am not a fool.'

'I know that, prime minister, but over the next few years a generation of girls will be coming to maturity who know in their hearts that their fulfilment as women lies in their freedom to choose motherhood, and they will not lack my sympathy if –'

'Isabel!' the prime minister howled, 'do something!'

'Seems to be a slight hitch with one of the cars. Old-fashioned things.'

The president's scepticism was palpable. 'We have a tight schedule.'

The prime minister's attempt to reply was aborted in a hum that became a high-pitched roar from far below in the street. The startled lunch guests flocked to the windows. The prime minister collapsed in a chair and covered his eyes.

A colourful sea of children swamped the base of the palace, and more were coming: rolling up Oxford Street and Charing Cross Road and Tottenham Court Road and all the little side-streets in between to converge on the towering building, shouting and waving. It wasn't a riot, it was more like playtime. Nonplussed policemen stood together in groups. Guns bulged on their hips – boys approached, asked to see them. Occasional tough guys drew batons, but the children merely examined them with fascinated curiosity. Police dogs were brought; the children patted them.

Police horses were fed sugar and had their noses stroked. Children climbed over parked cars, taking their shoes off first to protect the paintwork. Nearing the palace, they stopped running and sauntered, or sat down and ate sweets. Many carried banners or paper lollipops. There was just one slogan: 'The Women are on Strike!'

The president asked, 'What is all this?'

'A traditional festival?' the princess suggested faintly.

'Don't be alarmed,' said the prime minister.

'I am not alarmed,' said the president.

'What do they mean?' wondered one of the wives.

'On *strike*?' read another, 'Well! I won't say I haven't been tempted myself.'

The party turned back from the window. David Laing was at the koffee pot, helping himself. The princess took the pot delicately from him and offered the president a refill. 'Now,' she beamed, 'I wonder what all this is about.'

Laing sat down and stretched himself. He yawned and scratched his hair. His moodiness seemed to have lifted. He was bitter and glib. 'It's obvious. They don't like their terms of employment. Can't say I blame them much.'

The president's face was purple. The prime minister laughed. 'It's a practical joke. Never let it be said that our women lack a sense of humour. Always saying, aren't you, that the only time we appreciate the work you put in is when you, ah, don't.'

'Quite,' said a wife.

'A joke,' said another.

'You think you can control productive coitus among that lot?' the president demanded of the professor.

'The tour is still on,' the prime minister said, 'it's just that, er, you may see some mild disorder.'

'It might be interesting for you, Mr President,' said the princess.

The president indicated that there would be no tour. The party would proceed to Dover. He added that on his not-infrequent visits to the underdeveloped world, governments made it their business to ensure that he was not troubled by protesters in the street. Had he come to London to fight his way home through unruly children? 'What's the matter with your women – or your men for that matter?' he demanded, glaring with such challenge at the prime minister's crotch that the princess blushed and busied herself with a crease in the tablecloth. The president became ribald. 'How far does it go? What else do your women refuse?'

The professor spoke softly to Peel and Laing. 'The Europop project will run into difficulties if the women are not co-operative.' He shook his black locks.

'Yes I expect it will,' said Laing.

'You said they would be.'

'They will,' said Peel.

'Oh yes,' said Laing, 'they'll co-operate. They're all in favour of it. They don't know what it is yet, but –'

'They obviously think they do,' said Peel, 'Professor, you have my assurance. The trouble-makers are a tiny minority. Their leaders will be dealt with, and then – is something funny, Mr Laing?'

'Don't you understand? They don't have leaders.'

'What nonsense. This thing was led.'

The Europea party swept to Dover in sealed cars through back streets.

'You were a lot of help,' Peel stormed at Laing, 'What in hell are you smiling at ?' His composure was shattered, his eloquence gone. Clenched white, his fists pounded his knees.

'Nothing, I'm sorry, it is serious I agree, it's just . . . well, you have to laugh. Whoever they are, they've called our bluff.'

'I have heard,' said Peel, 'that in some parts of the world they reduce population growth at a stroke by aborting girls. Works wonders over a generation or two.' His teeth showed. 'Why the hell didn't you think of that, prime minister?'

The mass media had always reserved a special tone, somewhere between smirking glee and moral outrage, for stories about feminists. Now embarrassment was added. The premature departure of the visitors was a serious business. 'These women cannot realise what they have done.'

All day crowds of children kept turning up at stations and terminals and ancient monuments, in universities and parks, hotel lobbies and laboratories, offices and factories. When it became clear that their mothers intended leaving them overnight, the prime minister ordered that they be taken to women's prisons. That would shame mothers out of their nonsense. The women prisoners were reported to be enchanted, the officers rather less so. The children kept scampering along corridors when it was time to lock them into cells, wanting bedtime stories and carrots and drinks of water. Then the men in men's prisons started demanding their share of the children.

Next morning the prime minister ordered firms to give fathers time off from work to go and collect their children. But many men could not be spared, and, besides, no individual knew where his children were. The women had been away all night. The Department for Family Welfare set up reception centres staffed by girls from Young Families of Tomorrow. The children's behaviour at the centres was impeccable. They said please and thank you and ate nicely. When the younger ones cried they were comforted by the older. But they would not give their names.

The princess agreed to go on television.

'The hearts of my husband and myself go out,' she said, 'not just to the children who have been abandoned, but to the women who have felt driven to take this step. Not everyone will agree with me for saying this –' in a glass box at the back of the studio Peel and the prime minister glanced at each other over Laing's impassive head; she was departing from the script they had given her '– but the needs of women are still not adequately respected by policy makers. There is still, er, lots of discrimination. But this is no solution. You have made your point. You are not bad women. It is late. Your children are bedding down in strange homes or wriggling to find comfort on the hard floors of large dark halls. Their courage forsakes them as they long for a mother's goodnight kiss. Come and take them home before irreparable damage is done. At my personal request a group of MPs will meet with your leaders, and they will give, I promise, the most sympathetic . . .'

Laing said, 'They don't have leaders.'

The princess said, 'Was I all right?'

The reply was lost in the shouts of children invading the foyer downstairs. The princess's aides had to advance before her to clear a passage.

Fascinated foreign correspondents asked, 'What will you do with the children?'

'Nothing,' said Mr Peel.

'You will let them starve?'

'Of course not,' said Laing and the prime minister together.

'What is it costing you to keep them in reception centres?'

'No comment.'

'What are the demands of the women?'

'This is what is so absurd. We don't know. They haven't even said who they are.'

But sharp-eyed newsmen had spotted the half painted-out graffiti, and wondered what it all meant. Mr Peel cut in on their speculations in a tone of hurt surprise that it was really necessary to go into all this. There were plans, he explained, to let in a few foreign demographers to collect figures on the British birth-rate. That was all. The women had got hold of the wrong end of the stick and reacted hysterically. As usual.

Although a few hundred women had trickled back here and there by the end of the week, public indignation was running high. Any woman of child-bearing age seen on the street without children in tow ran the risk of being stoned, spat on or refused admission to public buildings or transport. Some reported attacks by gangs of men who threatened a repetition if the women did not go back to their children. The policemen wrote down the details carefully. Then they said, 'Are you sure you didn't ask for it?'

For safety and support, striking women were banded together in pre-arranged houses and feminist squats, carefully stocked up with food. They knew each other, they had been planning together for weeks. Now they had long, hungry hours to talk.

The women who were in FAMILY tried to explain why, and the women who were in women's liberation tried to understand. Then it was the other way round. Everyone was kind and cautious in what she said; concern for the children never took long to surface.

In a packed flat in Collindeane Tower, Lynn ventured: 'Maybe it would be useful for us to try and understand why *we* feel so responsible.'

A girl about Jane's age who had abandoned a very young baby in a hypermarket but who was losing courage, turned on her. 'What do you mean, we? It's all right for you. Your daughter's grown up.'

'Yes. She's probably looking after yours.'

'What?'

'Your daughter?'

'She's a Young Family of Tomorrow person.'

'How come?'

'It's not so rare, rebelling against your mother.' There was a pause. Lynn's anguish was showing, *but it's not me, it's not me that needs support.* 'She's just got married to spite me, she was going to wait, she said she'd give us time to come round and like Martin but when she found I was involved in . . . in all this she said she wouldn't live under the same roof . . .' She forced a smile, a change of subject. She looked at the young women. 'I always wondered what you'd be like.'

'Who?'

'The new generation.'

'And are you proud?'

Lynn said yes but she didn't know.

At other times they discussed organisation, leadership. The FAMILY women were used to agendas and votes. They admitted that nothing had convinced them so effectively of the need for resistance as the defection of one of their founders. The feminists explained that they thought loose organisation was more democratic. It was better to take individual responsibility than to be swayed by the views of some cult-figure.

They were hungry for news. They had none of their own. The FAMILY communications networks were closed to them, feminist contacts chaotic. A firm report that one group was weakening would be followed by indignant assertions of hundred per cent solidarity. Tales that rapists had invaded a squat spread panic; counter-rumours bred hope and doubt. They discouraged each other from taking note of the mass media news, but it was all they had.

It told them that many fathers had fetched their children from the reception centres, but, on delivering them at school had been told that the authorities were taking no chances on a repetition. The schools were closed. It told them that young children had therefore to go to work with their fathers, which fathers didn't like. Children impaired their concentration. Firms set up creches and playrooms and let fathers work special shifts, but the pay was less, even before child-care costs were deducted. Even with care, the children disrupted the working day. Their demands could not be predicted and they were used to undivided attention. They missed their mothers. They wanted cups of milk, dispensed by father and only father. They played and chatted in office corridors, whining for paper to draw on and turns on transmitting machines. They fingered goods in shops, and disappeared, exploring, down burrows on building sites, and whole operations had to be held up while they were extricated. They turned awed eyes on the world of work in which daddy lived, and asked questions. In one factory a child stood by a production line and pointed at a gadget of which a man had been making a thousand a day for seventeen years and said, 'What's that for?' The man said, 'I'm blessed if I know,' and went to find out. Sometimes a toddler was spotted sliding down a conveyor belt and emergency switches had to be pulled.

And that was just the very young. Older children roamed free. They played ball games in churches and took rides on public transport without paying. Or they stood around in gangs, frightening people. When broken windows or piles of litter were spotted anywhere, people knew who to blame.

'It seems they're being looked after though,' the women told each other, 'in general.'

'But when are we going back?'

The government promised a statement.

A FAMILY woman said, 'If they make the slightest concession I think we should go back.'

There was agreement. 'Yes, we must allow them room for manoeuvre.'

But the feminists held fast. 'You talk as if we should be grateful for anything they give us. We have our demands. Benefit for all mothers. No selectivity. And no experiments. Women all over the country are holding out for that –'

'How do we know? How do we know they don't want to compromise?'

'Because it was agreed! It's a decision! We can't set ourselves up as leaders and negotiators just because we're in London!'

The FAMILY women were restive. 'How can you say it's a decision when there's no mechanism for changing the decision?'

'How long is this going on?' the prime minister demanded, 'We're an international laughing-stock, a nation brought to its knees by some tiff about who should change the nappies.'

'Yes, why can't we get back to real arguments?' Laing said sarcastically.

'I don't know what's got into you, Laing.'

'Why don't we just give them what they want?'

'We've offered to see their leaders.'

'I'm inclined to agree with Mr Peel,' said the prime minister, 'the whole thing is getting beyond a joke. Do you think you can handle it, Peel?'

'Yes sir.'

'Then I'm sure Laing will have no objection if I ask you to.'

'None at all,' Laing growled, 'you want me to resign?'

The prime minister flapped. 'Of course not, my dear chap.'

'Not yet,' said Peel.

This time Peel did the broadcast. He preceded it with several hours in the film archives and several more ordering technicians around in the editing rooms. Now he wore a shiny suit and his FAMILY badge. His hair was combed and the rims of his nails were white. He sat in the studio and waited for the signal to speak. The broadcast began with close-up film of babies crying, from the irrational howls of the newborn to the unhappy sobbing of toddlers. The wailing and shuddering persisted in the background as Peel leaned forward on the screen, his eyes sincere but stern.

'It's a sad sound, isn't it?' His voice glittered. 'I know it tears at my heart. Can you hear *your* child, you mothers out there? It's been said – it's been scientifically proven – that a true mother can spot her own child's cry in the midst of thousands. And we've had no difficulty making this film over the last few days, I can assure you.' The volume went up on the crying. 'Over the past few days, isolated areas of the country have suffered a unique and particularly unpleasant form of social disorder. I say particularly unpleasant because it has been directed against those least able to retaliate – little children. Look again.' Now the film showed five-and six-year olds, limp and bewildered.

'I can only express surprise and relief that more suffering has not been caused. It's well known that separating children from their mothers, particularly in traumatic circumstances such as these, can do lasting damage, and this remains to be seen. What of the damage now? Well, the girls of Young Families of Tomorrow have rallied round and coped magnificently, and so have the fathers. A special tribute to the fathers. And of course the overwhelming majority of mothers who have remained at their posts, as it were, have helped by taking in the little strike orphans, as we have come to call them.

'Yes, it is thanks to them that more little limbs have not been sheared off children playing unsupervised on factory floors, that more small bodies have not been fished out of canals or found in the gutters of main roads. Thanks to them that we haven't had much more to deal with than tears – though there have been plenty of those.'

Now the screen split down the middle. On the left a child shedding tears. On the right a 'spinster' with a bun and a women's liberation symbol on her flat bosom.

'And what is the reason for this tragedy? The women, we are told, are on strike. Very nice. They think that because an enlightened government sees fit to reward them for their efforts, they have no more responsibility than ordinary workers. Such a position would not have been reached, need I say it, by ordinary, loving, maternal, patriotic women acting on their own. No. Their minds have been poisoned by forces not far to seek. By counterfeit women who do not know what it is to mother and are thus able to see mothering in terms of cash and strikes. Is that you?' A birth – a real one, but clean and majestic, an awed mother touching the baby not yet out of her body, a complete circle dissolving into a silver coin. 'Is that how you see it?' Now his voice trembled with theatrically controlled anger. 'I fume, you know. I fume with indignation, with vicarious indignation . . . I share the anger that many of you must feeel when you realise that not only have you been hoodwinked but that those who have hoodwinked you have arrogated to themselves the title of *The Women*! The Women! These, I think, are the women of Britain.' FAMILY processions down the years. Women getting married. Women cleaning floors, helping old people across the road, lying beneath the men who were having violent sexual intercourse with them. 'These, you, are the women for whom they most certainly do not speak, women fully deserving of your Benefit, which will be withdrawn pending thorough rehabilitation from any mother who does not resume normal duties within twenty-four hours.'

Peel paused for drama, then became gentle. 'I am sorry if that seems severe. It is the only language some of these persons understand.

There is one more point. Some of them have been putting it about that there is some kind of science-fiction conspiracy to put contraceptives in the drinking water or some such thing. You know, I do wish you would get your facts right before you get into such a state.

'The facts are that there is a world population problem, and this country is going to contribute to its solution. We have been specially selected because of the specially responsible attitude of our mothers. It's an honour, for goodness' sake! All we're going to do is provide some information for surveys and so forth. It's a bit complicated to explain and it's not settled yet. But you may rest assured that nothing is going to happen to *you* without your understanding and agreement . . .'

The relief in many of the strike centres was palpable.

'There we are then,' said the ones who wanted to go back.

'What do you mean?' said the hardliners.

'No experiments. We've won.'

'He didn't say anything about selectivity.'

'And we mustn't give in to threats.'

Some women left quite openly. Others wanted to check that their children hadn't suffered accidents; if they were okay they would come back. Others sneaked out secretly. The feminists tried not to be despondent. It couldn't go on for ever and something had been achieved – hadn't it? Something had been proved – hadn't it? Nothing would ever be quite the same again – would it?

Peel extended his amnesty three times. Rumours abounded. The government was turning children loose on the streets. Children had strayed on to an airport runway and been mown down by a jet. Families in Europea were offering foster homes. Ships equipped with toys and nurseries were preparing to depart from Dover.

Everyone tried to keep it friendly as the last of the FAMILY women left Collindeane.

'You will stay in touch, won't you?'

'Of course, and I'm not going back to cleaning the floor more than once a day I can tell you.'

'I mean, we do have things to say to each other.'

'Oh yes . . .'

The tower seemed very empty. Emptier than ever before.

'Some of our own women have gone too,' Marsha noticed.

'Yes,' said Lynn.

'Will they come back?'

'I don't know.'

'Have they all joined FAMILY?'

'I don't know.'

The Protection of Women Act reaffirmed family values as the moral bedrock of the nation. Views subversive of those values were subversive of the state. Women must not band together for the purpose of propagating them. Public expression of sexism (defined as hatred of women in their natural role) was an offence.

Lesbianism became illegal for the first time, and heavy penalties attached to the unqualified practice of medicine.

But the PoW Act was not all stick. There were carrots too. Benefit went up for those women entitled to receive it. And the princess was involving herself personally in a new programme to reverse the injustices that had led to the recent unpleasantness (to which further reference would not be made). Benefit or no Benefit, it had to be realised that the housewife's lot could be a hard and lonely one. She was prone to isolation, prey to doubt. It was good for women to come together. A Europea grant would allow FAMILY to expand its helping centres so that every woman in the country would be registered at one. Depending on her age and status in life, various services would be offered. Domestic advice, sexual counselling and help with birth control would be available. They would be the agencies for the payment of Benefit and the administration of rehabilitation (now called Domestic Education) programmes. There would be the usual hints on fashion and cookery, and creche facilities for women who had good reason to leave their children for a few hours. The centres would be called Women's Centres.

Peel felt sure that the president of Europea was impressed by his speed and thoroughness but would not show it.

'The point is,' Peel explained, 'getting them all under one roof.'

'All right, but what about The Women?' he spoke the capitals, 'as opposed to the women.'

'You're getting those,' Peel grinned.

'What?'

'The ones we're rehabilitating. Ah, domestic educating. We send them to Europea, live in carefully selected homes for a bit of work experience. Bit of free help for your wives. Bit of the other for you from what I've heard.'

'No.' The president was not amused. 'Not in our homes.'

'Factories then. Food processing.'

The president permitted himself a flicker of interest.

'They are not popular places to work.'

'Women are good at food processing.'

The organisation known as The Women was declared banned, and a special detachment of investigators was formed to root out the leadership. Flippant colleagues dubbed them the Sex Police but they took their job seriously. They spent a lot of time interviewing former strikers who, back now in the bosoms of their families and registered at a government Women's Centre, were easy to persuade to give information. They had many stories as to where the leadership of The Women lay.

Hundreds of women were dispatched to Europea for six-month courses. Some took their children, others were allowed to leave them with approved foster families. A magistrate trying some women for performing an illegal medical procedure offered them a Domestic Education course as an alternative to prison. There was no law or precedent for the offer but it stood. And the example was followed in other courts.

Feminist pamphlets were impounded as sexist. There were more and more attacks on women going unescorted on the street. Sometimes the victims were devout adherents of FAMILY; The Women were clearly to blame. Sometimes they were feminists, but who was to say the attacks were not stage-managed, particularly when they stopped short of rape? Court orders were taken out in the name of dead landlords and long defunct local authorities for the repossession of squatted buildings.

The fashion industry responded to the new mood of femininity by creating a new Olex textile which was spun thin like lace. Long frocks, ruffs and collars were all the rage. Olex lace had to be washed by hand but it didn't matter because red hands were thought alluring. Special creams could be bought to enhance their colour.

Sex therapy at the government Women's Centres proved popular. Many women who had abandoned their children now suffered deep guilt and their marital relationships were impaired. They were told to remember the strike (if at all) as a bad dream. Latest research showed that complete passivity of mind and body were the pathway to pleasure in women. If sensations in the clitoris distracted from the joys of intercourse it could be excised, but this was not generally necessary; a correct attitude of mind should be enough.

It became dangerous to picket the Women's Centres urging women not to register. Gangs of police and other men were never far away. And meanwhile the government was running a massive campaign to fit contraceptive pellets in every woman of child-bearing age. Special badges advertised who was wearing one, and the devices were removable on demand, more or less. Many famous women (some post-menopausal but keen to show they were not afraid) testified to their trouble-free up-to-dateness. It was the younger women who remained cautious, and so photogenic girls were sought who would have them fitted and appear on posters, smiling as reassuringly 'after' as 'before'. Star of the publicity drive aimed at engaged girls was Jane Carmichael, nee Byers.

At last Britain went into Europea, all its flags flying.

It was the strike that had made up Jane's mind. Until then she swore she'd been trying to find a way to peace through the antagonisms that lay between her and her mother. After all, whatever Lynn might think, the FAMILY message was always that a child's duty to love and respect his parents was second only to a mother's duty to nurture her children.

It was ironic too, considering Lynn's dislike of Martin (she'd dislike any man having the nerve to love her daughter, Jane brooded) that it was he who had led Jane to reconsider her attitude to her. 'You really hate her, don't you?' he'd said once, and it was not just his manifest disapproval that had stopped her short. It was that word *hate*. Lynn herself had made the same accusation when Jane first joined YFT. It was four years ago but she remembered it well. She had been wondering how to tell Lynn she'd decided to join, and had let her come upon her admiring herself in her new uniform. The jacket and skirt were skilfully designed. They made a flat bust look round and softened angular hips. The green flattered her red hair and even her pallor looked intriguing rather than pitiful.

Lynn had cut right through it. 'What on earth are you wearing?'

'You can see.'

'Where did you get it?'

'You don't have to be embarrassed about me getting charity. There's no charity in YFT, we just help one another.'

'And hate your parents!'

This had hurt. And the same charge hurt again, years later, coming from Martin. She didn't hate Lynn. She just sensed resentment and returned it. At least that was the only explanation she could think of now, as an adult, for her admitted perversity as a child. The treatments for her illness had been the classic opportunity for conflict. The memory made her blush a bit. She'd realised much earlier than she let on that they were a life-saver rather than a skilled scheme of sadism dreamed up by Lynn to make her life a misery, yet she'd got into the habit of sulking and martyring herself and enjoying the attention this earned. What an appalling daughter she'd been! What would she do if she got one the same?

Happy in Martin's courtship, she made a special effort to be helpful and polite to Lynn. He encouraged this. When they got married he wanted a big ceremony with at least the outward signs of approval from both her parents. She started respecting Lynn's political opinions and concealing her suspicion of Marsha's visits. She was welcoming to Jim and read books that enabled her to have useful conversations with Derek. Once she even got Lynn to admit that Martin was quite a nice boy even though she wished Jane would take up Derek's offer to pull a few strings and get her at least a year of university education before she married. Jane said she wouldn't need it. Some sort of peace reigned.

And then came the unbelievable news that over half the nation's mothers had walked out on their children. Deliberately, cold-bloodedly, as a political gesture. And not only did Lynn approve, she had helped organise it. Even Derek seemed to have had a hand in getting the information, sour though that fact would make the feminists if they did but know! It was the sickest thing Jane had ever heard of, and she walked out too.

Martin had been stern and anxious. 'Whatever they have done,' he said, 'They are still your parents.'

'I won't go back.'

'Where will you live, then?'

'With you, I'd hoped.'

'Jane!'

'Married I meant.'

'I had hoped your parents would be at our wedding.'

'If they are,' Jane said fiercely, 'I won't be.'

So they married fast. Martin was reluctant and embarrassed: FAMILY was encouraging the practice of long, chaste engagements during which girls should attend preparation classes. If a girl attended these after her wedding rather than before, everyone assumed she'd had to get married. This was another reason for Martin's suggestion that she have her contraceptive pellet fitted before the wedding with full publicity.

Now Jane wasn't sure how she felt about being married. She didn't know what she'd expected from sex (she had ignored everything Lynn had told her) but it certainly hadn't been this combined sensation of being fantastically important and yet not there at all as Martin prodded and pumped away. His bossiness as a husband didn't worry her unduly, it was the underside of his strong sense of responsibility, and he only bossed her to do things that she accepted as her job anyway, like housework. She knew she wasn't very good at housework yet but he had a nice sister called Astrid who often popped in, full of advice. What did worry her – embarrassed her, though she told nobody – was the way she kept wanting to wake up in her own bed at home. It wasn't that she was unhappy or regretted getting married, she just felt childish and homesick. She had pooh-poohed the importance of a ceremony, of parental approval; now she felt that the transaction of her marriage had not been properly completed, that she had been kicked out (or had flounced out) of the world of childhood, without being properly honoured as an adult.

Martin had just finished giving her her physiotherapy. She got up from lying sideways over cushions, feeling slightly sick as she always did, and a mixture of aroused and grateful and humiliated at her husband's willingness to take this on. Her poor old ribs. It was a wonder they were still there.

She started to cough to clear her lungs. What a disgusting business. Yet he stayed with her for company. Just as Lynn had. Jane wanted to avert her eyes from her own body on these occasions, yet the people who loved her stayed. Would she be able to love like that? Well, she'd have to.

'Thanks,' she muttered.

'It was a pleasure.'

'You'll get tired of it.'

'On the contrary. It'll save me beating you.'

She smiled, a bit disturbed. 'I want to have this pellet thing taken out and have a baby,' she said.

'What, now?'

She pretended to consider. 'Tomorrow would do.'

'You've only just had it put in.'

'That was for the posters.'

He frowned. 'We'll do whatever you want, love. But why?'

'Why?' she shouted, 'Why do you think? Don't you want to?'

'Of course I do. But it's preferable not to have children in the first year of marriage, it's been proved by statistics.'

'I've always wanted to be a mother,' she said. It was true. Well, if she was fair she had to admit that the first time she thought of it was in a skirmish with Lynn. Lynn was always saying 'What do you want to be when you grow up?' and Jane used to go through the normal answers – a doctor, a nurse, a journalist, a professor. One day, almost at random, she'd said, 'I just want to be a mother like you,' and Lynn had tried to hide the pursing of her lips as she turned away. But Jane had noticed and stored it up as a weapon. In time it became a real wish. She wanted babies, lots of babies. She'd loved the brief time when they used to go to Collindeane because there were babies and children there, and then the time in the reception centres. Children's questions were so fabulous because they made you wonder about real things. Why are trees that way up? Why can't I see words? Why do sounds stop and where do they go when I can't hear them any more? Say *why?* and people will talk to you. The child wants to be talked to and reassured. The adult likes to be confirmed as superior and knowledgeable. A partnership. Sealed by *why?* So many exquisite little symmetries in the bond, Jane mused, yet these mad feminists talked and acted as if motherhood were no more than a job!

Why did Lynn have her if she didn't want to look after her? But she had looked after her. But she'd resented it so. But she hadn't resented it, she'd been devoted. But . . . oh damn it. She was grown up now. She was off Lynn's hands. Lynn could do anything, cavort with lesbians in a clapped-out block of flats if that was what turned her on. And Jane would have a baby. And the circle would be completed. And Jane would go to Lynn and say, guess what, you're going to be a granny, and there would be peace between them.

Next day she slipped disdainfully through the feminist pickets and into the government Women's Centre.

'Excuse me,' she said to the clerk who sat on a tall stool picking his fingernails, 'I'd like to make an appointment to – er – ' She hunted for the right word, surprised at herself.

He glanced at her breasts. 'Starting a family?'

They really ought to have women to staff these places. It was bad enough for an emancipated, articulate girl like herself, who knew her rights; some women would feel intruded upon. 'Hope so. Hardly worth having it put in in the first place really, but I, er, did it for the posters.' She nodded at the pictures of herself on the wall; she'd hoped he would recognise her. 'How long will it take?'

'That's up to you, my dear.' He leered. 'Or your husband, should I say.'

'I meant getting it removed.'

'No time at all. It's a simple operation, you can do it in a lunch hour. Make a day of it though, it's best. Name?'

'Carmichael, Jane Carmichael.'

'I'll look you up.'

By what right did he *look her up*? They really should have women . . . he was pressing keys on a humming lighted board. The board covered a box which contained information on all the women registered at this Centre. The box coughed and spat and emitted a tapeworm of paper. The man ran his bitten fingers over whatever secrets it contained. Jane felt dirty, as if he held her underwear. She shivered.

'You don't appear to exist,' he said, smiling with a mockery that was only partly directed against himself.

'Of course I do.' She frowned. 'My maiden name was Byers, if that's relevant.'

'Of course, of course. Come back tomorrow.'

Suddenly she was afraid. She shouldn't have given her maiden name. Maybe they'd match it with a list of subversives and find Lynn. Maybe they'd tell her she wasn't suitable. The thought formed: *what business is it of theirs?* It was disloyal. She brushed it away. The man was still fiddling with dials and buttons.

'Byers?'

'That was my name.'

'Any hereditary illness in your family?'

She turned very cold. Her voice came out as a croak. 'I have cystic fibrosis, but I'm –' The man's face stopped her. Stupid, humiliating to plead. She knew what was coming.

'CF, eh?' He moved to the other side of the box, pressed different keys. 'Must've been well looked after to last this long.' Another strip of paper oozed out. He read it and smiled the smile of a man who has solved a knotty problem. 'CF. You're in a different category, never occurred to me, you looking so well.' He was reproachful. 'I don't suppose they'll recommend removal in your case.'

She said quietly, 'Who the hell do you think you are? I demand to see a doctor.'

'Suit yourself. Tomorrow? But I'm telling you, you're wasting your time. You'll find other outlets, bright girl like you. They're trying to wipe out these illnesses, you see.'

9

Terrorists

Someone said kindly, 'Go up and share lookout duty with Judy, Marsha.' It was necessary of course. Judy couldn't keep her mind reliably on one thing and she had taken some little girls up with her which suggested some game was in the offing. But Marsha knew this wasn't the only reason. Judy wasn't the only person who needed looking after.

Marsha's feet were heavy with the long climb, and her chest ached. The physical failings of middle age were such a boring nuisance; back in the old days she could take these stairs two at a time. Her breath came fast and her blood beat in her ears. What would it matter if her heart stopped altogether? Who would be worse off if she bent dizzily over a banister and it broke and she smashed spreadeagled on to the stone ground floor? Well, the women would if she did it right now because she was meant to be keeping watch, but what about later when she was off-duty? Who would care? Not Lynn. Lynn wouldn't even notice.

Her toe caught the lip of a step. She slipped, barked her shin, sobbed. She forced her legs to lift higher than they needed, as a punishment.

What did I do wrong? she wailed inside, then mocked viciously the cry of the thwarted lover. What had she done wrong indeed? How could she ever do anything right? When even people sensible enough to fall in love with members of the opposite sex and backed up by a culture, an etiquette, a religion, whole industries, whole fictions and mythologies, whole genres of joke telling them how to behave, when even for those people things went wrong occasionally (*just occasionally* she added bitterly, thinking of millions of couples down the years at their ceremonies swearing 'till death do us part' and then swearing it again with a new partner, and again with another). *What chance is there for us?*

Why waste time and tears on straight women anyway?

She'd been so careful. She didn't know how many lovers Lynn had had in her life, or even if there had been any other than

Derek; but she was damn sure none of them had been as ethical as she was. There were many forms of pressure that could be applied in a women's community to a straight woman who spurned the love of a sister to run home to her husband, but Marsha had tried none of that. Nor had she presumed upon the greeting kisses and congratulatory or sympathetic hugs that were part of the women's normal life together, even though Lynn seemed to like those as much as anyone. She'd made sure that their bedding lay close together when Lynn stayed nights (the roads being unsafe after dark) but she'd felt Lynn's tension like beams through the darkness when the couples around them started shifting and whispering, and held off. Was that right? Had it really been tension? Was that conversation they'd had the day the news of Posy came forgotten, or had it just been to comfort her? Last night, at last, she'd thought not. She'd laughed at herself – the tension had been her own. Now she wondered.

How had it happened? In the end not by seduction, not by blackmail. Just gentle frankness. The departure of the strikers had left empty spaces in Collindeane Tower.

'You know I love you, Lynn.'

'Yes, I know.'

'Is it the same for you?'

'I don't know.'

'Can we try?'

Lynn sighed. 'I don't want to think of you as an experiment. What are you laughing at?'

'Lynn, you're so wonderful. I'm the one who's supposed to feel guilty.'

'God damn it!' Lynn was shouting, the corners of her eyes were wet, she was laughing and her fists were clenched. 'Why is it that whatever we do we feel guilty?' and they hugged each other and didn't let go. It was a sweet polite night. Once Lynn raised herself on to Marsha as if to mount her, then exploded into laughter and fell on her side, hiding her face. 'I'm sorry, I forgot.'

'Is that what you do with Derek?' said Marsha – unforgivable, but Lynn forgave. 'What's Derek doing in the women's tower?' she demanded, and it was an answer Marsha could not work out her reaction to because it said *I'm not thinking about Derek at this moment Marsha, so you don't have to*; but it also said *what Derek and I have is safe from the likes of you, otherwise I wouldn't be here*.

They slept. Marsha woke when it was still dark and felt Lynn's soft hand on her.

'Fascinating,' Lynn murmured.

'What?'

'Your body.'

'Same as yours.'

'Not really.'

Lynn yawned. 'No wonder men like us so much.'

'Never mind about that. Come close.'

'You're shivering.'

'It's a bad time of the night.'

'What time?'

'Three o'clock. Bad things happen. Time stops, People die. Your heart slows down, you know? Police raids happen at three.'

Lynn said, 'The guards will warn us.'

They lay together. Marsha stiffened. 'What's that?'

'I didn't hear anything.'

'There it is again.'

Lynn repeated her owl noise and snorted with laughter.

'Shut up, you'll wake the bloody hens.'

In the morning they were tired and sunny-eyed and slightly drunk. They volunteered to shovel chickenshit and spread it on the window boxes. 'Fancy eggs for breakfast?' asked Marsha, and Lynn said, 'mm.' The other women turned a blind eye to the great bowls of yellow curds they prepared for themselves (one egg per woman per week was strictly the ration) and they ate and nudged each other like puppies.

When did the mood change? Marsha remembered a moment of stillness. One minute Lynn was wiping a bit of bread round her plate with her fingers, scooping up egg. Then she stopped. It was as if a film had changed mid-reel. She picked up her knife and fork and cut the bread delicately. Marsha raised an eyebrow. Lynn met her glance and looked away.

'Lynn.'

'What?'

'What are you thinking?'

'Nothing.'

'What is it?'

Lynn spread her hands. 'I don't know.'

'You didn't like the experiment.' Marsha tried to make her voice light.

'It's not that.'

'Ah. You did like it.'

'Yes. I did, but that's not . . .'

'It's all right you know,' said Marsha, 'I've been assuming you'd go home.'

'Yes.'

'I can spot a woman who doesn't want to shovel any more chickenshit.'

But Lynn stayed till all the nesting boxes were clean and the wood of the floorboards was clearly visible. 'You can power engines with this stuff, you know,' Marsha remarked. And Lynn said, 'Oh really,' and the moment froze.

Someone called that Lynn had a visitor. Derek, Marsha thought. But it wasn't Derek. It was Jane.

'Jane's come *here*?' said Lynn, her eyes wide.

And then what a touching scene! Marsha couldn't bear to look and couldn't turn away. The return of the prodigal daughter – falling on her mother's neck, floods of tears all round, more joy in heaven for the lamb that was lost and is found etcetera. Jane wailing and coughing: yes, yes, the feminists had been right all along, FAMILY was a monstrous organization, the Europop project an abomination, and all the women coming rushing to the sound of tears and listening in sympathy and welcoming Jane to the fold – and Marsha just watching, numb –

And Lynn tactfully shepherding the girl into a quiet room and not saying, 'You come in too, Marsha, you're one of the family now,' but closing the door on her – giving her a kind, woman-to-woman you-do-understand smile, yes, but closing the door on her nonetheless –

And later, when Marsha was pretending to find more chickenshit to clean, hearing Lynn and her blubbering daughter helping each other down the stairs – and feeling murderous anger, a wish to hunt out Derek (whom she liked, damn it, and never wanted to hurt or compete with) and say: *look! She wouldn't leave me for you, you know! Just for that snivelling brat!*

'Are you off then, Lynn?' she called, her voice casual, strangled. Their eyes met, and again that woman-to-woman, can't-you-see-she's-upset, don't-make-it-more-difficult-than-it-is look that was worse than a rebuff. 'Are you coming back?'

'Of course.' Lynn's voice was too bright. 'I'm taking Jane home so we can talk things over.'

'See you then.'

And then there was nothing, only a great blank of pain and someone saying, 'Go up and share lookout duty with Judy, Marsha.' Someone kind. Someone who knew the top of the building was the best place to be when you were glum, surveying the suburb and the city beyond it and the dizzying tiers of windows in the diminishing column beneath you and knowing it was full of women who were their own women.

At the top of the tower in the leaking cavern that she called the woom (after the error of a child) Judy Matthews, robed and veiled, lit thirteen scarlet candles on a red velvet cloth spread across the floor, diamond-shaped.

She hummed as she placed things in order, and laughed, little ripples of giggle swelling into hysteria which frightened her till she had to comfort herself. The light was dim, the windows were covered, the walls were draped with red and there were vases of crimson roses that Judy cultivated while the others were bothering with beans.

Someone whispered outside the door. Someone tapped.

Judy frowned. 'Just one minute, honey. You got to be patient.' She surveyed the room. She asked herself, 'Is that okay? Yes, that's okay.' She opened the door. Twelve little girl-children, red-dressed from head to toe, filed in, subdued and very reverent.

Judy's face tensed and relaxed as they took their places round the diamond. They crouched. Doing as they had been taught, each girl made of herself a red bundle, knees drawn up to her chin, hands folded round her crotch. Judy positioned herself at the head of the diamond. She sat flat, her bent thighs horizontal, her feet returning to meet each other. She raised her arms diamond-like over her head, her elbows pointed with sharp symmetry. Her fingertips touched.

A giggle escaped from a child. Judy turned a terrible face on her, then smiled. The girl blushed. 'Are we ready?' Judy said.

She started to hum. The girls hummed a few notes lower. Judy stood and her hum became a chant. She chanted the names of fruits and flowers and herbs, months, seasons and festivals, goddesses and heroines. Suddenly she approached one of the bundles and kicked it.

'What is *this*?' Her voice was mighty with contempt.

The other girls got up and made great play of pretending to

examine the bundle, asking each other:

'Is it dirt?'

'A vessel of sin?'

'A thing of – of – '

'Filth and corruption,' Judy hissed.

The bundle giggled. 'Really,' said Judy.

'Identify yourself, or shall we burn you at the stake?'

'Rape you?'

'Break you on the wheel?'

'Veil you?'

'Slash your holy cli – cli – '

'Clitoris!'

' – clitoris, close you and sew you?'

'Hide you in a nunnery?'

'Sell you in marriage, enslave you with a baby every spring?'

'Poison you with untested drugs?'

'*Speak*!' they commanded in unison, 'What are you?'

The bundle lifted her head and proclaimed: 'I am *woman*.'

'Prove it!'

The girl raised herself to her knees. She parted the front of her robe between her thighs. She was naked underneath. Her genitals had a soft covering of blonde hair. She reached between her legs and pulled on a little thread that hung there. A red dripping sponge emerged. She held it up triumphantly. All the girls clapped. She laid it on the velvet.

'Is it holy blood?' Judy intoned.

'All womanblood is holy blood.'

'Is it magic blood?'

'All women are magic.'

'Is your monthly bleeding sickness and weakness?'

The little girl sat back on her heels and frowned with the effort of remembering.

'It is strength and knowledge. It is not to be afraid of men who shed the blood of others, my body sheds its own. It is . . . it is to know my power to create life. It is to know the hour and the day and the season from my own . . . my own . . . '

'Rhythms,' Judy said, 'Very good.'

'Rhythms.'

'What do you ask, this day of your maturity?'

'Sisterhood and love.'

The girl passed among her friends. They kissed and hugged

her, and gave her presents. They gave her an egg, a feather, a hand-made jewel. Then they began to dance. Each girl shed her robes and danced naked. The robes made a red pool of cloth in the middle of the room, a pool that grew and disappeared, disappeared and grew, as the girls pulled and threw off the robes.

Judy clapped her hands. They rushed to the walls and tugged the drapes. The candles were put out. The walls were white. Daylight dazzled. And the twelve girls grinned and nudged each other and breathed hard with relief and gave tips to the girl whose day it was.

'Watch yourself and you'll learn all about your body. You'll be able to detect illness long before doctors can. Or pregnancy. Then there are things we can do that doctors have never dreamed of–'

Judy put her arms round two girls.

'Once,' she said, 'We made believe we were sick and bewitched at this time. Unclean. It was our way of getting a holiday, because they forbade us to milk the cows or go to bed with them. Lucky for us! Remember that–'

Footsteps interrupted her. The door was wrenched open. Judy glared. Marsha stood there, pale and puzzled.

Judy gasped. 'The favourite of the goddess!' She fell on her knees and signalled for the girls to do the same.

Marsha said curtly, 'You're supposed to be on watch.'

A girl said, 'It's my menarche.'

'Tough.'

Judy leapt to her feet, spitting like a cat. 'You speak that way in this holy–'

'I'm the favourite of the goddess. I say what I want.'

Judy began to moan. Marsha's eye fell on the swirl of drapes, the roses and the candles, the anxious children. She didn't know what had been going on but it looked special. Judy ought to know that play and lookout duty did not mix, but still – 'I'm sorry. Happy day. Now go and help your mothers.'

They trooped out.

'It should be a joyful time,' Judy said sullenly.

'Yes,' Marsha went to the window, 'it should.' Seyer Street stretched below. You could see right into some of the houses through the dilapidated roofs. People still lived there, mainly the proliferating Hindleys. Usually you could see them, playing or brawling or chatting in the street. Today the air was thick and still. Marsha wanted to cry.

At her elbow Judy whispered, 'It will be good when they come at last. There's too much fear now.'

'We won't stand a chance. We're not armed.'

'*Armed*? We're magic.'

'Magic.'

'*Magic*.' Judy's face was radiant. 'Magic. And they are fools who attack us in the source of our magic.' She pressed her hands over her womb.

Marsha sighed. Her whole body ached. The pleasures of last night had been wrenched away like a pulled tooth. Something moved at the far end of Seyer Street.

She watched with interest as two low-slung shiny green armoured vehicles started to lumber towards the tower. They were only insects. Behind them policemen crept, but they were only insects too, less than insects, maggots.

'We ought to give the alarm,' she said, as if it was an interesting idea she had just thought of. She did not move. The policemen formed two rows facing the tower, leaving a space for the vehicles to get through. They crushed the barbed wire like tangles of hair. When the front wheels hit the vegetable patch Marsha flinched and ran.

'Invasion, attack, emergency!' Her voice was wild, not her voice at all. 'Invasion, invasion, it's police, it's men!' She looked down the long tightening coil of the stairs; curious faces looked back. They'd seen. They were in position. They were ready (even the menarche children) with their pitiful ammunition. Marsha wondered: should she jump? She felt no fear – she just couldn't imagine oblivion being so near when she felt so full of life. She might as well, though. They would manage – if at all – without her. So obsessed with her own problems, she hadn't even made herself useful on her shift as a guard.

Wind gusted from the woom. Marsha went back in. Judy stood by the open window undressing, looking upwards.

'My moment has come,' she said.

'Come away from there.'

'They will never take me. The goddess will raise me to herself.' Judy continued to unwind her clothes, a long, wide, red strip bandaging her body in great loops. It went under her arms, between her legs, round and round like wool unravelling. Her body was straight and brown, and thin with hunger.

'Judy – '

Marsha caught her attention.

'What's that?'

'This? This is a water pistol.'

Judy laughed softly and rolled her eyes. 'What will you do? Spray them?'

Her question hung in the air as she jumped. She jumped so high from the window that Marsha had to wait to see her fall. The sloughed-off red garments lay where she had left them. Marsha could not move. She closed her eyes, not to see Judy's face as she realised the goddess was not going to lift her. From far away she heard a cracking thump of sound and then another as if the body had bounced. The building froze with horror beneath her.

Answering Judy's question she said slowly. 'No. This is for somebody else.' She took off her own clothes and started to wind the warm red bandages around herself.

'You took my tower,' said Marsha. She had snapped the little yellow cylinder into the gun and now she was pointing it into David Laing's face. It had been easy to get away. The police had responded to Judy's fall with an electronic voice saying that anyone who left could go free, they only wanted to repossess the building which was structurally unsafe. Prepared for this, the women ignored it; they knew of the gangs who would be waiting round the corner, predators who followed the eviction squads like carrion crows, rapists, kidnappers and moralists with scores to settle with women who had dragged the nation so low. But Marsha had slipped out anyway, winding and unwinding her red robes, raving and staggering and muttering imprecations to the sky, brandishing her gun.

The women had tried to stop her, thinking her maddened with shock. But she slipped through their fingers. In the street men approached her but turned away in disgust from her haggish grin and wild laughter. She ducked round the corner and was gone and never saw what happened next.

Even the police and the women missed its beginnings, it was so unexpected. It was like an old cartoon film, the way the doors of the Seyer Street houses collapsed flat off their hinges and ragged men, women and children roared out. At first the women in the tower thought they were police reinforcements, but the air filled with war whoops and whistles and the crash of sticks on pans and dustbin lids and the cry 'Hindleys to the rescue! Leave our women alone! Hindleys forward!'

The men waved clubs, the women threw slippery oil, the children flung stones with accuracy and without mercy. The police were astonished to find themselves trapped between tower and street.

'Leave our women alone!' Oh the Hindleys had had a joke or two (some a bit near the bone) about the weirdos in the tower but Seyer Street and its environs were their territory. Besides, there were matters outstanding between the government and the Hindley family.

The youngest of them knew the story of how poor grandmother Hindley had died in middle age – starved herself to death, she did, because some busybody do-gooders had told her she was too fat and went on about it till she stopped eating altogether. 'I prefer it,' she'd repeated as she wasted away. Grandpa Hindley's eyes still misted over when he told the tale: 'I kept telling her she weren't too fat for me. A fine stately woman.' The social workers had been sent on their way shortly after, and the government soon stopped sending visitors to look at the street. And when Benefit became selective, it was Seyer Street's proud boast that not one of its women was considered eligible.

The Hindley children had grown up regardless, and filled the street with their own badly-behaved offspring – they were a force to be reckoned with! They were a clan, a community – there weren't many lorries they couldn't hijack, there weren't many fortifications they couldn't scale into a hypermarket in the middle of the night! Grandpa Hindley, a mighty age, rolled around the street in an armchair to which the grandchildren had nailed wheels, and directed operations. 'A Hindley man's a family man,' he liked to say, just to hear Patsy's youngest pipe up: 'What about the girls, grandad?' 'A Hindley woman's a fighter,' he'd twinkle, and now he urged them on as they charged up Seyer Street, screaming and waving weapons, till the surprised police withdrew for further instructions. Four Hindley youngsters picked up Judy Matthews' broken body, covered it with clothes of their own and delivered it to the door of the tower.

Meanwhile Marsha was insisting on admission to David's office It was not easy. Security was tight, strange women were suspect, and even though she'd dropped her mad act as soon as she was out of sight of the police she knew she was trembling and high and her voice was coming in rushes. She sent up the message. 'Tell him I've changed my mind about his proposal,' and word came back that she was to be let in, much to the surprise of the guards who insisted on searching her. But she had been right on one thing: they were reluctant to probe too closely a middle-aged lady's knickers.

David was dwarfed by a huge bare desk. She was a flame reflected in his eyes. He was going grey. His gold spectacles pressed so tight on the bridge of his nose that they must almost cut the flesh. The room was dim. He didn't look as if he'd been doing anything much.

'You took my tower.'

'What's that,' he said, 'a water pistol?'

'No it isn't.'

'Let me see – ' He started to walk round the desk. He was treating her like a child. He wasn't frightened.

'Get back.'

He shrugged, sat down as if it didn't matter. He glanced over her shoulder. She felt the presence of someone and followed his eyes. Nobody. The room was empty but for the two of them. And in that second of turning he could have disarmed her. She must take hold –

'You took my tower. And Judy Matthews is dead. And Lynn's daughter –'

David said in social worker tones, 'I'm sorry about that. But my latest reports say the police were beaten off.'

'Liar.'

'Marsha, if you're planning to injure me in some way, please do it. Your hand's shaking and it's making me nervous.' He really did think it was a water pistol. 'Your clothes are rather curious.'

'They're Judy's clothes.'

'I could lend you a coat. I could get you some hot coffee at least.'

'Don't keep trying to change the subject. I've come here to kill you.'

A door opened behind her. This time there was no mistake. Two uniformed men blocked the opening. She panicked and hid the gun. David asked them to bring coffee and a warm garment. When they had gone he said, 'You'll never make it as an assassin, Marsha. There's a little emergency button I can press with my foot. That's just one of my tricks.'

'I don't care about getting caught.'

'You care about making yourself useful.'

'You bastard.'

'You see, political assassination only makes sense if the victim is a lunatic, a genius or an autocrat.'

'You've given it a lot of thought.'

'Yes. The only other purpose it serves is to make an otherwise ineffective person feel heroic.'

'For just that I could kill you.'

But the moment had passed and she knew it. She felt tired and foolish. Someone brought coffee and a sort of dark overall. It covered Judy's robes and the red flames vanished from David's eyes. It smelt and didn't even make her warm. She cast it off. She sipped at the coffee. It was the real stuff. Its smoothness was almost unpleasant; after a time of drinking koffee your palate learned to brace itself and the experience was tolerable.

'I take it you have nowhere to go.'

'If the tower's safe – '

'But you've failed in your mission. You won't want to go back there.'

'Will they try again?'

He shrugged. 'Depends how important we decide it is.' She had the feeling of a trap closing. 'Cabinet ministers have very large flats. It's assumed we have wives and things. Why don't you come and stay for a few days, sort yourself out, sort me out. No strings. No one would need to know.'

She laughed wildly. Went to kill the bugger and ended up living with him. And saved Collindeane Tower. It would shake up Lynn's ideas for a start. What an alliance! Well – it was what he'd always said: her compassion, his common sense . . . the tears ran down her cheeks. Through them she realised he wasn't sitting at his desk any more. She panicked as his hand closed on her wrist.

'Give me that – '

'David don't fool around, it's not a toy – '

He wasn't fooling around and he knew it wasn't a toy. His face was set as he fought her. Her hand clamped on the trigger. She struggled to point it – where, which way would be safe, which way would protect them from burning in this confined space – 'David it's not an ordinary, it's not a bullet – '

The wave of hot air knocked her backwards. Her skin singed. The desk fell, protecting her. She closed her eyes but the pillar of flames that David had become glowed through their lids, vapourising him as he stood. All kinds of sound beat round the inside of her head, the click of the gun, the whoosh of flame, hissing, crackling, but not a sound from David, not a scream. The screaming she heard was all hers.

'You misled us,' the professor stormed at Mr Peel, now Secretary of State for Family Welfare.

'I think not, sir.'

'You told us your women would accept the project. What do we see ? Mothers on strike and political assassination.'

Peel was contemptuous. 'Political assassination. They were lovers.'

'Lovers!'

'Years ago, but you know how it is. Hell hath no fury.'

'Mr Peel, that weapon is well-known among foreign terrorists. Where did she get it?'

'She's helping police with their enquiries.'

'And her associates?'

'The place is being dealt with. Finally.'

The professor drummed his fingers. 'We are going to have to rethink this, Peel, we really are. It is a pity. This country would be so suitable in many ways, but –'

Peel started to whine. He hated the indignity but he cared for the Europop idea. It fired him. He was wild at being thwarted. He wanted to be the man who made birth policy rational. 'Professor, you're worrying about a minority, and we're dealing with them. We're dealing with them! Haven't you seen our figures – well over half of all women are registered at their local Centres, numbers going up every day, the childbearing ones fitted with pellets –'

'Yes, and they are simply removing them if we advise against pregnancy! We have told them it is an appalling and dangerous business but some of your women are so obsessed with motherhood they will take any risk –'

'Professor – don't be insulted. How can I put this?' Peel was earnest, boyish, 'Basing the project on getting those things inside women and keeping them there – well. Isn't it a bit primitive? Isn't there a simpler way?'

'There is, yes.'

'And what is it?'

The professor sighed. 'It's stage two, and ultimately of course it is the solution, hopefully worldwide. But we have to win public opinion in stages.'

'You amaze me.' Sensing he had the moral advantage, Peel let his eyes glisten with contempt. 'If we have it in our power to solve the population problem, how can we not do it? Tell me, at least.'

Some other time, the professor promised, and took himself off. Peel's mind was full of other things. Word came that it was all over at Collindeane Tower and he called his car to take him to see. His brain was on fire. Beggars rushed the speeding vehicle; it was usual but today his contempt was virulent. It was not need that he despised, heaven knew – any man could be down on his luck, and need sharpened the wits – it was the refusal to see it that way. The utter lack of self-respect that led a man to beg. The outrageous assumption that because you wanted something you needed it, and because you needed it, it was your right. The giver of charity was selfish. He did it because it made him feel good.

His car whispered up Seyer Street. The hovels of the gangs who had so unexpectedly and so effectively defended the tower from the first eviction attempt (and thus necessitated the use of gas) were being flattened and scooped up by excavators. They were a health hazard.

And the tower. He stepped out of the car and looked at it. The attack had not changed its shape but it looked frail, bent, shy as a naked woman hiding behind her hands. Broken boards in the lower windows took the shape of teeth. Fluids poured in defence from the top still dripped down the building like tears. There seemed to be a lot of bodies on the ground, roughly covered. Here and there a face showed, frozen in an agony of suffocation. Some of them were children dressed in red.

'It's outrageous,' he muttered.

'Sir?' said a policeman, hurt.

'Not you. It. That it was ever built.' The policeman was about his own age. 'They used to put the poor to live in those, you know, and thought they were doing them a favour.' He collected his thoughts. In his official voice he said, 'How did it go?'

'Quite straightforward, sir.'

'And the, er, occupants?'

'Many left voluntarily.'

'Good. The others?'

'Some arrests, sir.'

Peel glanced at the draped bodies. 'Injuries?'

'Those were the ones that left voluntarily. They jumped when they smelt the gas.'

'Is it clear to go in?'

Peel approached the building. Debris was being loaded into skips. Men carried the skips in a human chain to a disposal truck, loads and loads. Would it never end? How long had the women been there to accumulate so much junk? Rugs and wood and dead chickens. The truck backed away, low with weight; another advanced, crushing a heap of rubbish. Peel held up his hand. The van stopped, the driver sighed; Peel rummaged in the rubbish, identified the soft brown tail of a dead dog. He took the dog in his arms and delivered it to a policeman who wrapped it in a rug and laid it with the women. Peel proceeded into the base of the tower.

He paled and gagged, then was hastily flippant. 'Don't think much of their housekeeping.' The policeman laughed excessively. 'Saved us a lot of bother, sir, dropping it all for us.' Peel smiled but wanted to be sick. The mess on the floor (so nauseously thick you could not even see the floor) suggested some giantess going berserk in a kitchen in hell: earth had been thrown, and manure and smashed eggs and sponges soaked in blood (he gagged again at the shape of the sponges, knew what the blood was) and buckets of shit, human and animal and bird; and cooking oils and milk (milk from what animal, dear god, or was it . . .?) and treacle and jam and beans and their liquor and honey and urine and candlewax, and, clinging to the stickiness, feathers and flour and leaves and the petals of roses and dear god the smell! His nose sought the lingering sourness of the counter-insurgency gas as relief from the sickening, organic musty intimate smells of women and their works. One thing he decided; the men who had dealt with this would get medals.

He started to climb, marvelling at the state of the place. Daylight shone through cracks in the walls, bricks were missing, window-frames barely met. Forgivable in an old building, he supposed, but he understood that this one had been falling down since it was built, destroyed from within by the sainted proletarians it was built to 'help'.

The figure of a fleeing woman grabbed his attention. He flinched, hid, peeped – but it was only a curtain bulging and swaying at an open window.

Up he climbed. The height was no hardship to him, he was fit. But keep families in here – nowhere to play, steps to haul prams up, neighbours to disturb! Only a planner with no requirement to please his customers could come up with such a thing. If people had wanted to live in tower blocks, they'd have built them for themselves.

He reached the top and his thoughts were coming clear and fast with the freshening of the air. He looked down on the flat street. The former inhabitants would have to go somewhere. They could not be jailed or rehabilitated forever.

What, then, did one do with . . . he hunted for a phrase, remembered only *the wrong rats* . . . those who would not pull their weight? The great dilemma for politicians who chose to make such people their business. Peel knew some history. You could leave them to starve, but there were dangers in having a class with nothing to lose, even if, left to themselves, they would breed themselves out. (Maybe it should have been done . . .) You could ship them off to camps and kill them *en masse* but that was inhumane. You could make a fortune writing books to prove they were not to blame but that was amoral. You could spawn a leviathan welfare industry. Or you could do none of these things.

The Victorians had known a thing or two, and if they had only had the courage of their clean, logical convictions the chaos of the welfare state would never have come to be, chaos which David Laing had loved to lambast and ridicule but for whose return Peel was sure he yearned. Take his squeamishness over withdrawing Benefit from mothers who didn't deserve it, for example! And all the time swearing he didn't believe in handouts!

Poor Laing. Peel genuinely regretted his end and the manner of it. But he could not be looked to for sense. He was of the soft generation, of the post-war guilt-ridden child-obsessed baby boom. They rode a roller-coaster of gratuities: free milk, free cod liver oil, free schools, free medicine, free grants to go to college . . . it was Peel's view that the trauma of the seventies, the sudden realisation that the party was over and they couldn't get what they wanted by slapping on the label *rights* and howling, had blighted that generation for life, had rendered them incapable of understanding how life works.

Night follows day. Illness follows infection. Want follows idleness and destitution improvidence. The Victorians had understood. He leaned on the brick wall on the roof of the tower. It was solid. The Victorians too had put up buildings for their poor – but they had made no pretence that they were offering desirable residences!

'We should have tried it years ago,' Peel thought, and added (not realising he spoke aloud) 'We did try it years ago. And what was the result? A nation more prosperous and inventive than at any time in its history. Before or since.'

'Let go of me.' Marsha's wrists were bound rigid with thick cuffs of light, tight metal. They were high over head, stretched and tied to a stick fastened to her back. Her ribs ached. Hard fingers had searched her, inside and out, and when she tried to wriggle away from their discomfort, fists cuffed her. No one had asked her anything. They kept saying, 'You'll talk,' as if she had refused. What had she to tell? She couldn't remember what had happened. First she was going to assassinate David, then she wasn't, then she did. Except that she had a feeling she didn't. She didn't want to think. Thinking brought back his flaming pillar of a body, boiling in speechless agony.

'Stop pushing,' she pleaded. With her arms up like that she could hardly breathe, yet her voice sounded polite. She might be standing in a bus queue. She couldn't understand why they kept pushing her. They surely didn't think an assassin (they thought she was one, she wasn't sure) cared about escaping.

Even when she had the plan to kill him (which she had abandoned, or had she taken it up again?) she didn't remember planning an escape. All she'd felt was hatred. All she'd heard was Posy urging that for once in her life she should get off her ass and stop waiting for a nice collective cop-out compromise decision and go ahead and bloody do something outrageous, spectacular, cruel and stunning, to match the enormity of the seizure of the tower. All she'd heard was the contempt in the voice of the guerilla woman. All she'd heard was her own voice: *you'll always be an interloper in Lynn's life. However much she tries to do the decent thing you'll always be her bit on the side. You'll never be as legitimate as the slimiest, smuggest, most casual boyfriend*.

Now she felt numb with the shock of death. The one man who'd fucked her didn't exist. He hadn't even left a body.

She was manhandled past a window. She glimpsed her face, tomb-white. Behind it her thoughts seethed like maggots, untouchable.

They untied her and put her in a small dark room. She could feel neither walls nor floor, her limbs were numb. It was warm and airless and dry. A blink of light dazzled her and was gone. It let her see a hole in the floor, maybe two inches across. She was meant to pee in that, she supposed. Typical. Or was it a secret escape route, could she pick and wear away at the sides of it, rubbing with her fingernails till it was wide enough for her body? The light flashed again and again. The flashes got faster till her eyes did not know if the light was on or off; the light mixed with remembered darkness, darkness with remembered light – she moved her hands before her eyes – the movement looked jerky, like very old movies. Her body seemed to disobey the orders she gave it. The walls of the cell moved in to crush her, then out of sight. She panicked. Shadowy waves rode up and down. She was in a ship. She was going to be sick. She tried to aim for the two-inch hole but it would not stay still.

'Count the waves.'

The voice came from the four corners of the room but she saw nobody. A spasm hit her feet and rattled her teeth, more un-nerving than painful. That voice again:

'That was a grade one shock. There are ten grades. Count the waves.'

Her eyes tried to follow the waves up the walls through the dazzling strobe light.

'Count them.'

'Fifteen.'

'Wrong.'

'Twenty now . . .'

'Wrong. Go on counting.'

'Why, if it's always wrong?' A shock juddered up her spine. 'Fifty-two! Fifty-three!'

'Wrong.'

She was always wrong but as long as she tried to count there were no more shocks. Sometimes they pretended they would let her sleep but when her eyelids met, electricity made her stomach heave. *I'm being tortured, it's too funny, I'm being driven mad.* She made her brain stop counting waves while her voice shouted random numbers. Her brain tried to figure out why she had assassinated David, since sooner or later she was going to be asked. And she needed to know for herself. A towering block of windows rode the waves and figures fell crashing from the windows and she cried. *Why are they torturing me, I've nothing to deny?* She welcomed the electric shocks and the pains from her bonds because they were real and distracted her from the mad seasickness of counting waves.

Hours or months later when they took her into another room for interrogation she maintained her balance only with difficulty as she proclaimed, 'I am the goddess.'

'You're the ringleader?'

'Goddess.'

'And who's yer visible presence here on earth, goddess?'

'Posy.'

'Posy who? Describe her.'

'I have never seen such a powerful woman. A rock of flesh. So much flesh – ' Marsha's head nodded. They let her sit.

'Where is she?'

'Anywhere, she could be anywhere.'

'D'you want to go and count waves again?'

'I don't know where she is, she goes everywh – '

The interrogators closed in. 'So it's international?'

'Women all over the world will rise up, Posy says.'

'Is that where you get the guns from, Posy?'

She described Posy for them, every detail of her body and her work and her manner and her beliefs and how they would know her. They wrote it all down.

They took her to another cell, a still grey box. She saw waves but they could have been inside her eyes. No one talked to her; bland food appeared through a hatch. She supposed she would have a trial soon. She looked forward to it. It would establish what had happened. There would be a jury. She would walk into court and see Lynn on it, smart and discreet in a ladylike hat. She practised the imperceptible smile they would give each other, and the hug when she was acquitted.

But would there be any more hugs, after that celebratory one?

And would she have a defence counsel?

And would she be able to appeal?

She watched her body to tell the time. Two months she guessed . . . but stress could disrupt periods, and besides, at her age . . . When they stopped altogether was it merely menopause, or had time stopped, or had somebody raped her . . .

'When am I going on trial?' she demanded of the bowl of pap.

'You? You're unfit to plead.' The hatch rapped shut.

She was not to be tried, then? Or sentenced, or released? She was only fifty-one. What if she lived to be a hundred? She heard animal noises in her cell and could not believe they came from her. She was given books she did not want to read and the chance to hear taped music. One day they said to her,

'We're going to let you out.'

They let her out into a grassed-over yard. Wild-eyed men pressed their noses against the glass and leered and gestured silently. She guessed she was in a men's prison. Or asylum. Of course. They wouldn't want her mixing with women.

'Run about now! Take exercise!'

But she wanted to be back in her cell. Had she been useful? The world thought her mad. She quaked. By killing David she had brought Peel to power. Posy came at night like a gentle giant. 'Of course! You'll go in the herstory books – it was heroic, it was fabulous!'

'But was it any *use*?'

Posy winked and hugged her. 'They haven't caught me yet.'

She decided to hunger-strike. After all, the suffragettes did it, and got let out. Marsha didn't expect to be let out (she didn't even want to be – it would foul things up for Lynn) but she wanted a visitor or a letter or evidence that someone cared.

'No one's asked to visit you,' they said.

'That's a lie.'

'Or letters.'

'But the whole women's movement is . . .'

'Women's movement!' they scoffed, 'There isn't one. Not any more.'

She shuddered at their certainty. Was Lynn all right? It was astonishing how long you could go without eating and not feel ill. A week, two, three . . . But what if they didn't know? What if no one out there knew she was hunger-striking? What if the government were pleased to be saved the bother of executing her, what if that was why she was here? She thought she heard women singing and imagined them hunger-striking in solidarity with her at the prison gates. *Go away, go away, save your risks for something else.*

A dish of stewed beans appeared at the hatch with thin shreds of meat. They smelled good, they were evidence that someone cared, even if it was only the clerk who'd have to fill in an extra form when she died. She ignored them. She lay still, saving energy, wondering why her body could not get the idea that it wasn't meant to survive.

She lay two days with her eyes shut and smelled the beans rotting. When she opened her eyes a cardboard box lay by the dish. It had been examined but they had sealed it up again. As if she were a child.

It was light. They hadn't, they surely hadn't sent an empty box to torment her . . . the little spray of twigs and leaves and hard berries that had been in Posy's funeral garland fell into her thin hand. Their faint scent caught her starved senses, shooting her sky-high like a drug. Guilt caught her throat. She should have saved them from the tower herself instead of rushing off like that. (Maybe she wouldn't be here now if . . .) She searched for a note. Maybe they'd taken it away. Maybe a love note between women was too subversive. Maybe there hadn't been one.

Her famished fingers were alert, skimming the box. They felt slight indentation. She tilted the box to catch the light, and read (as if someone had leaned heavily on the box to write and the words had cut through) 'You were useful. Love, Lynn.' And as she looked again she saw that 'were' had been crossed through and replaced with 'are.'

You liar, you liar! Or did she mean, you are at your most useful when you are out of the way? She examined the dried berries. Never eat strange berries, they may kill you or render you sterile, invisible, mad. She sniffed them. She smiled. When they brought her fresh beans and meat, she ate them, keeping the berries for company.

Isabel Travers' honey-blonde hair waved softly over her haggard early-morning face. She had not made up yet. She looked from the newspaper to her husband, half asleep, teeth hanging out, pushing at his breakfast. Breakfast was rather a grand name for the wet pulp, but she had sworn that as long as her legs would carry her round a kitchen and as long as Alan could raise a spoon to his mouth, he would not want for hot food. She liked to serve beans in their dark juice in nice white dishes, monogrammed in green.

She looked back at the close lines of miniscule type in the latest government announcement. How could an old person with failing eyes be expected . . . she wavered with her magnifying glass and realised that this message was not for old people with failing eyes.

'DEPARTMENT FOR FAMILY WELFARE – EUROPOP

'An action-research programme will begin immediately with a view to giving British women the benefits of the latest research on parenthood-planning. Special encouragement will continue to be given to women showing high standards of mothering. Potential mothers wishing to draw state Benefit will also be given the opportunity of volunteering for the following pilot projects:

'a) ACCELERATED REARING. To ascertain the feasibility of raising children to adulthood in less than the traditional 15–20 years, suitable mothers will be invited to accept prenatal procedures and early intensive education with a view to equipping sons for professional qualifications in their early teens.

'b) SKILL AND SOCIAL PROGRAMMING. Behavioural science has long been concerned with the extent to which characteristics (aggression, sex-roles, genius, etc) are innate or learned. Mothers will be treated to ensure the birth of identical twins. One twin will be removed from the mother at birth (after full counselling) and raised in a neutral environment. The other will remain under carefully controlled social and familial influences. Comparisons will be made to ascertain . . .'

A low moan escaped from Isabel's lips. Alan grunted and jerked his spoon. Beans fell on the floor with a soft plop. Isabel bent closer to the paper; the lines swam together.

'c) SEX RATIO PROGRAMMING. This long-term multigenerational project will give women the right to choose the sex of their unborn baby. Researchers will seek to establish the correlation between the proportion of females in the population and national fertility rates . . .

'Further projects (cloning, extra-uterine gestation, &c) will be announced in due course.

'Women wishing to participate will be given priority for the removal of contraceptive pellets and the payment of Benefit . . .'

Veins stood out on Isabel's white temple. Her arm stiffened – she thumped the table.

'You must talk to Peel,' she said.

Alan stared.

'Peel. *Talk to him.*'

'Ha! Peel!' Alan started to mutter to himself, bean juice staining the white stubble on his chin.

'He must know that this was never – '

Alan mouthed, 'Europea – '

She wasn't listening. 'The effect would be devastating,' she said, 'if we were to denounce – '

'Rubbish!'

'Alan, why is it that you are so lucid when you wish to contradict me and senile when I want to *discuss* something?'

He looked at her in astonishment. She could not remember when she had last raised her voice to him. He grumbled: 'He'd call us sentimental old has-beens, mourning our lost potency.'

'I never had *potency*,' she retorted, and he was back in his dream.

How had it happened, she wondered as she peered at the newspaper, trying to find a saving clause, something that would tell her she had misunderstood, how had it happened, this descent from an ideal of family life, to control and contempt? *Same thing*, she heard the feminists hiss, and knew she could not go to them, even if she wanted to, even if she knew where they were.

There was a truth and a rightness and a homecoming that they refused to acknowledge, in submission to the male. Outward submission, that was. When it came to it women had ways to get what they wished – and a woman whose husband was secure in the belief that he was the boss could be more 'liberated' than one with an insecure man fumbling between equality and guilt. Didn't the sex act say it all? It was hard to believe, watching Alan's senile slobbering, but her flesh could still tingle and weep at the memory of nights of voluptuous surrender – the pride and gratitude of feeling his strength and aggression melt into tender care for her delight. The wild thrusts of the man impaling her like prey, and the love and mercy in his face – didn't that synthesise it all, wasn't that what it was all about? And how could there be joy in it if the strength and the aggression and the mercy and the love were all melted down into politics?

The feminists didn't understand. But then did she?

What would the government do next – especially if there was resistance, if the improbable feminist-FAMILY alliance that called itself The Women turned out not to have been repressed? She shuddered to think of the years ahead, of more and more clumsy mannish interference in the chemistry, the poetry, the checks and balances of sex and creation. The Women had called her an oppressor when all she sought was to claim and safeguard the female empire!

She'd often wondered, over the years, how much her own sterility (a mystery, the doctors said) was the result of some botched political plan by men . . . radioactivity in the air, perhaps, or a pollutant in the water supply.

Alan made a clumsy movement with his spoon and sent more beans scattering over the floor. She sighed deeply and reached to pick them up one by one, each bean leaving a sticky smear. Her head rested on the edge of the table. Her golden hair slipped and fell off. The hair underneath was a short white cap, and the back of her head looked winsome and young like a boy risen wet from a swimming pool.

10

Planned Population

The Europop researchers had always known it would be many years before their work produced results that the scientific community would recognise as significant. Even if Accelerated Rearing did create fourteen-year-old nuclear physicists, there would have to be enough of them to rule out the possibility of random genius; many dozens of pairs of identical twins would need to reach adulthood before firm conclusions could be reached on nature versus nurture; and of course the Sex Ratio Programme would not bear fruit in the lifetime of its architects.

The researchers had been carefully chosen for their sense of mission and dedication, and were well paid to compensate for the lack of status that shorter-term projects with earlier conclusions would bring their peers in other fields; but sometimes they grumbled.

'We won't be around to see the species when every rogue gene is obsolete.'

'We may, we may. The professor may yet abolish death.'

'Then we'll be out of work. He'll have to abolish birth to make room.'

'And then what will the Tummies say?'

'Tummies' was a little joke they had. It had been coined by a journalist at the time of the mothers' strike. If there's a strike, the journalist had quipped in a column, there must be a trade union. The trade union of mothers. TUM. It didn't take much wit to move from that to Tummies, especially if you thought for one moment what you were talking about. It avoided paying the strikers the compliment of taking them at their own assessment: The Women. Now Tummies was popular parlance for any recalcitrant women. In the government Women's Centres it was shorthand for those who got pregnant without permission or were otherwise unco-operative.

There weren't many but there were enough to be irritating. Organized feminism – The Women – appeared to have been wiped out. Thousands had been sent abroad for rehabilitation and returned with the wind taken very much out of their sails. Skulking back to what they thought of as 'their' communes, they found themselves invited to enter Welfare Hostels, minimal accommodation for the truly destitute with conditions expressly designed to encourage them to seek an alternative. If suitable, they could get married, have babies and draw Benefit. Or they could take domestic employment in private homes.

Many succumbed or disappeared; the post-entry economic boom had allowed Benefit levels to be a real incentive to women to behave themselves. The whining of the Tummies was not organised resistance, just perversity: 'I'm not one of The Women, doctor, but I don't see why I shouldn't have another baby when I want one.' The doctors tried to be philosophical about the fact that it was always the feckless, difficult women who took this line. The ones whom one wouldn't really mind having an extra baby or two were always the ones who stuck most meticulously to the population plans made for them, and whose contraceptive pellets remained firmly in place until permission was given for their removal.

The Europop workers considered appealing over the heads of married Tummies to their husbands, but Peel warned them off. It would go against the grain of the British male to be instructed on any aspect of his sex life by foreign scientists; it was a small miracle that he hadn't openly objected already! It was far better to use propaganda to remind men that the twin bounties of pellets plus Benefits could relieve them finally of any anxiety concerning the consequences of sexual intercourse, and to hint that concern with family planning was rather unmasculine.

And so, when women who had agreed to participate in Accelerated Rearing suddenly protested that their children's babyhood was being taken from them, or refused at the last minute to give up the second identical twin, or confounded all predictions by opting for girls in the Sex Ratio Programme, or sneaked off to backstreet practitioners when Women's Centre doctors refused to remove their pellets, the Europop workers tried not to worry, tried to see it as teething troubles, looked more closely at their counselling techniques and put pressure on Peel to step up the propaganda of the New Family Movement.

Peel was less confident. The professor buzzed and bleeped him over airwaves at odd hours of the morning to rant that the programme was expensive and it was money down the drain if random breeding continued to be allowed. 'It confuses the figures, Peel. And it is bad for the morale of those who are co-operative.'

Peel wasn't sure, either, that The Women had been wiped out with the ease and thoroughness that their silence suggested. Someone was still doing illegal operations. Someone was still sowing discontent. Just because you couldn't see them it didn't mean they weren't there. The nastiest diseases could be clobbered by drugs and appear cured, when in fact they were continuing their lethal work deep in the body, unheralded by symptoms until it was too late.

Whenever he saw an unaccompanied woman, he wondered . . .

Whenever he heard a tale of female recalcitrance, be it in a Welfare Hostel, in some man's home, in a Women's Centre or a Europea factory, he wondered. He decided he'd liked them better when they were visible. For who could tell? When a tearful girl asserted her right to fulfil herself through motherhood, who knew which side she was on?

The refurbishment of FAMILY – now the New Family Movement, open only to those whose loyalty and morals were above reproach – was long overdue. The emphasis had to change from sentimental concern for individuals to the Family of Man. 'The Family of Man has ruled this planet for only a short span in the history of the universe. Are we here to stay, or will we waste our resources, destroy ourselves? Let us show, by planning and self-control, that we *will* stay! And let it be the proud boast of this nation that *we showed the way*!'

The NFM ran processions: mammoth spectacles now, transmitted from whichever city originated them, to giant telescreens in other urban centres, and piped into private homes. Here was a sick deformed monster – not a real one of course, that would be inhumane, but a constructed parody of a human being with bent limbs, watery skin and the clownlike features of the hereditary-mad. Watchers were encouraged to give free rein to their feelings – hiss, boo, turn away, vomit, feel no guilt. Guilt belongs not in natural reactions (does not the lioness mercy-kill her deformed cub?) but in those of us who have permitted such travesties to be born when we could have stopped even their conception.

Films were shot on to walls of buildings, humans with black skin stretched thinly over poking bones, picking fields bare like locusts. 'The way of the future? Not for Europea!' And fat white people lounged in a modern city for contrast.

Smiling women operating machines that cleansed the air. 'Chained to motherhood? No longer!'

Peel was almost as pleased with his public information films as he was with his Welfare Hostels. They at once cleared the streets of trouble-makers and encouraged workers to accept the jobs that Europea offered. This in turn made the president better disposed to the British in general and Peel in particular. The president had been scornful that a man with a ridiculous ministry called Family Welfare could claim to have the answer to labour troubles, but now Peel felt he was well on the way to a prestige job in Europea City.

Of its own momentum, far more effectively than any public information film could engineer such a thing, fear of the Welfare Hostel entered popular culture. Teachers could warn difficult students: 'You know where you'll end up.' 'Go to bed, or Mr Peel will come for you,' mothers could tease. 'Better than a stay in a Welfare Hostel,' trade union negotiators could console their members over a watered-down pay claim. A whole new genre of sentimental fiction (particularly popular with the ladies) chronicled families' struggles to keep from the disgrace of the "ostel". 'Little licit' became a term of abuse addressed to a child; it referred to the illicit babies, those conceived outside the plans of the Women's Centres, who frequently ended up in the Hostels, with or without their mothers, since no Benefit was payable and families with illicit children often found it hard to get jobs or homes.

The use of those conspicuous old tower blocks ensured that

many people could view a Welfare Hostel from the windows of
their homes; and churchmen were pleasantly surprised that the
visibility of immediate retribution revived an interest in hell, even
in so sophisticated an age. Religion took a new hold, particularly
among those who did not regard themselves as candidates either
for Welfare Hostel or hell.

It was Peel's duty to visit a Hostel now and again. It would be a
very solemn occasion, the inmates lined up by age and sex in their
loose Olex uniforms with the name of the Hostel's catchment area
stamped on the shoulder. He would listen courteously to their
complaints about food or conditions, then point out that the doors
were open. Sometimes he would list job opportunities, or suggest
that the destitute might turn to their own families for support.
Finally a pretty little girl would present a bunch of flowers, a
ceremony which reassured Peel that he was not turning hard, it
touched his heart so.

It amused Peel to hear the demands from political dissidents
(grown vocal and cocky in the boom, yet easily dealt with by
selective offers of employment in far-flung regions of Europea)
concerning the Hostels. He considered it instructive, the way they
made more fuss over minimal provision than they ever had when
there was none.

If there had to be Welfare Hostels, the dissidents loved to
argue (missing the point entirely) did they have to be so inhumane?

'No one has to go there,' Peel would reply quietly.

Did they have to be painted inside and out in garish, restless
colours, with lights that always burned? Must the inmates wear
stigmatising uniforms, did the interior walls of the flats have to be
removed so that people were kept without privacy, like goods on
shelves? Did the most personal details of life have to be bound with
rules, like talking and movement and visits to the lavatory only at
set times? Did families have to be shattered, one man's wife forced
to lie with another man's husband and the children rotated
between different sets of adults until they didn't know who they
were? Peel noted the objections but had one answer. 'They can
leave at any time.'

Lefties complained about the work the inmates did. Great bales
of industrial laundry were brought from Europea in ships, overalls
and tarpaulins stained so deep with caustic dirt that skin would
come off scrubbers' hands before it would budge. It was rumoured
to be make-work too; the laundry was sent to other Hostels to be

made dirty again. 'If they don't like it, why don't they seek work outside?' Peel would enquire; anyone could turn up at a channel port with identity papers and get put on a boat. Passage was free and destinations seductive: the Mediterranean coast, millionaires' playgrounds.

The lefties had their answer, of course, most notably in the shape of a half-caste young firebrand called Jim Matthews, who'd been there. 'The visiting workers are assigned to factories where no one else will go. Sun and millionaires' playgrounds there may well be only a few miles away, but the visiting workers are not to know. We sat in clockless, symmetrical barns in thick protective clothing. Nuclear energy installations are the most voracious users of British male labour; we sat at benches radiating from a central tank and packed god knows what coloured powders into heavy lead cylinders. Workshifts ended and began at all hours; you had to undress and be scrubbed by men with brooms, then taken by closed van to visiting-worker hostels, row upon row of tiers of bunks in another circular barn, till you dreamt all night in lines and circles. Board and lodging are docked from wages at source and there's precious little left . . .'

When they weren't complaining about the conditions in the Welfare Hostels, the dissidents fell back on the cost. If the state could afford to maintain people doing make-work in tower blocks, why not give them the money instead? Let them keep their lives together? Peel smiled. And when he heard that Matthews and some of his chums were getting together to form a political party that would revive the old Department of Health and Social Security, he could only laugh wildly. He was particularly entertained by reports that their inaugural meeting had ended in disarray when some historically-minded females pointed out that the old DHSS had discriminated against women, and refused to accept the male majority's plea that they agree the *principle* of reviving it and leave the details till later. Still, the social security party gained modest ground, and Peel began to wonder whether priority should go to allowing the women to wreck it, or finding out who they were.

Now that Lynn stayed at home all day, hunched over piles of paper at the kitchen table, writing letters that she never knew if Marsha even received, Derek decided he'd preferred the past. She'd been more with him when she spent time at the tower with

Marsha and came home guiltily eager to be as nice as possible, than now when she was around all the time but seemed not to notice whether he was.

He'd almost got used to the idea that she was in love with Marsha. She'd been sparkle-eyed like a teenager, she'd made him feel like a parent, she'd even made him feel that it was patronising and dismissive of him not to feel threatened, as if he didn't take women's love seriously enough; but now as he let himself into the house and saw her, her body still, her eyes and wrists racing across the page, just as he had left her this morning, just as he had left her when he went to bed last night, the only thing greater than his anxiety was his feeling of being shut out.

What did she write in those letters? What did the prison censors smack their lips over? Her disappointment that even now Jane wouldn't turn against FAMILY, insisting with tears pouring down her cheeks that they were right, it would be anti-social for her to try for a child and she must just study hard to be a good wife and help her paragon of a sister-in-law, Astrid, with her children? His own shortcomings as a husband? Ah well. There would be something new for them now.

'I've lost my job,' he said.

She went on writing. *Derek has lost his job*? It occurred to him that she hadn't heard; it occurred to him that he hadn't really spoken. He said, leading up to it gently, 'I've been asked to go to another of those conferences.'

'Designing another new continent . . .' she murmured, not looking up, 'Well, I'm utterly confident . . .'

'I said I wouldn't go.'

'Why?'

'Because I didn't want to leave you.'

'She seemed surprised. 'Why?'

'Like this.'

'Why?'

He sighed. 'I could have made up lots of reasons, especially as I know why they asked me. Its one of those year-long gatherings of geriatrics in Rio or some such place, during which time they get someone else to do your job as a tribute to your indispensability. Oh, I've seen it coming – pointed remarks about making way for a younger man – but do you know what I said? I said, I don't want to leave my family at this time. Like newly-weds with a baby.'

'How touching,' said Lynn.

'Lynn, please stop writing.'

'I'm not writing about you.'

'I know, but . . . oh, don't be angry.'

She put down her pen and covered her writing with a sheet of blank paper. 'I'm sad, not angry. I never wanted to be an emotional drain on you.'

He laughed and put kisses all over her inert shoulders. 'Some drain.'

'No, really.' She reached up and took his hand. 'I used to think any woman who lost her man by expecting him to sort of live for her, deserved it. Maybe that was why I was so scared about having babies, I thought I'd depend on you too much.'

'You? You never depended on me for anything.'

'Did you want me to?'

He sat down and closed his eyes. If there was one thing that still unnerved and excited him about her it was her insistence that he analyse his feelings. It seemed like second nature to her – to all women maybe, maybe that was why they were saner and madder than men – and he'd tried to learn. 'I suppose it would have been nice to be able to show you you had nothing to worry about, but that's a power trip too and no excuse . . . poor Lynn. What did you think I was going to do to you when I was your lord?'

'It doesn't matter,' she said crossly, and went to the sink and started swilling round koffee tins to see if she could make him a cup. He went after her and hunted for his voice.

'Anyway, that's all over now. I've lost my job.'

'Derek, don't be silly. Go to your conference.'

'I told you. It's just the preamble to firing me. A year here or there . . . I prefer it this way.'

'It's your politics, isn't it? Your subversive wife. Ah, it's not even that, I'm not a proper subversive, but some of my best friends –'

'It's my age.'

'Bullshit. You've given your life to that place. Here, do you want this? It's dregs.'

'What about you?'

'I'm up to here with it. We will be all right, won't we Derek?' She hated her whining, wheedling tone. 'I mean, of course we will. What will we live on?'

He struggled for words. 'That's the trouble. There's peanuts in the staff pension fund. And when they halved my salary — we never finished the payments on the house. I mean, I didn't.'

'You were right the first time.'

'I could hardly hold you responsible for my failure as a breadwinner, could I, not after –'

'I'd prefer it if you did.'

They sat looking at each other, bright-eyed with disbelief. They talked of little things and Lynn put away her letters to Marsha. They ate and went for a walk. The evening was light and there was a high wind.

'How do you get admitted to Welfare Hostel anyway?' said Lynn flippantly. Derek must have been thinking the same thing, his answer was automatic. 'You let the police catch you begging at an airport.'

'Bit undignified for a professor and his lady. There must be a more decorous procedure for the middle class.'

Without deciding where to walk, they ended up picking their way through the rubble of Seyer Street.

'I wonder what happened to the Hindleys,' said Lynn. They were both keeping their eyes firmly on the surface of the road to avoid tripping.

'I wonder what happened to our house.'

'Got knocked down.'

'I meant the bricks. D'you think this is one? Oh Lynn, we're going to have to ask Jane and Martin to help us.'

'I won't.' She raised her eyes to the tower. It looked fragile but it always had. The repainting was nearly done, dead, dazzling white. The cracks up the side were almost picturesque. Each line divided and subdivided. Like a family tree. Opaque glass blocked the windows, thick blind eyes. 'I'll go there, I don't care.'

They stood with their arms round each other and looked at the tower for a long time. It was very still against the racing clouds. A dog trotted round its base, lifted its leg and pissed. 'I know how you feel, dog,' said Lynn. Derek laughed. They were about to turn and go when a high window opened and a rope was lowered. For a long horrified moment Lynn thought they were going to hang somebody.

Another window, another rope. Then complex operations trying to join the ropes in the wind. Then a cradle that looked about as sturdy as an orange box was lowered. Two small children, stiff and passive with fear, were put into it. Tins and brushes were handed to them, and as the cradle swayed and bashed against the walls of the building eight storeys up, adults could be seen behind the windows shouting encouragement and instructions on how to paint.

'Beats picking oakum,' Derek muttered, but Lynn was gone, beating on the door. A bored man in a uniform said, 'Yes?'

'Don't you know how dangerous that is?'

The man looked up. 'Those kids are light.'

'You mean starved. And terrified.'

'You their family? Come to take them away?'

'I'm – I'm a journalist –' Lynn warned.

The man pantomimed quaking with fear and Derek came up behind her and gently took her away, not letting her look back at the swaying cradles.

Martin and Jane were brisk and kind.

'Of course you must live with us.'

All the discussing and arranging went on between the men. The setting was a polite dinner together. Lynn and Jane just nodded silently, avoiding each other's eyes. Lynn felt an odd indignation. She'd relinquished control of her life on the understanding that Derek would retain it; now she felt betrayed. They were doing sums. Men were so clever at sums. Martin had a good salary. Derek's pension from the university was small but not to be sneezed at. Jane took in clerical work at home and Lynn could probably help with that. Jane and Martin would give up their place, which was too big anyway for a couple on their own, and move in with the Byers; wasn't that just the sort of eventuality their home was designed for? The men noticed the women's silence, tried to fill the air with domestic arrangements, compromises between privacy and co-operation, but their voices became high, fast, inept.

'It isn't fair,' said Lynn at last, looking at Jane, 'on you, I mean. You want your own place.'

'Only a child,' said Jane steadily, 'expects life to be fair.'

'No, but we should have had more children, to sort of share us out.'

'Next time Jim turns up we can get a few quid out of him. He hasn't got anyone to support.'

'In any case,' Martin pointed out, 'You're my wife's parents, and how would I feel if you went into a Hostel?' Lynn stitched on a smile and rebuked the uncharitable thought that what he meant was *how would I look*?

Jane said, 'There's something I'd like to talk to Lynn about alone.' Lynn quaked and felt humiliated as Martin drew Derek away. What was this going to be – some pious speech about unbreakable obligations of blood?

'I want you to help me,' said Jane.

'Help you what?'

'Have a baby.'

'Jane – '

'No, listen, Do I or don't I have a right to have one?'

'I would have said yes. You would have said no.'

'It's wrong, they can't mess about with women's lives like this.'

'No.'

'I always wanted a baby. If I can't have a baby, what am I for?'

'Lots of things.'

'Like punching holes in cards for Europea plastics, or – '

'No. Not that. Finishing your education.'

Jane turned away. 'Forget it.'

'Jane, I'll help you do whatever you want. But you do know the risks?'

'You know where I can go, don't you?'

Lynn didn't. Her mind started ticking off the loose threads of the feminist networks that might still exist: women who had not been imprisoned or rehabilitated or housed in a Hostel. Someone would know someone whose friend . . . damn these informal networks! If you were in you were in, but if you were out oh boy were you out . . . and yet it was best, for secrecy. 'I'll find out for you, Janey.'

Jane sat down suddenly. She looked thin and weak, and her hair, which had got redder as Lynn's faded, was pale too now, like hay. Lynn wondered if Martin was looking after her properly, if she was getting all the right foods and tablets and having her physiotherapy sessions. She didn't ask. Jane turned to face her.

'I hope I get a nicer kid than you did,' she said gruffly. And Lynn, pretending to misunderstand, said, 'There's no reason to think Martin's a CF carrier, is there? And if he isn't, your child should be okay.'

Weeks of guarded chats with strange women outside hyper-markets or rummaging in the dustbins of the rich finally won Lynn the address of a woman who would remove contraceptive pellets with hygiene and secrecy. The women who told her would not give their own names. Lynn said, 'Who are you all?'

'Just say the women sent you.'

'With capital letters?'

'Who's writing?'

'But is there something organised? I'd like to be part of it.'

'It looks as if you're part of it already.'

And Lynn had to be content with that. Sometimes she felt exhilarated, excited. At others she chided herself for being romantic and childish. All that was going on was that a lot of individual women were taking individual stands. There was no organization. It was demeaning rubbish to use words like revolution or resistance.

The woman who had agreed to operate on Jane turned out to be the ex-nurse wife of one of the Europop doctors. Under cover of sex therapy classes she helped up to a dozen women a week begin unauthorised pregnancies. Lynn went with Jane, but Jane didn't want her there while the operation was being done. Lynn was given a room to sit in, and some women came and sat with her and played music and chatted in ways that were soothing and communicative but steered off specific identities or information. She felt glad; if they were looking after her this well, Jane need have no worries. She couldn't resist asking, 'Are you The Women too?' and they smiled deprecatingly and said, 'Aren't we all?'

Lynn shrugged. 'Maybe.'

Jane was pale and wobbly-legged for a day after the operation, but she kept insisting it was nothing. 'There's nothing to it, mum. It didn't hurt and it hardly bled. It was just fear. As long as I relaxed, it was okay. That was why it took so long, they were talking away all the things I'd read about pain and dangers. It was nothing, nothing at all.' And as if in proof she missed her next period, and within a few more weeks was boasting sore breasts, morning sickness and half-hourly visits to the loo.

They had a party to celebrate the pregnancy once it was established beyond doubt. Martin dropped an earlier pose of righteous anxiety and was frankly delighted. Lynn thought she had never seen Jane so affectionate and cheerful, which was a pleasure in itself. She tried to look forward to the bewildering idea of being a grandmother when she wasn't used to being a mother yet. She focused on her daughter, who for all her smiles was still unwell and was going to have to get through her pregnancy with the minimum of medical help, and on the tiny foetus, the growing child that was a little licit, an outcast before it was born.

Lynn never came nearer to believing in a goddess than she did a week later when the Department for Family Welfare dropped its latest bombshell.

No further contraceptive pellets would be inserted in women, and any woman who wished to have hers removed could do so. They were a primitive method of birth control, not wholly reliable, and caused unpleasant side-effects. Furthermore, the DFW was concerned to reduce casualties among women who had sought illegally to remove them and had been admitted to hospitals in their thousands with lacerated wombs.

Besides, pellets were no longer necessary. The ultimate in trouble-free contraception had arrived. A small amount of contraceptive chemical had been placed in all the nation's reservoirs. The chemical had been tested for one hundred per cent effectiveness and freedom from side-effects. The outward manifestations of women's menstrual cycles would remain unchanged, as would their ability to become pregnant after a short course of antidote tablets obtainable from government Women's Centres.

Lynn and Jane were together when they heard the news. They were sewing a shiny new textile into baby-garments for a Europea combine; it was slightly better paid work than punching cards. As it should be. The unpleasant material was so slippery that it seemed alive, squirming from the needle and resisting scissors. It also gave off a mist of fibre which irritated Jane's throat. A battle with Lynn to stop her doing it altogether ended in a compromise, Jane would do half an hour with a mask on and then sit before an open window deep-breathing.

'It looks as if I was just in time,' she said, 'they'd never have let me. How could such a thing have happened?'

'It's Peel,' said Lynn, 'he's mad.'

'Maybe if David Laing hadn't – '

'Be quiet. Individuals aren't important.'

'But why did no one hear of it? Don't things go through parliament any more?'

'I'll find out.' Lynn spent a day in a library with parliamentary reports. When she came home her voice was steely. 'Yes, it's been through parliament.'

'When?'

'Twice. Once in a debate on the water supply. They were rubber-stamping procedures for putting in purifiers and vitamins.

No argument of course. Then just after midnight, Peel put in an amendment. "Or other therapeutic substances." No argument.'

'And the other time?'

It came up in a debate last week. There were about six members in the chamber, and to judge from the report they spent most of the time cracking jokes.'

'What was the debate?'

'Women's role in the modern world.'

The Byers and the Carmichaels divided up the house equitably, adjusting the walls upstairs and sharing the downstairs. Martin was out at work all day and so was not expected to do housework. Derek said he would do his share, and help with Lynn and Jane's sewing or card-punching, but Jane argued that he should not have to.

'You're retired now, dad. Write a book or something.'

Lynn scowled into her mirror. 'I will not be a mother-in-law.'

Derek sat miserably making notes and in the end Martin found him a job answering a man's telephone. 'It's not much,' Martin said confidentially, 'but it'll get you out of the house.'

Lynn and Jane were getting on quite well; the only friction was over what Jane called Lynn's fussing. Pregnancy had wrought wonders with Jane's health, she had never been so symptom-free, and she was furious when Lynn went behind her back and persuaded Astrid to overcome her embarrassment at an illicit pregnancy in the family and pass on to Jane the advice and information she herself obtained at her ante-natal classes. For Astrid was very excited and proud to have been chosen as one of the first women to be given a set of green translucent capsules to swallow to overcome the sterilising agent in the drinking water and enable her to produce a baby engineer.

'Astrid's so damn smug,' Jane would grumble, and Lynn had to agree. And in a way it did seem foolish to introduce anxiety where none existed before. After all, Lynn remembered, she herself had given birth to Jane with only Derek in attendance. Hospitals were being run down then with the spending cuts, and mothers-to-be had faced two choices: either to go it alone or to face a highly technological, heartless, cost-cutting baby-production line.

She remembered as if it were yesterday. There'd been no classes of course, but she'd read books and made sure Derek read them too. He'd shaped up honourably to his duties and permitted himself to be lectured: 'I know what they're like, these hospitals. They want you in and out between nine and five, tubes in all your orifices and no husbands getting in the way. Well I want you there. I'll need an ally so I'm telling you now. There are to be no anaesthetics that I do not specifically ask for. I will not be induced unless a doctor looks me in the eye and tells me it is medically necessary. When the baby is born it goes to me or you first for a cuddle and a chat before it gets whisked away to be disinfected and put in a box, and it's not going out of my sight till it's got its little name-tag on.'

How naive they'd been! Doctors forcing attentions on them had been the least of their worries. They'd accepted the rather insulting advice that as an 'elderly primagravida' Lynn should come into hospital as soon as labour started, but it had been dark and deserted when they arrived at four in the morning, and they'd found a spare room with a bed and Lynn had got into it, hoping some official wouldn't bustle along and be angry. On the contrary; the exhausted nurse who did eventually look in seemed relieved and grateful that they were coping.

Derek had gone exploring and reported vacant rooms, nurseless wards with mattresses folded on unused beds; and occasional, ill-looking mothers labouring alone with moonlight on them.

Now all that seemed like the good old days. As an illicit mother-to-be, Jane was entitled to nothing: no advice, no care, no labour wards, no Benefit. Lynn and Derek and Martin had conferred about it late one night, and Lynn had gone off hunting again for women who could help in an emergency. Women washing clothes in one of the commercial laundries gave her a name but stressed that for security reasons it *was* only for emergency use. This time Lynn asked no questions about The Women.

Meanwhile Astrid visited relentlessly. It was not for her to comment on the risks her brother was allowing Jane to take, so she didn't. She tried to keep conversation as light and optimistic as possible, concentrating on plans for her own baby. What an honour to be chosen for Accelerated Rearing! She was having special oxygen treatments to develop her unborn son's brain, and a regime of exercises. And the pills she had to take! Vitamins and proteins and – well, she was sure she rattled when she walked! Did she rattle? She was sure she could get away with asking for a spare bottle if Jane would like –

'No thanks,' said Jane.

'Well you should be having lots of milk. Would you like some milk?'

'That would be kind, Astrid,' said Lynn firmly. Jane glared.

'Let me look at your teeth at least,' said Astrid, and Jane sighed and opened her mouth. 'And I know this sounds silly – but are you reading to him yet?'

'Yes, I've started him on the theory of relativity.'

Astrid flushed. 'I know when I'm not wanted.' And after a few more snubs, no amount of apologising from Lynn would bring her back.

As the time for the birth drew near, Jane found she had only one fear and that a shameful one. She didn't want her mother with her. She appreciated that Lynn was trying to be helpful, indeed was being helpful. She felt guilty about how she had treated her in the past, and the enormity of maternal responsibility was beginning to weigh her down in mind and body; nevertheless, she didn't want Lynn being kind and useful when she was open and vulnerable. The idea was embarrassing. She felt like crawling away to have a child in a forest.

And as for Lynn's wanting to rush off and find hordes of her old feminist buddies – well! Didn't they realise, damn it, that birth was a natural event?

As it happened, she was alone in the house with Derek when the first contractions came. The first he knew was when she looked at him rather vaguely and remarked, as if to herself, 'It doesn't hurt. It isn't pain. It's a strong female muscle limbering up for use.'

'Have you started?'

'I think so.'

Derek dropped the book he was reading and started flapping around.

'Dad for heaven's sake, you've done it before!'

'Yes, but – '

Somehow it had been different when it had been his own. He remembered, of course he remembered everything, that sense of crushing responsibility to be strong for Lynn, to protect her from doctors. He hadn't been in the least bit frightened of the baby or the birth ¬ he'd been much too busy quaking about taking stands against hospital officialdom. How could you argue with a doctor who had all that knowledge? It had been all right of course, and the baby had come right there on the hospital bed with doctors and nurses only rushing in to take their bow, as it were, after the final curtain-call; but now he longed for a doctor and knew he wouldn't argue.

'I expect Lynn'll be back soon.'

'Dad, you're the only person in this family who's ever delivered a baby.'

'Yes, but – '

'I don't want her here.'

'Oh now Jane – '

'When it gets near please send her out to get those women of hers.'

'That's only for emergencies.'

'It will be if she's here.' Jane winced. '*Please*, dad.'

He sighed. He felt like whipping her murderously as a spoilt ungrateful brat. And whoever heard of a man delivering his own grandchild? Grandchild! Absurd! A grandchild was a fluffy clean creature pawing your white beard, not a squirming animal counting on you to get it into the world!

By the time Martin came home, Jane was well into the first stage of her labour. Everything was fine as far as Derek could tell. He'd re-read all the childbirth books but it wasn't necessary. He'd found he knew them by heart.

Jane gave off calm energy. She might have been a veteran. She sat, lay, squatted or walked around. She chatted, concentrated or let out complex moans which would have been alarming had they not ended in beatific smiles.

Her optimism affected Derek. He reminded himself how natural it all was, felt sure it would soon be over, guiltily hoped Lynn would not arrive. He felt almost professional in his competence, understood how doctors just let it happen and then took the credit.

Martin's faced appeared round the door and panicked. Jane's contractions slowed and she seemed to feel pain. 'Be calm, be calm,' she scolded her husband, 'You know what to do.'

He remembered that his planned role was to keep her relaxed. He kissed her and rubbed her shoulders, sometimes letting his hands creep shyly to her breasts. He told her stories. Jane winked at her father. They both knew who needed relaxing.

But as the contractions grew stronger she tried to hide her mounting agitation. Derek held her hand and told her it had been the same at her own birth. It was getting late; the room was darkening. Martin reached out for the lights but Jane was furious.

'Have some respect for my eyes, damn it!' And her eyes seemed to blaze.

Derek said calmly, 'Lynn was the same.'

'Is someone taking my name in vain?'

Lynn couldn't have picked a worse moment to arrive. Jane shrieked, 'Get help, get help!'

Derek whispered to Lynn, 'I think you'd better fetch those women.'

She looked at him. 'Is it an emergency, then?'

He gave up. 'Of course not. She's in transition and she's scared. And she wants you out.'

'Well,' Lynn took a deep breath, 'fuck that.' And she walked softly and deliberately to the far end of the room and sat in a chair facing away from Jane.

'I'm here,' she said, 'if you want me.' Then she started to read.

'I think you should get ready to push now,' said Derek.

'Oh I can't,' said Jane, 'I'm so tired.'

'You'll have the baby soon, don't forget,' said Martin, 'I can see her pretty head.'

'You do it, I can't,' Jane moaned.

'Come on now,' Lynn heard Derek coax, 'Lynn, come over.'

Lynn fought with the pride that wanted Jane to ask her but there was nothing, only tetchy little moans. She stood up. Jane was half sitting, half lying, her husband cuddling her. Derek was bracing himself against the wall for one of her feet to push against. The other foot hung in the air.

'Come on love, push against me,' said Lynn, taking hold of the foot. Jane opened her eyes. 'I'm good at that.'

Then there was nothing but energy between them and in the room; Lynn and Derek held hands and looked down into the dark straining tunnel of their daughter's body. Beneath the stretching opening and the wet black head Jane's skin looked white and ready to rip.

Derek whispered, 'Should we cut?'

Lynn wanted to laugh. '*We*?'

'You.'

'I don't want to do that.' Instead Lynn reached down and touched the taut flesh, caressing and willing it to soften and stretch. Just as it seemed impossible, just as it seemed that a ragged tear would reward Lynn's reluctance to cut, the head was born with a little gush of blood and fluid and after that it was easy – a couple more pushes and the baby fell plop like a fish into Lynn's hands.

With the cord still pulsating they laid the baby on Jane's flat soft stomach. It was a little girl – Lynn thought – the genitals were rather an odd shape – huge confused labia – what an irony if – but no, this was normal, she remembered reading it was normal for a baby's genitals to look odd. Life and growth would determine sex. This was a baby girl all right.

Jane let out a long groan as her body relaxed.

'Cry, why doesn't she cry?'

'Stupid, she's okay. What's she got to cry about?' The baby was making little speaking noises as if she scorned to cry, and looking round with wide-awake eyes.

Derek and Lynn and Martin stood round Jane's belly and admired, counting the baby's fingers, admiring her shell-like ears and the tone of the cries that she was deigning to give as if she realised it was expected of her. Jane's flesh quivered and shifted as she hoisted herself on to her elbows.

'Is this a private birth,' she said, 'or can anyone join in?'

She was all smiles.

A month later, Astrid went into the shiny new maternity unit annexed to the Women's Centre.

She was pleased that things had gone well for Jane and that the baby seemed fit. Still – none of this earth-mother stuff, dining-room obstetrics for her! The most sophisticated machinery in the world would help her, and the baby's engineer-brain would receive stimulation from the moment his head popped between her legs.

Her labour was going well. She was sedated. Wires from machines sent her body into spasms at intervals. She tried to count them but her head kept going woozy.

Foreign doctors stood over her.

'Astrid is a model mother having a model birth.'

'Is Astrid going to have a big family?'

'She'll see how she gets on with this one . . .'

Fluids dripped into tubes, cylinders disgorged their contents into Astrid's supine body, she was floating beneath the surface of thick music.

'. . . excited to be chosen . . .'

'. . . professionally qualified at fifteen . . .'
'. . . what is more wasteful than childhood . . .'
'. . . curtailment . . .'

Astrid's eyes glowed with drowsy pride. Then she felt something stop.

It was an unpleasant sensation, like swimming under water and unexpectedly hitting the bottom. She sent a message to her face to plead with the doctors, but they seemed quite satisfied with their machines, which continued to drip and tick.

'Astrid looks unhappy about something.'

'He'll soon be here, Astrid, and saying his ten times table as like as not.'

Astrid never saw the baby. The look of horror on the face of the young medical student at the end of the table was enough, as he hauled something out of her. She struggled to shout the message her body gave her that something had gone terribly wrong, but a black gas mask came down over her face, and its enveloping circle became her world.

She woke in a silent room, whimpering for her baby. The medical student was by her bed, his face as white as his coat.

'Where's my baby?'

'He's in intensive care, dear, please don't worry.'

'Don't lie to me, you know he's dead.'

The medical student covered his face. 'That's what they told me to say.'

'What do you want?' she screamed as she saw his tears and his pleading eyes, '*Me* to comfort *you*?'

'He never lived.'

'How can you say that? He had a job!'

They kept her in a room by herself, to spare her, they said, the sight of happy mothers with healthy babies. They told her she was too ill for visitors. She knew she was not ill, and she wanted nothing so much as to see a happy mother with a healthy baby. It might hurt, but it would disperse the sense of cold death that weighed like a stone in her womb. She slipped out of her room and walked corridors in the moonlight, and from every locked room came the sleepless sobs and pacing of women. There was no sign of any babies.

A doctor chased her back to bed, locked the door. An hour passed. She heard a scrabbling sound and a woman's voice whispered:

'You in there, love?'

'Who is it?'

'Just one of the women. What happened to yours?'

'Dead.'

'It's a blessing.'

'What do you mean?'

'Some of them are living. Did you see yours?'

'No.'

'It's a blessing.'

It was happening everywhere. Throughout the country, babies were being born with deformities so gross as to make some of them unrecognisable as human. The best of them lived eight hours.

Explanations poured in from Europop. Undetected factors in the women's history. Infectious bug, something in the air. The high quality of ante-natal care that had ensured the birth of babies who might otherwise have been aborted spontaneously as damaged foetuses. Each story sounded thinner than the last to the nation in panic. Panic turned to fury with the realisation: *it must be that stuff they put in the water.*

'Impossible, impossible,' soothed the professor, 'it was thoroughly tested. Sometimes the eating habits of expectant mothers –'

'You can't blame them now, man!' Peel screamed, 'What have you done?'

'Is there some additive or pollutant in your water that I was not told about?'

'You're passing the buck, professor! It was up to you to check!'

Some hastily-conceived experiments with female rats provided the answer. The contraceptive chemical alone could not be blamed, and neither could the water. But the third arm of the lethal triangle was the drug in the antidote. Harmless by themselves, the three had come together in women, rendering them unsuitable as vehicles for the carrying of unborn children.

11

The Women's Day

'For all of us,' wrote the professor, 'our potential to do good is matched by our potential for disaster if we err. So when you judge me (I seek to evade nothing) I plead that you be no harsher than you would be on a professional mistake in yourselves – even though, in your case, the consequences may be slight, your mistake never found.' After writing that he hanged himself, and his body was secretly disposed of.

The Europop project was disbanded. Participating scientists raced into print to declare the suspicions they had had all along. The project's funding was transferred, as compensation, to the British government, and international charities sent parcels of clothes and cosmetics and messages of condolence to the bereft mothers. Educational trusts offered bursaries to enable those who were suitably qualified to bury their grief in a new career. The suggestion was made that babies might be imported from under-fed parts of the world to benefit from the dammed-up maternal love and breast-milk of the British; but the mothers in the under-fed parts of the world were reluctant. 'Let our infants starve with us!' seemed to be their mood, (anthropologists noted with interest the primitive suspicion of a nation of barren women) ' – even if they are what the British mothers want, which we doubt!'

The British mothers looked as if they wanted blood. Women's Centres were ransacked, sometimes burned. The mobs seemed unled, spontaneous, disorganised and wild, but they were thousands strong and the police had little heart to resist. The Europop workers, for the most part, escaped; native or foreign, they were lifted out in special planes.

The government considered using sections of the Protection of Women Act to restore order, but psychologists advised that it would be better to allow the women to work through their sorrow in whatever way they chose.

Mornings found streets dug up and rows of sticks with discs on top driven into the mud; each disc bore a child's name. The police simply diverted traffic. Women in red robes were spotted holding ceremonies of memorial over these makeshift graves in the middle of the night; and ministers of many religions began to find their places of worship desecrated with blood and mud and plants, and tiny twin pools of water, as far apart as eyes in a woman's face.

Every woman affected got a tasteful card from the royal family, 'to let you know we are thinking of you at this difficult time.'

Abortions were offered to women still pregnant. Some refused, never wanting another doctor or instrument within miles of them, or feeling the infant moving inside them and knowing that it was safe, had been miraculously spared. The doctors noted sadly that it was always the softer, more unstable women who thus refused to accept the evidence of science, the ones who took it most hard when the birth came and they found there had been no miracles, no one was spared. There were some anxious moments when a few of the monster babies looked like surviving, but none lasted longer than a day.

Mr Peel resigned and left the country in a Europop airlift. No one would touch his job, and indeed the name of the Department for Family Welfare could not be uttered by anyone who hoped to remain in politics. The Social Security Party was guiltily glad to find its ranks swelling: the consensus was that an entirely new approach to social and family policy was long overdue. The disaster had been an inevitable consequence of placing human affairs too low on the national agenda. Besides, the nation's children were now especially precious – no one could say how long it would be before more could be born, and the behaviour of their mothers over the next few years was likely to be – well – unpredictable. An old-style social security system also seemed attractive in view of the waves of revulsion now conjured up by the Welfare Hostels. In a booming newcomer to a supercontinent, they could be seen as a triumph of sense over sentiment. To a nation in mourning, they were an outrage.

Jim Matthews had been a founder member of the Party, and his star was rising fast. He discussed the new ideas with Lynn.

'It's almost the old Beveridge idea, mum. People pay contributions and then they're covered for unemployment, sickness, old age – and – *and* don't interrupt. Er, please. And motherhood. It'll be an insurable risk like any other. Women'll be treated fairly, in their own right, not as appendages to some man. What's wrong with that?'

'Nothing.'

'There'll be none of this conditional nonsense. All mothers will have money of their own. And if it's expensive, that's too bad, the government must find the money. If the nation wants children it can damn well pay for them.'

'Lynn raised dull eyes. '"The nation" can't have children,' she said, 'whether she wants them or not.'

'No, but I mean after all this chemical business has been sorted out. We must look to the future. We must plan.'

'Population is the louse in the ointment of planning.'

'Pardon?'

'Oh, nothing. Who wants children anyway?'

Jim said, 'You'd be surprised. You should hear some of the men. I think they're worried about their classic bone structures being lost to posterity. But seriously, there is talk that twenty years from now we could be in a bit of trouble if we're sort of missing a generation of workers. Hardly the point, I say – ' he added stoutly, 'but – '

Lynn burst out, 'Even now the best that they can come up with is that motherhood is an *insurable risk* and – now shut up, Jim, it's my turn – having to find excuses for doing things for women in terms of children, "the nation" and men feeling disinherited!'

'I didn't – '

His repentant face defeated her. 'Wherever their real sympathies lie. It's a good scheme, Jim. Is it yours?'

'Oh – planning groups. You know.' He fidgeted. 'We'd love to have more women in the Party, mum, but they don't join.' She shrugged. 'The men feel responsible,' he went on, 'Well, the ones I know do. They don't know how they can make amends, but they want to. What do the women want?'

'I don't know, Jim. Why don't you ask us?'

The all-party parliamentary committee that was drawing up plans for a social security system that would deal fairly with women and meet the needs of the modern era, proclaimed The Women's Day. The London Eurodome (there was one in every capital city of Europa, a vast people's palace for the use of any people's organisation, a symbol of Europa's commitment to progress through democracy) would be the site of a conference. Ten thousand women were to come and say what they wanted. They were exhorted to be just, warned to be realistic and promised that serious note would be taken of what they said. The government promised that no bugs, journalists or stool-pigeons would be planted; and the conference could continue into a second day if necessary.

Selecting the ten thousand turned out to be a problem. The old FAMILY organisation could hardly be used; feminist networks were in disarray and technically illegal. So the parliamentary com- mittee reopened the Europop Women's Centres for one day and told women to go there and vote for delegates. The response was apathetic. The government shrugged and sent off free transport vouchers.

The night before the conference the princess (who had been invited to attend the Eurodome but was not going) delivered an address to the men of the nation.

'Tomorrow,' she said, smiling sadly down from screens in homes and city centres, studio lights gleaming in the dampness of her eyes, 'tomorrow you are going to have new duties because your wives will not be at home. I understand that even those women who have not been chosen as delegates are holding meetings of their own, so in anticipation of the problems this might cause, The Women's Day is being declared a national holiday at my request. Care lovingly for your youngsters – perhaps even turn your hands to a little spring-cleaning as a surprise. Furthermore, do not assume that the women will necessarily return in a frame of mind to resume their old roles where they left off. I anticipate – indeed, I hope for – nothing less than a quiet revolution.'

Meanwhile Lynn Byers was putting reluctant finishing touches to the opening address she was going to give at the Eurodome. She had been furious when she received the invitation.

'This is your doing,' she fumed at Jim.

'We were all asked to suggest names. I thought, well, you're not a mad radical and you've lived through this without taking sides –'

'Good God!'

'Well, someone's got to do it, mum,' he said reasonably.

'Possibly, but it doesn't have to be me, I wasn't even going. And it doesn't have to be someone appointed by the government.'

'I'm hardly the government.'

'You don't know anything about women's meetings, Jim. They'll probably decide they don't want anyone to chair it.'

'He spread his hands. 'Okay,' he said, for the tenth time, 'if that's what they decide. But how can ten thousand people decide anything if there's no one to say, right, the meeting's open, what do you want to do?'

Ten thousand! She quaked. Still, he was right, and maybe this was all she could contribute. What should she say? But no – *should* did not come into it, what could she say? Only what she felt. And if other women responded to that, that was okay, and if they reviled and overthrew her, that was okay too. She didn't even know what she hoped for, but it was not what she saw when she got to the Eurodome.

Only a few hundred women for a start – sitting in ones and twos in the serried ranks of chairs, docile and dwarfed by the great white egg of the ceiling. Like a slide-show in her mind she saw still pictures of the women's conferences of her youth. The endless tables selling badly-printed literature. The women hugging each other and nothing ever beginning on time. The random motions, appeals for solidarity, intense workshops, furious indignation if anyone suggested anything so reactionary as an agenda or a time-limit on speakers. The exasperation and ecstasy – but this pitiful gathering might be new girls at a school awaiting the arrival of a strict mistress. Was it their age, their background? They seemed to be a mixture. They seemed to be in a state of shock. Or maybe they were intimidated by the place. The dome had a sort of muffled feel to it. It was too comfortable – you felt manipulated, as if the whitish feel and colour and taste of the air were signalling comfort to your brain while bypassing your senses. As if you were being soothed by music you could not hear. Yes, maybe that was it. Or maybe the respectful silence (as an absurd little escalator carried her five feet up on to the platform) was the lull before the storm, and as soon as she opened her mouth there would be an organised coup.

She gazed out into the expanses of the hall, striped with empty chairs, wondering who could be organising anything. Her eye lighted on Jane, who hadn't wanted to come (being one of the lucky ones, being mother of one of the youngest and healthiest babies in Britain, but who had agreed when Lynn said it would make her less nervous) and she smiled encouragingly. The slide-show started up again – there was Posy (why on earth should she think of Posy?) gibbering with impatience and yearning to take the lead; there was Marsha calming Posy down; there was Marsha chained to a bed in a cell . . .

'It seems a bit silly,' Lynn tried, 'for me to shout. Why don't we all move a bit closer, up to the front – ' She wasn't shouting, she didn't need to shout. The hall's acoustics were perfect and there was no sign of microphones. Her voice rolled round the glistening walls like marbles on a drum. 'Can everyone hear me all right – ?' No one moved except to nod, yes, they could hear her all right.

In a minute, she thought, the doors will open and there will be a radical feminist takeover. Or a bourgeois-liberal feminist takeover. Or something. This can't be all! A lady in a fur coat was looking at her watch; Lynn should have opened her mouth to speak two minutes ago.

'I've come – I want to ask your permission for me to chair this meeting. The first session, that is. I want to make some opening remarks. May I?' Not a flicker. Maybe she'd got it all wrong. Maybe she had to take command. Jane caught her eye, mouthed 'Water?', fetched her some. Jane seemed to be the only person alive out there. 'My name's Lynn Byers.'

'Byers. Is that your father's name or your husband's?'

Did she imagine it? She looked for the source of the question. The acoustics told her nothing. Every face was expressionless. She did imagine it. But just in case: 'My mother used to call me Lynn.' Silence. She wondered. The sort of person who asked that sort of question wasn't usually subdued so cheaply. She'd see. 'We've all come together in the wake of appalling tragedy to tell the government what we want them to do about it. I thought first we might take time to offer comfort to the sisters who've suffered. Perhaps if those of you who've lost babies could stand?'

A few stood, one of them Astrid, whom Lynn had not noticed. Had someone elected her as a delegate or had she just drifted along? She was pale as milk, numb and sandbagged with grief. The other women were the same. It was an embarrassing moment, utterly misjudged.

The voice that had spoken before said, 'Some of us may prefer not to.'

Lynn said, 'I didn't mean – '

'It's one way to get cosmetic unity, of course.'

Lynn's eyes were quick and she spotted her attacker while her lips were still moving. At first she thought she knew her; then she realised she could be any of the Collindeane daughters: seventeen or eighteen, frail but steady-eyed in her thick patched coat and boots. She was small but swamped her chair by sprawling her limbs, as if contemptuous that such a paltry piece of furniture should aspire to contain a woman. Her hair was red – *but not as red as mine was*, Lynn thought, looking straight at her. Just as she was seeming to wilt another voice, kinder but no less determined, said, 'It's a good idea, Lynn, to remind ourselves of the dimensions of the atrocity inflicted on women by men, but I think some of us find it a bit intrusive.'

Not even trying to identify the second speaker, realising it was only a matter of time, Lynn started to speak.

'I belong to a generation that remembers when governments didn't put chemicals into the drinking water to stop women having babies. On the contrary. Once you decided to have a baby – or once you had one, deciding didn't always come into it – that was your business. So much so that when you were looking after it, you were assumed to have dropped out of the life of the nation altogether. *Not economically active* was the term they used. If you were inconvenient enough not to have a man to support you while you were being not economically active they gave you your keep – on the same basis as the long-term unemployed, otherwise known as idle parasites. Now, to call the long-term unemployed idle may have been technically true, if less than charitable, but as most of you know, to call the mother of young children idle is a downright lie.' There was a slight spattering of applause. Lynn hadn't expected it, but she was glad; it was the more conventional-looking women applauding, the ones who might once have been in FAMILY. The red-haired girl's hands were still, though; flat on her knees. And her eyes and lips smiled gentle warning.

'If you were married, of course, you got nothing. Well, you didn't need anything, did you, if you had a man to support you. Whatever the terms he set for your support, whatever he required you to do, however often he beat or raped you, whatever it did for your self-respect to go crawling to him for pocket-money after your twenty-four-hour day of economic inactivity.

'So we stopped. We got fed up, we demanded the means to stop and we stopped. Some of us called it the women's liberation movement. We demanded jobs on equal terms with men, and proper birth control, and creches. Some of us chose to be lesbians – others wanted to go on living with men but as equals, not as domestic servants. We stopped, in other words, doing all the things that it has been taken for granted we would do till the end of time.

'A lot of people didn't realise this was what was going on, least of all us. It had plenty of names. Career women. Dual-career families, one-parent families, one-child families, no-child families. Latchkey kids, underachieving kids. The permissive society, decline of marriage, decline in the birth-rate. Abortion, divorce, pressure on the social services. What it boiled down to was individual women looking at what was expected of them and saying – no. I'm not going to do that.

'I've talked a lot. Do you want me to go on? Do you?'

She glanced almost playfully at the red-haired girl.

'Finish what you have to say, madam chairman.'

'So along came Benefit. The final solution. Pay women at home and keep 'em there. The last ditch stand of a welfare state that realised what it was going to be lumbered with if we gave up entirely. Plus, of course, the state realised – what we in the women's movement didn't, or didn't care to admit – that most women didn't want to give up entirely. Most wanted to have families and give them a lot of love and time. They didn't want to be taken for granted, despised, impoverished, ·discounted for doing it, but they had feelings of love for their kids and they saw family links could be good and strong and cohesive and they didn't see those feelings or those links as a male conspiracy . . . which was how many of us in the women's movement saw them, mistaking the way they've been exploited for the thing itself.

'That's what we've got to beware of today, sisters. Mistaking the way Benefit was exploited – and the horror that's come out of it – for the thing itself. Because what I'm going to do now is defend Benefit and I hope you'll hear me out. I'm not defending the reasons we were given it, or the way it let the Department of Family Welfare – sic, sic, sic! – think it had bought shares in our wombs – but the *principle* that people whose life's work is raising kids should be rewarded in the same way as people whose life's work is anything else, particularly as it's unlikely that that 'anything else' is more important or difficult than raising kids. It's a principle that our government's in a mood to yield, and I think that –' she raised her hand, 'yes, yes, whatever our attitudes to the government, whatever *alternatives* we're going to propose to government, we should keep it in the forefront of our minds. Because a social order that penalises good mothers for being good mothers won't survive and won't deserve to.

'Just one more thing.' Her face was burning. She sipped water.

Her voice was giving out. 'I don't suppose I need to say this here, but there used to be, and doubtless still are, people who think mothers should be content to be paid for their labours in the love of their families and the respect of society. Well, when we have a society in which love and respect are negotiable currency, that'll do. Until then –'

Astrid was on her feet again, swaying. She screamed: 'It won't do! I won't go through that again, not for love, not for respect, not for money, not for –' Lynn saw Jane go to her, put her arms round her. She saw the red-haired girl glance at her watch: *come in, Mrs Byers, your time is up*. 'What was that?' the red-haired girl sneered, 'a party political broadcast?'

Don't you shake your red hair at me, young lady, Lynn flashed back, *I'm not impressed*. She said, 'I'll stand down, if the meeting wants me to.'

The kinder voice she'd heard before said, 'Weren't you overlooking something, Lynn?' A black girl, same age as red-head, wide capable eyes and a halo of hair. 'You talk as if it's just a matter of deciding what's going to happen about Benefit and getting on with our lives. We can't have babies any more. Whether we want to or not.'

'I don't want to,' Astrid whimpered, 'and I won't.'

'We've been poisoned, we can't.'

The meeting was coming to life.

'We daren't.'

'It's all right for you, Lynn, with your grandchild – ' Who was that? It didn't matter. Someone had done her homework. It was only a matter of time now. A spot of resistance, though, would still be decent.

'Look, let's be realistic, about this poisoning business. I don't want to underplay it, but sooner or later they're going to come up with something –'

'But who's going to believe them?' Everyone seemed to be shouting now. 'When they come to us with their little green pills, tomorrow or next year or ten years from now and say, it's all right now, girls, we've perfected it and we've tried it out on beagle bitches and black women so off you all go and get pregnant because we're feeling broody and all our obstetricians are out of work –'

'And our population projections are going haywire –'

'After all, they only *say* they've stopped the experiments –'

'How do we know this isn't part of one?'

Lynn felt like a very old puppet that had played its last part and was ready to flop in a corner. 'Do – you – want – me – to – stand – down?' she shouted, and a soft voice beside her said, 'Yes,' and she looked into the green eyes and red hair of the youngster from the floor who thought this had been a battle and thought that Lynn had lost.

It was purposeful and humane, the way they ousted her; six teenagers, very calm and organised, half black, half white. She was shown to the escalator, hobbling like a crone. Jane stepped forward as if to catch her, offered her a handkerchief. She dashed it away but didn't object when Jane mopped her eyes. When she could see and hear again the kind black girl was speaking, introducing herself and the others who flanked her like a military junta. Her name was Cath. Like the others, she was a second-generation feminist; she had grown up in a women's community in the midlands; the others came from different parts of the country, including one from London, though not Collindeane, which Lynn found she minded.

'We are The Women. You are The Women.' You could see the capitals as Cath crooned and spat them. 'We are all The Women and this is The Women's Day but this is not The Women's Conference, if you take my meaning.'

Glances exchanged among her audience suggested they did not.

Cath smiled. 'You see, this meeting, with its chairperson – who is one of The Women – was foisted upon us, and we rather think women have had enough foisted on them for the time being. There are other things going on. The reason, you see, why there are so few "delegates" here today is that when women got together under government orders to elect them in the Women's Centres – which incidentally *are* now Women's Centres because The Women don't propose to move out of them – they decided they would prefer to decide things themselves. One of the things they decided was to send us here today – not as delegates but as messengers, and the message is to ask you to rejoin them, because that is the way The Women work out what is to happen now: on the reclaimed site of our oppression and with every woman having a voice.

'For example, here is something that will have to be decided by each woman. The sister – ' she nodded to Lynn, pleasantly enough. 'The sister thinks we should ask for Benefit back. Well, yes, that is all right as far as it goes – I'm sure that if we were going to have babies again we would be glad to have money of our own that we could pool to rebuild our old communities and make schools and playgrounds (they would be the same thing, of course) for our children – but the point is – *are* we going to have babies? Ever? The feeling at the other meetings, and here, I think, a few minutes ago, is that it can't be taken for granted.

'The sister –' Lynn again ' – referred to those who believe that mothers should be content with love and respect. She said that that would only do if love and respect were negotiable currency – and concluded from the outrageousness of the idea that women must regretfully insist on cash. But why? Why should we not build a society in which love and respect are – so to speak – negotiable currency? We have a lot of time, sisters. We have all the time we once spent on our domestic duties. Think what that means! We have the ultimate bargaining weapon. We will have babies again when we are good and ready; when our society is a fit place to bring them.'

Lynn had her hand up. The red-haired woman noticed and said, 'The government spokesman wants a word.'

'Please, I'm not,' said Lynn.

'Of course she isn't,' said Cath.

'Could we make one immediate demand of the government?'

'What's that?'

'Our political prisoners –'

'Must be freed. Of course,' said Cath.

The women didn't leave at once. They stayed, as Cath put it, 'to practise making demands'. She teased them for their modesty ('What do you mean, you want your roof fixed? Wouldn't you like a new house?') and mocked the way they asked for things for their men or their children ('What do you want for yourselves?'). When they got the idea it became hilarious: the still white dome frowned down on woman after woman demanding wealth or medical care or a world cruise, or rubbish to be collected from the tip at the bottom of the street; getting closer, giggling, then hugging each other and crying as they revealed wishes to be childless or lesbian or promiscuous or celibate; they wanted to love men, to farm them, to rape them, to be repaid by them; they were drunk and there wasn't a drop of alcohol in the place. At one point a woman said, 'Isn't this all a bit childish? I mean, let's be practical,' and Lynn thought *you're a braver woman than I am sister*, and Cath winked at the questioner and said, 'Men are the practical ones. They'll work out the details.' The questioner shrugged and smiled but left shortly afterwards; and Lynn left too.

There was no Women's Centre in Lynn's area; it had been burned; but light and voices seeped out of the old church hall across the street. Women were meeting there. Lynn slipped in, unnoticed.

'. . . . they'll say: what you demand isn't natural. We'll say: who defined nature? They'll say: we can't afford it. We'll say: oh? What have you been spending all the money on? They'll say: you undermine the family. We'll say: yes, and the state, and morality, and every other institution built on our unpaid work. Then they'll start to wheedle. They'll say: you must admit there's a population problem, and we'll say, when Europea stops hogging the resources of the world, if women and children are still hungry, then we'll talk about a population problem . . .'

Beautiful strong girls speaking to their rapt elders. Lynn found she was crying again.

'. . . they'll say: you must admit there's a difference between men and women. We'll say, yes, and we're going to find out what it is! We're going to find out who we are when we're not dependent on you and ruled by you. We're going to live free of you . . .'

Lynn whispered to her neighbour (a woman her age) about the need to free prisoners. The neighbour whispered back, yes, it was the first thing they decided.

Lynn worried about Marsha's homecoming. She hadn't known what to believe about tales of her being mad; and when it looked as if she might be in prison for ever, she hadn't even known what she wanted to believe. Now she knew she would need a lot of care (though she didn't know what kind) in a household of people already so screamingly polite to each other that some kind of dust-up must be on the way. Jane wanted to share the baby but not impose; Martin strove to bring in enough money but not pull rank as breadwinner; Derek helped everybody and felt guilty; Lynn supposed she was the emotional pivot and tried to make bright remarks and keep domestic wheels oiled.

Marsha was pale, still and frightened, but not mad. Her bones stuck out and she left trails of long grey hairs as she paced the house. She paced ceaselessly; sometimes she wanted a little space to be safe in, and then Derek and Martin would adjust walls in the top of the house to make a hideout, but shortly afterwards she would panic for open spaces and Lynn would walk with her through the streets.

'I'm the village idiot,' Marsha said once.

'Don't be silly.'

'Idiots are silly. Time and space were sort of . . . peculiar in that place where I was. You are good to me, though . . . all of you. It's like having a family. I wish Jane wasn't so suspicious.'

'Jane has a way of making people feel that when it isn't necessarily true.'

Visitors came in the daytime to welcome Marsha and bring her news of myriad meetings which they hoped she would attend when she felt well, and sheaves of leaflets that they were turning out, and news of plans for women's communities, women's farms, women's factories, women's shows. The other side of the news came over the radio. Unease, objectivity and hauteur competed in the voices of the male broadcasters.

'The princess said to day that she was pleased to see women working together to overcome their grief, and that she had no sympathy whatever for men left at home with the chores. "A taste of their own medicine," she called it. . . .'

'Scant enthusiasm has greeted the government's announcement that the London Eurodome will be the site of a massive skills-training drive for women seeking employment. No one turned up to enrol . . .'

'Our scientific correspondent reports that, owing to unusually heavy rainfall, the contraceptive in the water supply is losing potency at an encouraging rate . . .'

Some visiting women heard this while sitting with Marsha and Lynn and Jane.

'Thanks for the warning,' they scoffed.

'I'm going to get one of those caps,' said Jane, 'At half-strength that stuff might damage a foetus. Who knows?'

'Or you could give up having heterosexual intercourse.'

Another day, the radio reported, '. . . has indicated willingness to make more funds available for research into test-tube babies . . .'

'Test tube babies, is it!' Marsha shouted. She was having one of her claustrophobic times, sitting downstairs with Lynn in 3 a.m. darkness with all the windows open.

'Ssh.'

'Test-tube babies! And test-tube uteruses too, no doubt! And test-tubes to change their nappies in the middle of the night – well, that's okay. Let them get on with it, they'll learn a lot. But no. Silly of me. A baby designed by a man will have no ass-hole. It'll keep all its shit inside.'

'Marsha please, there are other people in the house.'

'How prim you are. Why should you have to be peacemaker, mother? Why don't you just tell me to shut up?'

'I am.'

Marsha got up and closed all the windows with quiet speed. Then she lit the fire, an open fire with a rudimentary self-built chimney that was inadequate to its task. The room filled up with smoke and the smell of burnt street-rubbish. 'Are you cold?' Lynn asked mildly, but Marsha was staring at the flames. Triumph and horror writhed in her eyes as Lynn read her thoughts.

'Marsha, do you want to tell me about David?'

Marsha started to whimper, to nestle by Lynn's lap like a dog. 'Which would be worse, if I meant to do it or if I didn't?'

'Neither.'

'It was nice of you to send me Posy's . . . posy. I didn't get any letters.'

'I did write.'

'Posy always said we should go on strike.'

'But like this?'

'Where are you, Lynn? I mean, where are we?'

'What do you mean?'

'Last time we were together, we were really together.'

'And we're together now.'

'But you rushed away to your family duties.'

'I don't have any more duties.'

The fire was chewing sullenly on damp rags, thickening the air till even Marsha coughed and pulled away the fuel. 'The air's fresher near the floor,' she said huskily, tugging Lynn's hand and they lay down together.

'Were you waiting for me to make the first move?'

'I was waiting till you were better so it wouldn't be guilt or pity.'

Marsha felt she had been starving and had been given bread. Lynn felt Marsha as part of her own body. She just wanted to hold and assimilate – notions like undressing or arousing or admiring or coming seemed absurd tonight. There would be lots of time for that, but now it seemed trivial, demeaning against this coming together that was hardly sex.

'You don't like what's happening, do you?' said Marsha.

Lynn paused to be sure she knew what she meant. 'I just don't think it'll happen.'

'It will, if we make it.'

'You see, I'm not going to leave Derek.'

Marsha stiffened.

Lynn went on, 'I want you to live here with us. Derek must accept that. But I'm not going off to some commune.'

'Well,' said Marsha, 'that's it then.'

'Not unless you decide it is.'

'Just because your man is the great shining exception doesn't mean you haven't got a duty –'

'I told you before,' Lynn said, 'about duty.'

Marsha shrugged, lay tense. Lynn said timidly, 'Do you want to come?' Marsha murmured, 'Why, where are you going?' and by the time she realised her mistake Lynn was asleep, but she woke her up and told her and it seemed astonishingly funny so early in the morning.

They slept late, realising from Jane's pursed lips and fierce hold on her baby that she must come down early and seen them. Lynn felt she ought to say something but was not sure what. She was glad she hadn't when Marsha grabbed Jane by the shoulders and demanded, 'Why?' Jane stiffened and flared but Marsha didn't let go. Jane hung her head helplessly. 'I don't know.'

'Haven't you had enough out of your mother?'

'It's just . . . well, I live here.'

Lynn intervened. 'Is it Derek?'

'I suppose it is, partly.'

'Don't you think that's between me and him?'

'Yes.'

'When you've finished discussing me,' said Derek coming in and speaking far too heartily, 'may I just say I feel very privileged to be living with any women at all?'

'You don't mean that,' said Lynn.

'I'm sorry,' he said, 'it's the best I can do.'

The consultative document New Deal for Women was impressive, it had to be admitted. You might think that there were no men left, the way the new order was going to concern itself with the needs and desires of women!

Old age pensions, homes, hospitals, childcare centres, canteens and laundries would all ensure the state sharing the burden of their traditional domestic duties. There would be laws for equal opportunity, and these laws would have teeth. The absolute right of women to control their own fertility was acknowledged, and there would be Benefits for all mothers. The new fertility drug (in the final stages of testing) would be free on demand, and so, when the drinking water was clear of the contraceptive, would be the most modern methods of birth control. The women gave back their answer in a thousand marches and on a million walls: 'It's not enough!'

'What *do* the women want?' the politicians wondered, and begged for someone – anyone – to come forward and negotiate. But it seemed that the only way the government could communicate with The Women was by means of public announcements, and the only way The Women replied was with slogans and demonstrations and actions, the most common of which now seemed to be thronging into buildings of varying degrees of suitability (barns, government offices, second homes left empty by the rich) and setting up house.

'These places are a health hazard,' the government warned.

'Then give us somewhere else! Give us the Welfare Hostels!'

The government turned cagey. It was true that, with the alternative provision now planned for the poor, the Hostels would soon lose their purpose. But in whose name was this demand being made? Who would feel satisfied if it were granted? Next year, the scientists were almost sure, it would be possible for women to have babies again in complete confidence. In celebration of the first births, the government would hand over Welfare Hostels to properly constituted women's groups for properly constituted charitable purposes.

'You can't say fairer than that,' said Lynn. 'Really.'

'Who can't?'

'Well, I mean you can't expect a government to.'

It was a thick, dark night. Marsha was calm but sleepless.

'The government isn't in this any more,' she said.

'Oh Marsha.'

'It's true. Who's going to dare to be the first to conceive? This could just possibly be the end of the world.'

'Marsha, I hate to tell you this, but there are one or two women in the world who aren't in this country.'

'Yes, I *know* that. But our women are going to be the first to find a style of life that isn't defined by men having power over us because we have children. That's what it's all about, in the end. And when we find it, we may also find it's so delightful that we'll have the women of the world clamouring to bring back the professor and pour his fluids into their drinking water. And even that'll be unnecessary if they do what I recommend, which is to give up sex with men altogether . . .' She glanced at Lynn out of the corner of her eye.

'All right, all right.'

'All right, all right.' Marsha chucked her under the chin. 'The first thing we've got to do is re-take Collindeane Tower.'

Lynn yawned. 'What, now?'

'Yes.'

'Marsha, where are you going, please?'

Marsha had pulled on her coat and was fumbling around in a cupboard where they kept tools, making a dreadful noise. 'Where's my axe?'

Lynn sighed. 'Do be quiet. Here.'

'That's not an axe, Lynn, it's a hammer. Don't treat me as if I'm mad. Come on.'

'Where? Don't go out Marsha, it's late and cold –'

'Wear a coat then. Come *on*.'

It was a long walk. It was very windy and dark, the moon peeping in fragments from behind black lumps of cloud. Marsha strode with her head erect and long strands of hair whipping up with the wind. Lynn gave up arguing, trotted along behind, hoped she could keep her safe. If she wanted to do something really mad she wasn't sure she could overpower her.

When they reached the stretch of rubble that had once been Seyer Street the sky was beginning to lighten. The Collindeane Welfare Hostel tilted against the pale blue. Great blotches of half-painted white gleamed on its side like a skin disease, wrinkled with cracks.

'Poor old Collindeane,' Marsha whispered, brandishing her hammer.

'It ought to be pulled down,' said Lynn.

'*No*. At least not unless it's by us. Come on, sister. Charge!' Marsha lurched forward and stumbled. Lynn held her and their eyes met. The light in Marsha's was quenched by sheepishness. An official face appeared at a window, noted the two women with indifference, looked away.

Lynn said gently, 'We can't knock it down now, Marsha. There are people in it. And anyway, they'll give it to us eventually if we want it.'

Fire darted in Marsha's eyes again. 'We mustn't wait for them to give it to us. We must take it.' But all her energy was in her voice. She sat on a pile of bricks as if very tired. She glared at Lynn. 'I dare you!' she yelled, and to calm her Lynn said, 'Maybe if we wait a while some others'll come and help us.'

They sat together in silence watching the sun come up. It was going to be one of those odd mornings when it was in the sky at the same time as the moon, racing with the clouds.

Virago

If you would like to know more about Virago books, write to us at Ely House, 37 Dover Street, London W1X 4HS for a full catalogue.

Please send a stamped addressed envelope

Book Tokens

Give them
the pleasure of choosing
Book Tokens can be bought
and exchanged at most
bookshops